Nin

Nin

Cass Dalglish

Spinsters Ink
Duluth, Minnesota
USA

First edition published November 2000
10-9-8-7-6-5-4-3-2-1

Spinsters Ink
32 E. First St., #330
Duluth, MN 55802-2002
USA

Cover design by Kathy Kruger, Whistling Mouse Illustration and Design

Production:

Camila Aguilar	Sharee Johnson
Charlene Brown	Claire Kirch
Prudy Cameron	Joan Oswald
Joan Drury	Kim Riordan
Tracy Gilsvik	Nancy Walker
Marian Hunstiger	

Library of Congress Cataloging-in-Publication Data

Dalglish, Cass.
  Nin/Cass Dalglish.—1st ed.
    p. cm.
  ISBN 1-883523-39-7 (alk. paper)
  1. Mothers and daughters—Fiction. 2. de Pizan, Christine ca. 1364–1431—Fiction.
3. Porète, Marguerite, ca. 1250–1310—Fiction. 4. Electronic mail messages—Fiction.
5. Mothers—Death—Fiction. 6. Haifa (Israel)—Fiction. 7. Women poets—Fiction.
8. Feminists—Fiction. I. Title.
PS3554.A4325 N5 2000
813'.54—dc21   00-044056

Grateful acknowledgment is made to the following for permission to use material copyrighted or controlled by them:

Passages from Christine de Pizan's writings are excerpted, sometimes in slightly modified forms, from *The Book of the City of Ladies* by Christine de Pizan, translated by Earl Jeffrey Richards. Translation copyright © 1982, 1998 by Persea Books, Inc. (New York). Reprinted by permission of the publisher.

Acknowledgments

The creation of this novel has come at the end of a course of study that has led me to the farnear and back to the herenow. I am indebted to everyone who has made this journey with me. The list of pilgrims includes the members of my doctoral committee, Marjorie Bell Chambers, Joseph Meeker, Deb Dale Jones, Trudy Lewis, Sharon Mijares, Leroy Robinson, and Gladys Swan; and my consultants, Peter Benchley and Deena Metzger. I am also indebted to my careful readers and helpful critics, John O'Brien, Natasha D'Schommer, Christina Lazaridi-Manoledaki, Cletus Dalglish-Schommer, Howard Covitz, Judith McCartin,

Peter Koffron, and Boyd Koehler; to Daniel Reisman and Deb Dale Jones, who told me ancient stories, taught me the oldest of languages and exhibited patience with my learning of cuneiform; William Hallo for his scholarship on the women of Sumer and his generous help in locating texts; to William Scheide, who shared his unpublished work on the Marys in the Bible; Batami Sadan, who offered her understanding of Rachel Blobstein's texts; Oded Nave, for his knowledge of Maimonides; and Harry Aguado, who shared his insights on the writer as a political force.

I am indebted to women writers, living and dead, who were as often ignored as burned, as often forgotten as elevated in infamy, especially Hildegard von Bingen, Marguerite Porète, Christine de Pizan, ninshatapada, and enheduanna—the mother of us all. These women writers inhabit the novel, telling their own stories, touching on their own themes, using their own images and casting their own metaphors. I am grateful to Spinsters Ink for having faith in this book and to Joan Drury for the power, precision, and care she exerted through her editing stylus.

I am honored to have come to know many deities, including Inanna, Nidaba, Ninkasi, Nammu, Tiamat, and Mother Nature, especially in their incarnations as the tempestuously spiritual Lake Superior, her winds and her fogs; the rivers, gardens, rocks, forests, and the fires that rage at her edges; the gulls and geese who fly over her; and the bats who scatter from her hills at night.

I would like to thank my Grand Marais writing retreat support team, including my faithful head wild dog, Ušumgalana, who was with me every step of the journey.

I am also indebted to Louis Branca, my husband, who not only read and re-read my work but noticed I had gone to the far-near to write, was saddened by my prolonged absence, and came with food and water to help me back into the herenow.

To my mother Mary and all my mothers,
whether they be DeLacey ladies or Morgan girls,
and to my daughter, Natasha, who is both.

Obituary

"We are back from some sadness," my father told me. He rubbed Lake Memphremagog water and white sand from my summer-browned legs, shook the towel, and snapped it taut. "The rest we will talk about later. Right now, the important thing to know is that we are back."

My father's voice was deep and slippery, rolling over my ears like July heat steaming off the lake in the late edge of afternoon. He was telling me that we were back from some sadness. I didn't remember our going away, but he was saying the important thing was that we were back—he and I and my sister Annie, who was three and a half years older. He was telling me the sadness story because I asked, as I often did that summer, if I had a mother. Or why Aurelia, our cook, wasn't my mother, and where my mother actually was. Since we were back from the sadness, my father was saying, now was not the time to talk about mothers. Mothers and the rest we would talk about later. Now was the time to dry off and sit down at the picnic table because it was my birthday, and Aurelia had prepared supper, and she was unwrapping sandwiches from linen napkins in the white cloth-lined wicker laundry basket.

"The basket I carried you across the world in, Nina," my father said and looked away for a minute. My father was the only one who called me by my baptismal name, Nina, and then only when he wanted to be dramatic, which he was about to be. He lifted an aluminum cake dome by its see-through red plastic handle and smiled, and—like a magician pulling a rabbit out of a hat—he whisked off the dome and showed me a white meringue-covered angel food cake with four bright blue candles already burning.

"Dangerous," said Annie, who was almost seven years old and getting more reasonable every day. "How could you know you'd get her dried off and over to the table on time?"

I was telling this old story to my husband, Andrew, who was listening as he opened a bottle of Chardonnay and wiped a trace of cork off the green glass rim with the dish towel that was draped over his shoulder. Andrew and I always talked about the day's passing over a glass of wine as we made dinner, and part of this day's passing was the fact that I'd told the old story to my personal writing class that morning, before I gave them their final writing assignment. So there I was, retelling the birthday-and-return-from-sadness story to Andrew, and not for the first time.

"Yes. The back-from-sadness story," Andrew said and poured Chardonnay halfway up the cup of the long-stemmed, dark blue wineglass he took out of the china cabinet. Then he reached for the clear crystal glass and poured it half full with Merlot—bull's

2

blood, he called it, too strong for him, too musky, too animal. He handed it to me. We touched the lips of our glasses and drank.

Of course he knew the story well. I'd been telling him about that afternoon since we were eleven years old, that summer we came together in Vermont and fastened our imaginations on each other and never let go. Impossible? Romantic? A woman still connected to a man she'd known as a child? Yes, but that's a different story, a sequel, one that comes later, after the one I was telling Andrew that night about me and my father and the sadness.

"I was trying to get the students to think about their obituaries in a more thorough way," I told Andrew. I'd never given birth, and yet I felt like a mother as I stood in front of my class that day. "I felt as though I were leaning over a nest of creatures looking up at me from their chairs, questions in their eyes, waiting for me to stuff them with stories, waiting for me to help them remember, quick, before memory disappeared, and we forgot all over again."

"I don't know if poets should teach obituary writing," Andrew said and grinned. Andrew used his grin as a signal of play.

"Not enough student poets to keep me employed full time," I said.

He set his tall blue glass on the counter and walked around to the kitchen side of the dining-cooking-living space we'd made by breaking down walls. We had moved from Vermont to Duluth and taken jobs at the university, and we bought the old house on the hill above Lake Superior because we could see the water from the living room. I was accustomed to being near water. I needed the cadence of waves lapping, the gloss from sun skipping across wet foil, and the purification of air moistened by fog. After we bought the house, we took out every barrier we could between the kitchen and the six-foot windows at the front of the house so we could become a part of the hugeness of a lake that invited ore boats to float under its aerial lift bridge. That's what living in

Duluth was about, seeing the lake. Just like living near Memphremagog in Vermont, but in Duluth, people seemed to have worn a harder edge into the water—building highways, pushing barges, surviving cold. Nothing I knew was as big or as cold or used as hard as Lake Superior was used right there in the city. Not Lake Memphremagog. Not even Lake Champlain. Andrew opened the refrigerator and rummaged through the crisper until he found lettuce and tomatoes and a red pepper. He set them on the marble chopping block—a green slab we'd scavenged off an old fireplace in a mansion being torn down on London Road. He took a large knife from its wooden brick.

"And what effect did your family obituary story have on this term's batch of writers?" he asked. He was making salad for dinner. Salad Niçoise.

"They were quiet. Not one nibble on the story. I had to keep going. I told them the rest, how that was the summer I tried to find out why my household was different from everybody else's in Johanna's Cape."

Every day, I asked about my mother, and my father answered the same way always—we were back from sadness—until finally it was September, and my father became Professor Michael Creed again, and he was busy and couldn't be interrupted when he was writing and not when he was studying and not when he was thinking and not after supper or before and not in the morning before breakfast, or after. And so I stopped asking.

That's when Aurelia began to spin stories for me.

Like the one about my mother speaking every language on earth. She knew Welsh, Aurelia said, so after that, she could learn anything. She was English, but she was Irish and French, too. She had many names: DeLacey was one, and so was Morgan, her mother's name. It was the Morgans who were Welsh and something else, from somewhere else.

4

Of course, I asked if she was from the town called Morgan across the river, on the other side of the bridge that hummed under my father's car. The place named Morgan down on Seymour Lake, was she from there? Not from nearby, Aurelia said. My mother and her family were from far, not near. They were from far over the mountains. Aurelia liked to call my mother Fata Morgana. She said my mother was my father's Fata Morgana. What's a Fata Morgana? Aurelia said it was a woman made into a king by her magic and faith. A king? Yes, Aurelia said, a woman king. One who sings magic songs.

She said my mother sang with her own mother and her mother's mother and her mother's aunts, some of them old and wrinkled and white-haired. And my grandmother played the mandolin back in Glastonbury, and long ago, before the war, they used to gather into a band and play on Saturday nights on the front porch, and the dogs in my grandfather's kennel would howl. Where was Glastonbury? There, where Guinevere lives, Aurelia said, right there.

"What were you hoping your students would bite on?" Andrew asked. He was cutting the red pepper into the outlines of bright vermilion clouds, each one exactly the same width as the next. His eye was precise. His knife was sharp.

"It's in the obituary that we have our last chance at setting the legend straight, telling the tale the way it might really have been."

"Nobody asked how a woman could be king?"

"They accepted it, the way I did when Aurelia told me. Why not?" Aurelia set up the rules: there were women kings who sang and had magic, and one of them was my mother. "That's part of what I was getting at. Why give up the opportunity to set up the rules in your own story?"

It was pleasant to sit with Andrew in the kitchen on the nights he cooked, telling my day while he diced and tossed questions

5

into the narrative. That night, I'd do dishes. The next day or the day after, depending on whether we ate at the deli or the Mexican restaurant or came home to cook, I'd be chef, and he would tell stories. It had been that way for the twenty years we'd been married. Balance.

I took a slow sip of Merlot. "But think about it, most of the time we let other people make the rules. So much so that even our obituaries leave out the parts that count."

Take my mother's, for instance, and my grandmother's. Truth is, they shared one obituary, which I finally read—yellowed dry, breaking at the folds—when I was eleven years old and spent a week with my friend Ruth Farrell, who lived in a large stone house next to Stella Maris College on the shore of Lake Memphremagog. We lived in a bungalow about a mile away, on the town side of the college. And one day when Ruth and I were bouncing my suitcase down the oriental-carpeted stairs of my house, my father came out of his study and said the sisters at Stella Maris and Aurelia had told him that it was time for us to talk. I figured he wanted to talk about philosophy or poetry like we usually did at dinner. Ruth giggled, like she knew he meant to talk about sex and poked me with her elbow that was especially bony, so I told him I already knew everything, and he took a deep breath and said that was good and handed me the old, folded newspaper. He looked so relieved—I wasn't about to interrupt him. I tucked the brittle paper into the zipper pocket on the outside of my suitcase, and my father carried my bag to the Farrells' car. I didn't unfold the newspaper until that night, after Ruth and I opened the windows so we could hear the lake hitting the sand outside. We lit candles and turned off the lights and crawled under the comforter. That's when we opened the old piece of newsprint, expecting philosophy and poetry, maybe even sex.

Haifa Israel English Language Gazette

"Haifa, Israel," Ruth said. "That's across the world."

The date—July 20, 1951, the day after I was born—was at the top, above the headline that said, "American Professor's Family Killed Yesterday in Traffic."

"Shoot, Nin," Ruth said, "is this about your mother?"

I didn't know. I only knew about my mother from Aurelia's stories. I always thought, if I had an ordinary mother, I ought to remember her.

Ruth kept reading. "The wife and mother-in-law of Professor Michael Creed, a resident scholar at the Carmelite International College of Theology in Haifa, were killed yesterday when they stepped off the curb at Mount Carmel in front of oncoming traffic . . . "

The next line told their names, my mother's and my grandmother's—Faith Morgan DeLacey Creed and Grace Morgan DeLacey, both originally from Glastonbury, England—and the details of their deaths: Mrs. DeLacey died at the scene; Mrs. Creed, who lived a short while after the accident, gave birth to an infant daughter on arrival at the hospital.

"Jeez, Nin, that's gotta be you."

I was sure she'd find more in the creases of the yellow paper. I told her to keep reading, but what I wanted wasn't there. No physical details. Nothing about magic and singing and dancing and dogs howling at the band. Nothing more about the two women who died or the one who was born. There was more about my father and some about a priest. "Professor Michael Creed, who attended St. Albert's Carmelite College in Vermont and earned a doctorate in philosophy from Cambridge University, studied with the Reverend Louis Cadeaux in Vermont, USA, and again at the Pontifical Institute in Rome. Father Louis served as founding President of St. Albert's College in Vermont in 1939, when the Carmelites closed their College of Philosophy here and left Haifa because of the conflict. When the Carmelites reopened their college here, Father Louis returned to Haifa. 'I persuaded Professor Creed to bring his family here to spend a most remarkable year with us in Israel,' Father Louis said."

By the time I got that far into my story, the salad Niçoise was ready, except for the dressing, which Andrew liked to churn up in the food processor.

"Hang on," he said. "One minute." It was noisy, whipping garlic and capers and mushrooms in oil. He flipped the switch and held his hands over his ears and closed his eyes and counted like a boy playing a game. When he turned off the machine, he asked, "They bite yet?" He was talking about my students.

"I just kept going. I told them how Ruth read the rest of the obit, 'Mrs. DeLacey was preceded in death by her husband, Dr. Harold DeLacey, a veterinarian who died in Glastonbury, England, ten years ago. Professor Creed also has a daughter, Annie, who shares with him this moment of sadness.' And that's when Martha said, 'Finally, the howling dogs.'"

Andrew knew Martha. I'd mentioned her before. By the end of every term, I'd mentioned most of my students by name and maybe one or two other identifying factors—like Martha having brown-black hair and carrying a coconut for a purse.

"So Martha, all of a sudden, said, 'Finally, the howling dogs.' And Sara, the bright blonde who brought her paper here last week, she said, 'So that's the sadness they came back from.'"

"Nibbles," Andrew was cutting carrot sticks, and he leaned toward me and put one between my lips. I took a bite, and he said he liked the part about my staying the week at Ruth's, watching what it was like to have two parents in the house, a man and a woman. That was the summer he got there, to Johanna's Cape.

Andrew was Aurelia's nephew from New York. His parents sent him to Vermont for the summer when they went to the Amazon on

8

a photo safari. They said Andrew was too young to go along, even though he was eleven years old. And he never did get old enough for them. All the way through high school, Andrew's parents brought him to spend summers in Johanna's Cape so he'd be out of New York while they traveled. He stayed with Aurelia, my father, me, and Annie. And every afternoon, Aurelia sent us over to the Stella Maris sisters to study in the French garden behind the convent.

Aside from the nuns and Ruth—who didn't like Gregorian chant and never went to the convent to study—Andrew was my only childhood friend. My sister Annie wasn't friendly at all. She thought Andrew was ridiculous and gawky. She said we did nothing but giggle. But Aurelia said we shared a flare. Annie wanted to know what we had a flare for, but Aurelia said it was too early to know.

In any case, we were eleven that summer when I stayed a week with the Farrells and Andrew came to Johanna's Cape. And that's when we started telling each other everything. I told Andrew about Ruth's mother giving us a party tray with a little loaf of sliced rye cocktail bread and soft cheese. And about her putting on nylons and sandals and Midnight Blue perfume and coral lipstick and going downtown to meet Ruth's father for dinner at the steak house. Nobody in my house ever acted like that. That was the night Ruth's parents came back talking about my father.

"Should have told her years ago," said Ruth's mother.

Then her father said, "He's done a good job."

"But look how he left the child wondering."

"That's how intellectuals are. Not too good at details."

Andrew was dressing the salad and nodding his head. "So, that's the point. That's why you told the story. The point is, detail. Along with the fact your father should have told you about the deaths and your birth long before you were eleven."

"You're right. You and Mr. Farrell. My father is not good at this kind of biographical detail . . . "

9

"That was obvious from the obituary," Andrew said and grinned again, tossing another carrot stick to me.

"Precisely. There was nothing in there about them, the women, the ones who died. It was all about other people, and mostly about the men in their lives. So, I told the students their last assignment would be to write their own obituaries, and they must try to list incidents that ought to be included. I told them: 'If you don't know what ought to be remembered about your mother, your grandmother, or yourself, go find out.'"

The salad was ready. Andrew took a baguette from the oven, and I carried the plates and spoons and knives and forks and two paper napkins to the dining room table. He poured wine again, white for him, red for me. We sat and clinked our glasses one more time, a double-triple clink, and I was looking at his hands: they were large, not wide, but with fingers that were long and slim and I could see why it was easy for him to hold his camera and adjust his lenses, and I looked up at his face, and he was looking at my hands. It seemed like fiction—we'd been married twenty years, and we'd been lovers almost thirty, and we'd been childhood friends, and yet our hands were still appealing to each other. He did a photo series on my knuckles, and I wrote a poem about his nails.

"I still wake up saying 'My god, I love even your fingernails.'"

He looked away from my hands, into my face. "Talk to Aurelia. Maybe she knows more."

We always went to Aurelia to get the real story, but there was really nothing more Aurelia could add. Not now. Not like she had that summer, when I was eleven. Back then, I tried Annie first, but she didn't want to get involved. She said she'd rather let it go. She was trying to learn advanced math in summer school, and she found a family history project interesting for me, but not for her. So, I hounded my father until he finally gave me what he had under his desk in a metal fishing box. The box was locked. He took a key from his desk drawer and opened it, and a shelf popped up. It was divided into compartments for hooks and weights and things, but there was a gold ring in one space, a necklace made of small blue stones in another, two grey-yellow-brown stones the shape of eggs in another, and in the largest, a gold enameled stickpin with a carved brown head that smelled of roses. Under the rose stickpin, there was a stack of photos of a beautiful woman with brown hair like mine and eyes that looked straight at me like the eyes on the statues at the convent.

"It's time we hung these up, don't you think?" my father said. We found frames in the attic and tucked two, three, four photos in each frame. We enshrined her, my mother, all around his office and the downstairs hall, and he gave me three frames full of her for my room. I had some hanging on the walls in Duluth, and when I looked at her photos, her eyes still followed me everywhere I went. She couldn't take her eyes off me. My favorite was my mother standing at the front of a white boat: she was wearing a green linen suit jacket and a skirt to match, and she had a scarf tied around her hair; she was smiling; she was pretending not to notice the camera, but she saw me. At the bottom of the metal box was a piece of rope, rolled and twisted and coiled, a skipping rope with handles the color of cobalt and cord woven from red, blue, green, and yellow threads.

Annie and I fought over the skipping rope until my father said Annie had to give it to me because Annie had memory, which was something I would never have. And she said she would, but only if she could have all the other things. I agreed, except for the photographs, which Annie said I could have, especially since I'd hung them all over the house, and she could see them anytime she wanted. Annie said I made my father too tired for him to be fair. After that, I didn't ask him much, but I didn't have to worry about Aurelia; Aurelia never tired of talking.

Andrew sipped his wine. Then he set his glass on the table; he ran his fingers lightly across my knuckles, and he said, "Talk to Aurelia again. Aurelia knows more about us than anybody else."

She knew my father almost all his life. She was a cook's helper at Stella Maris when she was sixteen, and she went over to St. Albert's when the Carmelites came and started their men's boarding school. She was there when my father finished high school and college in six years and won a big award and went to England, to Cambridge, where he met my mother.

"I've talked to Aurelia for forty years," I said and took the salad tongs and refilled our plates.

"Aurelia's the one with stories. Like the one about your grand-mother's music, about her not stopping, not even when she was old, not even in Israel; about the church in Haifa where she went on Sundays; about her singing and dancing out on the porch in the summer."

I told Andrew I didn't think they had porches in Haifa, and maybe not in Glastonbury either.

"Why would Aurelia make up stories?"

"Because nobody else did." I took another nibble of Andrew's salad. His dinners were better than mine because he liked to plan food; he fixed dishes in stages so nothing was rushed. He was home that afternoon, working in the darkroom because his photography classes at the Ag school had ended. While his negatives were drying, he poached tuna for our salad instead of using canned; it was fresh and tender. I came home, changed into my running shorts and shoes, popped a new battery into my yellow Walkman, and disappeared for half an hour. I had to run. I had to drive the blood through my body, through my brain, drive the student papers out, let poetry in.

"Annie called again this afternoon," Andrew said, "while you were running. She called about the poem."

"I haven't done it yet." I broke another piece of baguette. I was flying home to Vermont on Saturday to take part in the celebration of my father's new Thomas Aquinas translation. I hadn't read the book yet, either. "I'll do it all this week, when I'm done with grades."

Andrew said he told Annie I'd be catching a midday plane, after my run, and Annie said I'd become addicted to motion, like a Holy Roller. She told Andrew if I arrived any later than 1 p.m., she couldn't pick me up at the airport.

That's because it would be Saturday afternoon, and my father would be serving his traditional tea for the sisters from the college. I could smell sweet brown Guinness pouring out of a Wedgwood spout. "Nothing like cold ale on a summer afternoon," I said.

In Annie's opinion, it wasn't the beer, it was the company, and as Sister Immaculata always said, the talk. Sister Immaculata, the oldest, died at Christmas, but Annie still talked about her as though she were just taking a nap. Sister Fides stopped teaching the year before, but she still joined my father for tea. And Sister Vera would be there, and so would this Sister Hildegard my father had written me about, this newcomer.

"Annie said if you didn't have to run around like a pagan every day, you'd be there to enjoy the company yourself," Andrew said. "But most of all, she wanted to know if you'd written the poem yet."

Annie needed clarity. She needed constancy. She liked to plan ahead, and she didn't like uncertainty. As long as I could remember, she'd been that way. Nobody in the family had changed much in the twenty years since Andrew and I left Vermont, except it used to be my father who would call for poems, back when I was in high school; he'd commission me to invent a poem for his teas with the sisters.

"Saturday, 3 p.m.," he'd say, "a poem to commemorate the Venerable Bede."

And I'd run to the library, search out Bede's obscure soul, doodle with words at the long oak table in the reference room, and snag his bulky spirit into verse. Aurelia thought it was nice the sisters stopped by, to see how the family was doing. My father said the sisters came to do academic work, to retrace the history of knowledge, to remember the history of the Church. Sister Immaculata, Sister Vera, and Sister Fides said there was no difference: the story of knowledge *was* the story of the Church. And my father would pour Guinness Stout from a Wedgwood teapot into the sisters' bone china cups, and they would touch the lips of their teacups together in a salute to the love of knowledge. I used to worry there was something sexual about my father's relationship with the nuns, some craving between my father and those three restrained mysteries. But my father didn't hunger for real women; he was happier with pristine notions like the religious arguments of nuns, Annie playing pure repetitive Bach, me reading the madrigal of the day. Disembodied thoughts—angels dancing on the lips of teacups.

Guinness was the only concession made to the carnal nature that united them all. For me and Annie, tea with lemon and a single spoonful of honey. The only flaunting of the corporeal was done by Aurelia, who thickened her coffee with fresh milk and three tablespoons of chocolate syrup, who made frequent tins of oatmeal and raisin cookies that she stored in the pantry and secretly fed me, along with shots of thick cream from the top of the milk bottle. It had been years since those days. My sister Annie had graduated long ago to sipping stout instead of honey-lemon tea, but she still wasn't at ease with her body. I used to worry that Annie was becoming an Albigensian, all that orthodoxy and so little food, but she insisted she practiced the via media, the middle way.

She was right about my missing tea, though. The day I flew home, I was going to be wedged between maroon and yellow seats one hour from Duluth to Minneapolis, another two and a half hours from Minneapolis to Newark, and an hour again up to Vermont. All that, before the ride north to Lake Memphremagog and Johanna's Cape.

I took the serving bowl and our glasses to the sink and came back for the blue plates and silver. "If I miss the bus, I'll rent a car," I said and left Andrew sitting at the dining table again.

"Annie's final words: tell her she's a whirling dervish. Spin and spin and spin." Andrew was calling out Annie's message to me as though there were walls between us, which there weren't, but we forgot sometimes.

"I feel like I have blood poisoning when I don't run in the morning," I shouted back. Annie didn't like me to shout. Annie was born when my parents lived in Rome and my father worked in Vatican City. The experience seemed to have made her antagonistic toward all but the most regular of practices. She hadn't altered her ways in her metamorphosis into Sister Augustine and back again into plain Sister Anne, the mathematician. I might have been regular, too, if they'd stayed in Rome, right there with the Pope. How could my father leave Rome?

"Think of all the famous souls your father would've missed." Andrew was there, slipping the half-baguette back into its paper sack.

I was rinsing dishes and talking about my students again, telling Andrew how I gave them Aurelia's description of the family's living quarters in the Haifa cloister. "Five old college rooms by the Mediterranean above Elijah's cave. My grandmother's at the end of the hall, then Annie's, my mother and father's, my father's study, and finally the large room close to the public gate— the sitting room where my mother read the French mystics. Aurelia said the mystics were friends of Teresa of Avila, and I asked her once—Aurelia, didn't the mystics and Teresa live in different centuries? Aurelia said they were friends nonetheless."

Aurelia described my mother making real tea for the sisters who strolled from the cloister to the laundry room, their sandals tapping softly against the shiny, brown tile floor. A cup and saucer, three-quarters full with Earl Grey, the rest milk and sugar, a scone, a dab of marmalade, but no clotted cream. No fat products for them.

"Did you tell your class her other stories?"

"About the car?"

"Why they didn't see it?"

"And the nun looking out the window?"

"And going back to Glastonbury?"

"And the way he came home?"

Yes. I told my students about the nun, the one looking out the window, who saw my grandmother gesture toward the sea. Perhaps it was the sea, the nun said, the beauty of the green water or the feel of its soft spray. And there was the man selling nuts on the corner who said my mother was looking toward the sky. So, it may have been the blue of the sky or the yellow of the sun that caught them. And the woman sitting cross-legged outside the church said they were stooped over looking at something in the street, both women, bending over, running their hands through the sand at the edge of the road. Something shiny caught the eye, she was sure, a jewel perhaps, diamond or ruby or maybe a piece of lapis.

And about the women being buried in Israel, the Holy Land, what better place? No relatives left in Glastonbury, no reason to return. But my father went back to Glastonbury, to the top of the Tor, to the place he and my mother embraced under St. Bridget milking the cow, under St. Michael holding the scales, where wind blew around them up from seven plateaus on the mound. He stood there with his girls, and wind blew up around him again. And then he brought us home to Vermont.

16

Aurelia met him at the train, took him home to the house the college gave him, and told him about the job waiting for him in the philosophy department at Stella Maris. Father Louis arranged it all. Father Louis, who had invited the family to Israel for a remarkable year, had once again arranged it all.

And my father, he was like nothing Aurelia'd ever seen, the way he traveled back from sadness—retracing the steps he and his wife had taken from Haifa to Rome to Calais to Dover to Glastonbury and then getting off the train in Johanna's Cape, Vermont, holding the hand of one little girl, carrying the other, the infant, me, in the laundry basket.

Andrew and I had been telling these stories so long we could trade verses, like choristers changing parts. Sometimes, we'd sit like that retelling other stories—stories Aurelia knew about Andrew and his family. Good stories, too, some of them happening on the same day, but somewhere else and to Andrew. We remembered which were his and which were mine as easily as we remembered which of us took photographs when we shared one camera and one roll of film. We stood in a moment together, but time stormed around us at different speeds.

"But none of the magic was in the obituary," I said, and I put the plates in the dishwasher. "I told the class, if I'm not careful, none of it will be in mine either. For instance, in my obituary, the scene on the beach with my father, that should go in there, and the day we turned my father's office and the hall and my room into a shrine of my mother's photos, and the fact that I come from a line of women who sang and danced and looked at the sky and the sea and stooped to touch the earth the day I was born—and the day they died—that's the sort of thing I want in my obituary. I want my students to find moments like those in their own lives and write them, in their obituaries if not before."

Martha said that's not what she wanted to know about me, not what she wanted to know about herself. She wanted to know about passion and love and sex, and what makes a woman weep. She wanted everyone who read her obituary to weep.

I told Martha she had it partly right, but she wanted to know about the passion and love and sex in my life. The man with the fingernails, she said. She wanted to know about me and the man with those fingernails. She'd obviously read my poem. I told the class this final writing assignment was something different, something solitary, a woman writing something about a woman alone. Yes, there was a man in my life, and yes, there was passion, and yes, there would be more love and passion again, but in that moment, I wanted them to write stories about themselves, each one, about herself, as a woman alone.

"And the men in your class?" Andrew asked. "What did the men say?"

"If there were men in the class, I'd include them. It's strange, but no men took writing this term, not even the usual one or two. So, I told them, women all of them, to pick up their pens and start writing about themselves as women wandering this earth, alone. This was a story about daughters and mothers and grandmothers—about us as the women we want to remember before we disappear."

I washed the wineglasses by hand so they wouldn't break, and Andrew took them from the dish drainer, dried them, and hung them upside down from the wooden rack in the cupboard. "You're thinking about going to Haifa again," he said. "Haifa in the summer, this year. I'm afraid you're thinking about going."

"I'd rather not," I said. "Not without you."

"I can't," he said and shook his head. "There's the photo shoot, and then they've got me teaching summer school this year. I can't cancel on them now."

"I'm only going as far as Vermont," I said. "Couldn't you come there?"

"Not next weekend."

I knew he couldn't. Andrew had already told me and my father. He had a contract to shoot five hundred photographs of the roots of native Minnesota flowers for the Ag school; the idea was to pull plants out of the earth, gently brush them off, photograph their roots, and replant them. For Andrew, it was like tagging deer or collaring wolves. The school was going to assemble the photos in a digital botanical catalogue.

"Your father's book signing is the day after the shoot starts. Can't go." He'd be at the experimental Ag station, deep in the Boundary Waters. "He understands. He said he'd be with me there, in spirit."

That was easy for my father to promise. He could travel places in spirit. For Andrew, who tugged now at my arm, travel always had to include body as well.

"They're expecting me. In Vermont, they're expecting me."

"Yes, but Haifa's on your mind. I have a feeling you'll find a reason to go to Haifa."

"Eventually, I'll need to. Eventually. I'll have to see what I don't know."

"Maybe you know enough, already. Maybe there's nothing more to know."

"Perhaps that's what I need to know. That there's nothing more." I took his hands, and he took mine, and we held on, me to him, him to me.

"There'll be no love," he said. "You know, while you're gone, there'll be no love, not for us, not for the animals, not for any creatures."

Sometimes Andrew stretched the point. And he'd been using a

lot of plant and animal images since he'd started teaching in the Ag school.

"I think I know the story," he said.

But I can see now that we didn't know anything about the story. Nothing at all.

I got up before five on the last morning of the quarter and used the old Pyrex pot to make drip coffee, dark and brown, and Scottish oatmeal, the kind you have to cook for half an hour until it softens. It was the morning Andrew was leaving for the Boundary Waters. Before he left, he gave me an enlargement he made of a photo of my mother and her mother and her mother's mother and her mother's aunts, the Morgan girls, on their front porch, ready to tune their instruments and start the music. I sat awhile with the photo, sipping coffee at the kitchen table and writing this poem.

Cave Drawing

Picture the sisters tuning
instruments on the porch
fiddle and mandolin and guitar
those Morgan girls etched on the wall
dancing around the piano
wild girls who play
in the neighborhood band and Grace
who sings on Sundays at her mother's church
and does the jig alone at night when fires light the den
her smoky feet
kick rhythm into breaks in the clay
sisters
meandering into the intricacy of the past
calling, crying, chanting

until the muteness comes
the smudge that covers their lips
so they can only whisper
verses
dried at the edges
ditties
discarded
history misplaced
and no one knows
the tune
or how to play
except the girls
still wild on this cave wall.

Pornography—or, Should Women Have Been Made in the Original Creation?

There were mornings in Duluth when clouds covered my car. They stuck to my windshield like ice. I turned on the heat in my old Volvo, and the blower crackled from a hairpin or a paper clip rattling inside. Two hours after Andrew's leaving, there was still cold fog. It felt like early November in Vermont; it didn't matter to my windshield that it was June. Moments were out of sequence, one exactly like the other, summer like fall. I should have noticed that. That could have been the beginning, but if it were, what exactly were the stages, the steps? I don't think this story had a beginning. There was all the talk of obituaries and missing women, my mother, my grandmother, and Andrew's worry that I'd make the journey to Haifa without him, and my first rereading of Thomas Aquinas in twenty years, and then the not being able to reach Andrew in person again for weeks. That time, even though I'm used to seeing my life in story segments, I didn't notice any beginning at all.

I am a college professor who writes, a writer who teaches, a professor-practitioner they call me now, a poet trying to teach students to tap into the truths they hold inside. Sometimes, like the day I told Andrew about, I made them write obituaries. Sometimes, I made them sit in the quiet. Sometimes, I made them write words on slips of paper and then spill their thoughts all over the page. Once, when I had a class full of cross-country runners, I ran with them—'round and 'round the track inside the mushroom-shaped canvas dome where the football team practiced in winter—we ran until we could run no more, until we could no longer escape our muses.

I pulled away from the house when the blower cleared the vapor off my windshield. Three blocks up, at the stoplight, a woman about fifty was crossing the street with another, an older woman, white-haired, small-boned under a puffy, quilted raincoat. There was wind coming off Lake Superior, and I thought the younger should have gripped the older, held her safe against the morning, but it was the older woman whose hand touched the forearm of the younger, lightly, tentatively, as though she might let go and float away at will. She held on across the intersection. The light turned—red for them, green for me—and I headed down the street toward the university: Thomas Aquinas to finish reading, a poem to write for my father. I envied those women their safe passage across the street; I envied the younger the existence of the elder. I wondered if they were daughter and mother. Or were they sister and sister, like Annie and I in years to come? I didn't think we'd ever shared a safe crossing, other than our trip back from sadness, which I couldn't remember taking. Would we share another crossing, if Annie were there now? If Annie were there, wouldn't she be asking about the poem?

Of course, Annie's request wasn't really out of line. Everybody knew I wrote occasional verse from time to time, wrote on demand for people. I wrote commemorative pieces—an ode for the opening of a new park, sonnets for friends getting married, nursery rhymes for each of their children, blank verse for an English professor who retired. Over the years, the poems drew enough praise that my agent suggested I collect them all into a book and call it *Poetry on Demand*. It came out in the fall one year, in time for Christmas, and it sold as many copies as Martha Stewart's new cookbook. In fact, it tied with *Women MBA's—How Not to Use Your Sex for Success*. When they reviewed me in *Vanity Fair,* an editor went a little overboard and called me a "female Cyrano."

Still, a yellow haze rose from a column by Roger Stone, book editor of the *Duluth Journal,* and an alum of Lake University where I taught. Back in '57, Stone had been editor of the *Lake University Guild Review,* the student literary journal, and he said fidelity to his alma mater drove him to phone me before he published. He was letting me know in advance that he was leery of *Poetry on Demand.*

"Can one write real poetry to commemorate weddings, births, divorces, retirements, and civic holidays?" he asked. "How can one do it? How can a scholar of any stature publish a book of rhymes written on request?"

I said all poems came from the same love, surprise, grief—words. I said a request for a poem was like a warm-up for me, a good stretch. I told him poetry came when I got the words moving. All I had to do was get the words moving.

"Special occasions make me move." I said. "I exercise with words."

"Exercise?" he asked. "Calisthenics?"

"Meditative calisthenics," I liked the analogy. "Pump up the words, that's what I do."

"Pump?"

"Pump and jump," I was playing with words, and I was playing with him. "Let words bump." In fact, I told him, writing was always easier if I lathered myself in a heart-pounding sweat beforehand. Run with thunder first, then lie down in the rain, like a river—pulse, push, pour toward the quiet pool beyond.

This conversation was a mistake. The next Sunday when I opened up the Arts page, there it was—in thirty-six point type. Stone called the book "Workout Rhymes," and he created a new label for me, too: Nin Creed, Aerobic Poet. "Pump-pump-pull-away . . .," the review began.

That aerobic label stuck. The student newspaper caricatured me, running in place while I typed. When one of the TV stations did a special on me, this weird guy started following me on my runs. He had an instant camera, and one day when I stopped to tie my shoe, he snapped a Polaroid and demanded I compose an instant poem for him on the back. My audience was shifting. Dicey sorts of people were following me. Well, not right then; they weren't there all the time, and neither Andrew nor I were alarmed enough to call the police. Not yet.

On the seat next to me was my open tote bag, a large cloth sack I called my "limbo" bag because I kept everything in it I wasn't ready to deal with yet. I looked at my father's photograph on the book jacket of his new translation of Aquinas, there, in the sack. He was waiting for me, for a performance requested by Annie but nonetheless commanded by him. Look at him, standing in the garden at the Aquinas Center, fit and strong, absolutely glowing. Paying attention to his mind all those years seemed to be paying off in the end, seemed to have preserved his body from wear and tear; my father the Thomistic scholar was in his seventies, and he'd just published his nineteenth book. The critics called it his best, brilliant without rival, but then, who was there to compete with him? Young philosophers didn't read Aquinas anymore.

The filter Andrew used when he took that shot gave my father a fine gloss, a whipped glaze of perspiration, evidence of raw humanity I hadn't expected but wasn't surprised Andrew found. There my father was, peeking at me from the limbo bag, reminding me I'd promised to compose a poem dedicated to Thomas for his party. Time was running out, he was saying, only a few days left.

"Of course, Father doesn't know anything about it," Annie had insisted on the phone the night before. "Your poem is to be a surprise, a bit of nostalgia. It was Sister Vera's idea. Get a poem from Nin, she said, just like the old days."

"Is he thinking about retiring?"

"Why should he retire? He's been Stella Maris' Thomist all his life. Is your poem done? You're not really upset about that little passage, are you? It's a party for Father; you could try not to be so political."

The "little" passage Annie was talking about was one where Aquinas says something about nature and its desire to create perfect things; except when it can't, and then it goes ahead and makes things that aren't so perfect—like women—who Aquinas says are misbegotten males. I had never questioned my father's arrangement with Scholasticism, and even now that I'd read this obscure passage as a grown woman, I wasn't inclined to spend our few hours together that weekend arguing. Besides, philosophy was his passion. Poetry was mine. On the other hand, I really did hope he had an explanation for that line.

"When I read those words now, Annie, I bring a new world to them. Hasn't he said anything about the passage?"

"He just translates philosophy, Nin, he doesn't make it up like you make up your poems. Is yours done?"

On its way to being done. I was in the Volvo, turning the corner into the parking lot. Exams were over; my grades were finished, except for handing them in; and students were still asleep—except the unlucky ones who had an exam during the last time slot at 8:30 a.m. that day. Now, just before eight, I was surprised at the number of cars in the faculty lot, fifteen or twenty already. I parked between an old brown Fiat and a newer red car, close to the entrance, across from a row of groundskeeping trucks. I walked across the quadrangle toward Lewis Hall. Peace. Silence. I wondered where the people who'd parked in the faculty lot were. There was nobody else in the hush around my building except John, the handyman, standing on the staircase, staring up at the gargoyle perched on the gutter above the main door.

"Look out there, Professor. The cold froze the bile out of that gatekeeper last night," John chuckled as some kind of yellow-green spit dripped from the gaping granite mouth above the door. "Thirty-eight degrees overnight," John pointed at the new pear trees the regents' committee ordered him to plant in the quadrangle, and he reminded me he'd been against putting in new trees so early in the season. He wouldn't do that at home, he said, always a chance of a cold wind right up until the Fourth of July. It had been warm the week before—lilacs blooming in Canal Park, red tulips here at the edge of the sidewalk, yellow daffodils. But last night a chill took over, and by morning John's flowers were soft as old celery.

"Cold," I said and shivered to show him I believed in what he was saying. "How is it inside?"

He'd turned on the heat "to get the chill off," he said, in the corner of the building where the professors' offices were because he suspected some might be working early in the day, last day of the term. He could do that in Lewis Hall, heat the offices section by section. The old building had fifteen separate chimneys that rose out of the roof, remnants of days when English classrooms were warmed by fireplaces. Now the chimneys were part of a zoned heating system, furnaces that could be controlled, corridor by corridor.

Inside my office, I plugged in the coffeepot I'd set up the afternoon before. The radiator hissed, and I smelled heat—damp and dusty at the same time, like the old soft-paged books my predecessors left, and I had never cleaned off my shelves because removing them felt wrong. It felt like pruning history, cutting up the lives of those who'd passed through that space before me. I couldn't clean them out of my past. There was a red-covered copy of the abridged *Golden Bough* that someone had jotted notes in—they say it was Saul Bellow who borrowed it when he was in Duluth running a workshop. And Allen Tate left a city map. It could have been an important piece of history, maybe a literary treasure, *Tate's Odyssey*, if I ever figured out what he was thinking when he marked the page, where he was going, with whom. I spread my things out on my desk: my father's book, scraps of paper to mark passages I might want to quote, my marbled-cover composition book. I opened the dark green cover and went inside to the white pages until I found one that was empty.

"Good Old Thomas," I penciled at the top—pens would come later, when I was sure. I took my red-orange cup over to the coffeepot and filled it to the rim. I gulped. Hot. I liked it hot, but it was too thin. I'd rushed the pot, poured it while the grounds were still floating. Now I could taste bitterness in the coffee grounds that caught on my tongue. I chewed them as I sat down.

Heat steamed the windows in my office and made the library across the way look like it was standing in a tropical rain forest: vines wrapped around the pillars, almost grown over them, dark and mossy and drooping. Then, for a moment, I thought I saw a face in the cold tropical forest—round, chubby, shaved at the edges, and topped by a furrow of blonde—it looked like Prudence Rodney's face under a broomful of hair, but I didn't expect Prudence to be peering out from behind library pillars at 8:00 a.m. She was a late-afternoon person. She was also the leader and official spokeswoman of the Radical Unbiased Student Union: RUBS-U they called it, students who were most alert later in the day, when they went to the warehouses on the other side of campus to encourage the production of music with a new, no-lyrics sound. A second later and Prudence's face was gone, tapered into library pillars. My imagination was playing with wilted vines dripping in the steam on my window.

I sat down at the oak desk in the corner to get started on my father's poem, took another sip of coffee, and gazed at his photograph there, on the book on my desk, one more book among piles of books. It mixed in, as Prudence's face had, as I did in that room. I could be set on the shelves, and I'd fade in. My hair was dry-book brown; my skin the shade I imagined my mother's— swarthy, like the old photographs taken before I was born, before traffic swallowed her up and left me to be raised by my father. He had such trouble speaking of her, but he spoke to her. I knew he did that, spoke to my mother's ghost. Once I'd seen her photograph and how much we looked alike, I understood what my father was doing when he surveyed me—not me really, more the air around me, until his eyes came to rest on a point in the middle of my forehead, until he acknowledged the other presence. I knew he was communicating with her when he looked at me like that, and I would stare back, unrelenting in my glance, trying to yank his soul into his eyes so that he would have to engage himself with me—and me alone. I could never catch him, however, and as I grew older, I began to wish I could talk to the companion he seemed to think I carried around with me, the beautiful sepia stranger in the pictures who faded into my own beige skin the way a lioness blends into a dusty hill.

I looked away from my father's photo, stood, and walked over to the file cabinet. Reading Aquinas at this stage was hard on me. It was making me wonder if my father had been staring at me all my life because he was checking to see if I was "misbegotten." Who was this Aquinas, anyway? I mean, I knew who he was. My father talked about him in some way or another in every dinner conversation all my life. In college at Stella Maris, we had to do eight semesters of philosophy, and that meant Aquinas and Aristotle and Plato and Socrates. No other courses offered. Back then, all I did was memorize theories, questions, answers. I never asked if Aquinas had a life outside his mind. Didn't he have a mother either? Didn't he have a woman whose knuckles he loved?

There I was, arguing the other side of the obituary question. First I wanted my students to consider the life of a woman's mind, and then I wanted something more than mind in this man's life story. I wanted to know what he did when he saw flowers. Did he like flowers? Did he go out in the fresh air? Did he enjoy food? Actually, I was trying to amuse myself—like a wild cat, dry, brown dirt kicking up around my feet, my writing hand ready to break into a slow deliberate trot, to quicken its stride, lope alongside, run and tumble Thomas' image into the dust, grip his words in my teeth, swallow, and write. Even so, the poem wouldn't come. I was trying to find something playful and celebratory, but reading Aquinas that morning was not putting me in a playful mood. Why did I wait until now to take this guy seriously? In my memories, I saw my father sitting at his old school desk in the sunroom at the front of the house, translating. I had no memory of shock at the words Aquinas used or the questions Aquinas asked, questions like, "Should woman have been made in the original creation?" I shouted the question out loud, and then, to myself or my father or his editors, I yelled in the same loud voice, "How could you be allowed to publish such a blasphemous question?"

"Blasphemy. Now that's a strong word."

I looked up and saw Harry standing in my doorway. Harry taught linguistics. His was the last exam of the term, scheduled to start in twenty minutes.

"Who's blasphemous?" he asked.

"Thomas Aquinas," I answered and waved the book in my hand.

"I wouldn't have expected it from you," Harry said. "Didn't you teach Rushdie?"

"That's different."

"Well, blasphemy being blasphemy, you wouldn't censor Aquinas, would you?"

"I'm not censoring."

"What are you proposing?" Harry loved words. He loved making people define them. He reached into the pocket of his jeans and pulled out a grocery store receipt. He'd written something on the back. "It's like this piece of graffiti I saw this morning. 'God=Dog.' It was written on the side of a church. Should anybody be allowed to write this? Shouldn't we ban the sale of spray paint?"

"You're talking about prior restraint, and Thomas Aquinas has never been restrained. He's had plenty opportunity to bargain in the marketplace of ideas."

"But now? Can't he even ask a question . . . "

"Well, of course, he's free to pose a question, and I'm free to call it blasphemous," I insisted.

"And the others? Ready to call them all blasphemers?"

Suddenly there was a noise down the hall, a squeal and a roar and a deep pulsating beat all at once. Over that sound came an unbearable chant, "RUBS-U, RUBS-U, RUBS-U-2 . . . "

Harry spun around and said he was getting out of there while he could, test in ten minutes. "Grab your books. Shut your door," he said. "Don't forget it's Remembrance Day. They'll snare you if you don't get away."

I grabbed my notebook and my father's book and slammed my door behind me. When the students turned the corner, we were gone, down the stairs and gone.

Remembrance Day is what we called the last day of exams, not because anybody was remembering what they needed to know for class, but because back in the early seventies there had been a sort of riot on campus, one that bubbled up out of frustration over Vietnam and loss of power and yearning for peace and general *angst* over the last day of the term. There had been fires, a small fire and a big fire, and there were stories of naked bosoms, students' and professors' bosoms, because they stripped off their blouses and bras and threw them onto the flames in sympathy with their brothers whose draft cards were burning. "Hell, no, we won't go," yelled the men. "Rah, rah, burn the bra," yelled the women. And the wind carried a fragment of a burning bra or a draft card or both, up and out of the bonfire and over to the trash bins at the side of the admissions office where one thousand already-acted-upon files had been discarded and soon began to smolder. No one noticed until it was too late that the Administration Tower was on fire. That's when fire engines, police dogs, and FBI agents joined the crowd.

"We never would have burned our bras if the press hadn't suggested it," a history professor who stripped told me years later. "I mean, bras never were the issue."

So the next year, Lake University established a day on which students could control the issue, or have a measure of control. It was to be the last day of the term, after the last exam was done. There were teach-ins, sing-alongs, read-ins, art sales, and by the time I started teaching there, Remembrance Day had become a food festival with tacos, enchiladas, falafel, pita sandwiches, and turkey legs. At noon, technology students who designed solar vehicles raced sun-powered go-carts around the quad. It was a celebration, and I liked it. Actually, that's why I'd gone to work in my office that day; that and the fact I had to turn in my grades. The spring quarter ran long, well into June, and I enjoyed the end-of-term enthusiasm. Harry wasn't ready to enjoy it because he hadn't given his exam yet. I retreated with him because the festivities really weren't supposed to start until after the last exam period, and I needed to get my poem written.

Harry and I made it out the door, and he ran across the street to his classroom. I took another set of stairs down to the tunnel that led to the basement of the library. It was quiet there in the stacks, and I found a long empty table next to the oak card catalogue. They'd moved it down there when the library was computerized, but I still used it whenever I looked for old books because I couldn't resist the sound of the drawers gliding open, the smell of old damp paper cards, the feel of dull edges slipping against my fingers as I paged through titles and names. What was I looking for now, standing there with the "Sch" drawer open in front of me? Schopenhauer? Did I want to revel in Schopenhauer's card or keep paging through to Scholasticism? It could be that Schopenhauer had said something equally as appalling as Thomas Aquinas, and if I were upstairs using the computerized catalogue the thought would never have occurred to me. Meanwhile, these oak drawers slid open and whimsically, promiscuously, made offers. I found a call number for Schopenhauer, went back into the stacks, and picked a book off the shelf. Women, Schopenhauer said, were members of "an undersized, narrow-shouldered, broad-hipped, short-legged race." And perhaps to clarify, he also said women were "The Number Two of the human race." I smiled.

34

Greg, the reference librarian, had been watching me. "I see you're finding everything," he said. I could tell he wanted to know why I was smiling over Schopenhauer, but he was wary of infringing on a researcher's privacy, cautious about the way he offered help. "Is there anything I can help you locate?"

"I'm looking for obnoxious things said about women by famous men," I answered.

"Well, you've come to the right place," he waved his hand toward the shelves, promised to find me more, and disappeared behind a row of books.

I took Schopenhauer back to my table by the card catalogue. There, next to my notebook, I'd left my father's translation open to Aquinas' question: should woman have been made in the original creation? What was Aquinas' answer? How had my father dealt with that line? I remembered Annie's quick defense again. He's just a translator. He doesn't make this up. He just puts it in English. What he put in English was that Thomas thought there were two ways to consider the issue. It seemed to Thomas that woman shouldn't have been created. After all, Aristotle pointed out that woman was misbegotten, and nothing misbegotten should have existed before "the fall." But then, Thomas argued with himself. He said nature produced females because of some outside influence on the male seed, like a moist wind from the south, and then he referred to Aristotle again: nature must have intended the production of occasional females because God was the author of nature, and anything nature did was intended by God, so woman *had* to be created, deficient as she was, because that was God's authorial intent. God the author—not the translator, not the photographer, not the reference librarian. God was writing this one, all alone. God the author. He writes it into the scene; we play by his rules.

Greg was back with a handful of books. "Here's Confucius, saying 'Women and uneducated people are the most difficult to deal with.' Is that the sort of thing you're looking for? There's also the Chinese proverb: *'Tsung fu, 'tsung fu, 'tsung tzu.'*"

"Which means?"

"Obey the father, obey the husband, obey the son."

"Number two of the human race," I said and opened Schopenhauer to the broad-hipped reference. "Look what I found in Schopenhauer."

"He sounds a lot like Luther." Greg was holding a small maroon book, the word *Tischreden* pressed into the cover, and as he opened it, a fleck of brown parchment floated to the floor. Greg flipped through the yellowed pages near the back until he found a series of short tracts marked with Roman numerals. "This one," he pointed at the letters *DCCXXV* and read, "Men have broad and large chests, and small narrow hips, and more understanding than the women, who have but small and narrow breasts, and broad hips, to the end they should remain at home, sit still, keep house, and bear and bring up children."

What was with the fixation on shoulders and hips? "Is this chest-hips-understanding thing a popular *non sequitur* or what?"

"Pretty clear who Schopenhauer was following," Greg said and went back to the stack of books he'd set on the card catalogue. "Here's a few more. You've heard of someone named John Chrysostom, around the year three or four hundred? Get this. 'Physical beauty is only skin deep. If men could see beneath the skin, the sight of women would make them nauseous . . . Since we are loath to touch spittle or dung even with our fingertips, how can we desire to embrace such a sack of dung?' And it gets worse. Augustine. Ready for him?"

I wasn't sure I was. "I'll read it myself," I said. "I mean, not out loud." I took the black cloth book from him and opened it to the

36

page he'd marked with a pink Post-It note. Augustine had written, "We are born between urine and feces."

"Augustine's stuff makes Luther's discussion of the nobility of dying in childbirth seem almost sensitive," Greg said as he handed me Volume 45 of *Luther's Works*. "To find that much only took nine minutes; I timed it. Spend the day here, and you'll really get depressed." Greg said he needed coffee before he read one more word. He said he'd bring me coffee, too, and a passage from Kierkegaard's journal about Scheherazade.

When Greg had been gone about five minutes and I had seven books open in front of me on the table, I heard the sound again, the screeching that had sent Harry and me running from our offices. They came from film history, out from behind Fellini, a crowd—a guitarist, a small person pushing a steel drum on rollers, another with a keyboard strapped as though it were an accordion, two people who appeared very tall because they were wearing trash barrels on their feet, downhill bindings holding them to their huge ski boots, one with a small chain saw, or was it a gas-powered hedge trimmer? And maybe ten more, all wearing the white faces of mime and curly royal-blue wigs and led by Prudence Rodney and Barbara Pierson, one of my students.

"Shhh," I whispered, "This is the library."

"Professor Creed," Prudence announced, "this is the anniversary of the 1971 Takeover, and we are here to commemorate the event." The squeal and roar and drumbeat of new music grew louder for ten, maybe twenty seconds, then stopped. Silence. Nothing.

Prudence, whose voice was gravelly like a voice that shouts at sporting events, had been yelling "RUBS-U, RUBS-U, RUBS-U-2" as she approached, but now she was as speechless as her army of mimes. Instead of talking, Prudence unfolded a letter, which appeared to have been typed on the university's letterhead and seemed to have been signed by the president of the university. She handed it to Barbara, who handed it to me. I read it.

Dear Faculty Member,

The Radical Unbiased Student Union has been granted permission to commemorate the 1971 University Takeover in a peaceful demonstration designed to raise funds for the dedication of a "New Music Room" to be housed in the Dorati Center for the Performing Arts. They have permission to take you to a "jail" that they have constructed for the day. There, you will be asked to meet your ransom by performing tasks such as lecturing on a topic, solving a math problem, conjugating a number of verbs, or in the case of a writer, creating a poem. (Professors of medicine and pharmacology will not be expected to dispense drugs.) Please get into the spirit and enjoy the festivities surrounding this positive commemoration of an event that is burned into the history of the university.

Sincerely,
Kevin A. Galtier, Ph.D.
President, Lake University

P.S. RUBS-U has guaranteed there will be no fires.

I gave Prudence back the letter and said it was great, I'd be out to see how they were doing as soon as I finished writing the poem I had to write for my father, as soon as I'd read passages from these seven books open on the table, books I was not enjoying much because, quite frankly, the authors were antifemale. But they weren't interested in my schedule.

Barbara Pierson took a round sticker out of her pocket, a sticker the size of a softball, white with red letters, that said, "Offensive to Women," and slapped it over the jacket of my father's book. Then she slapped another "Offensive to Women" sticker on Confucius and another "Offensive to Women" sticker on Luther, and slap, slap, another on Chrysostom and Augustine.

"Barbara," I was surprised. She was usually very polite.

"She's not talking today," Prudence interrupted.

"Why?"

"She's out to stop offensive speech."

"But why can't you speak?" I turned back to Barbara, but she said nothing.

"Nobody's ever been hurt by the voice of a mute," Prudence answered for her. "We've joined together, Barbara's group and RUBS-U, to demonstrate we have a similar cause."

I knew some of the students had joined a local group that had been visiting discount stores and slapping these red and white stickers on CDs they found offensive, but now, thanks to Barbara, they'd expanded to philosophy. And could I blame them? Wasn't this the material that invited women to be burned and their ashes scattered across millennia?

"We're out to rid language of all offensive words," Prudence said, "rid the world of offensive thought."

Prudence and her group started a few months before, demanding a lyric-free spring dance, and they hired a deejay who played instrumentals only. "No Karaoke is Good Karaoke," read a poster advertising the dance. And then RUBS-U representatives went to the faculty senate trying to get a speech code passed, one that would have established shunning as a punishment for offensive speech committed by students and professors alike. Since the shunning would have included not responding in class—neither orally nor in writing—the faculty came out against the code.

Barbara took a notepad out of her left pocket and wrote, "This is what you said we should do. Remember? You made us sit outside and listen to the earth raining silence."

"Yes, but I don't think this is what I had in mind." They were a carnival troupe of primal mutes, medieval Lollards, Ellen Jamesians. Not what I had envisioned when I suggested that my creative writing students sit in silence and listen.

Barbara had more quotes from me. "Be gently radical. Slip into silence like dusk into night. Hold loosely the reins of nothingness."

I said those things? I guess I had. They sounded familiar.

"We'd like you to come with us now, Professor," said Prudence, who was the only one talking.

Perhaps it wouldn't be any worse than the time I offered to be an inmate of the Cancer Society Jail at the shopping center; an hour to get the necessary pledges, and I would be back in my office working on the piece for my father. I really would rather have volunteered later in the day. I didn't want to be interrupted at that point, so I looked Prudence Rodney in the eye and asked, "What if I say, 'Hell, no. I won't go?'"

At that point, the screech and drumroll started again, and I felt myself being lifted off the floor, my feet running on air, not touching ground, making no progress, yet not being propelled out of the library, just held there, above it all, by mimes wearing trash barrels. I was being kidnapped by a circus.

"I expected more from a child of the sixties," Prudence was speaking again. "You of all people should remember what the Takeover was all about." She motioned to the mimes, and they set me back down.

"It happened in 1971," I said. I was at Stella Maris in 1971, a college student myself.

"So?"

"So that was the seventies . . . "

"Not necessarily," Prudence said. "A lot of the sixties happened in the seventies. Like Nixon. And Watergate. And the end of the war. And Jimmy and Janis." Things musicians understood, she said, and that's why so many student groups had joined with RUBS-U, to find a musical solution to speech problems.

Then Prudence asked me what I needed when I wrote poems.

"Memories, like Rilke says, of nights of love, and of women giving birth and of sitting beside the dying . . . "

"I mean like a laptop or something," Prudence said. "When you do these instant poems you're famous for. You use a computer, don't you?"

"I write in my notebook."

Prudence squinted at me, as though the word "notebook" were in another language. "Get with the 00s, Professor."

"The ooze?"

"Zeroes. Naughts. Ciphers. In this millennium, you publish on the web or your work disappears, just like in the dark ages. Don't you write your poems on a laptop?"

"You want poems from me?" I asked. "Words? Written down? Not silence?"

Prudence said they'd decided while I was in their custody, I would have to let my writing lie fallow, and people would pay to watch me *not* write.

There was fanfare from the mimes.

To me, it sounded like the literary equivalent of a soil bank, the federal program that pays farmers for *not* planting crops. "Why do you want me to bring my laptop, then?"

"Symbols," Prudence said, "symbols." Then she shouted, "Baby buggy," and the mimes who had held me in the air picked me up again. They grabbed me under my knees like I was two years old. Within minutes, I was down the hall, and Prudence and the musicians and the rest of the mimes were behind me. I was

41

carried like that all the way to the portico at the front of the library, where RUBS-U had erected jail cells out of wooden slats, and they opened a door—it was more like a gate in a very tall snow fence—and set me down inside on a bench next to a picnic table. Barbara dropped another note. "Sorry. We'll keep it pleasant."

She was normally a temperate student, and this silence of hers seemed to be causing her stress; in fact, she looked as though she might abandon her embryonic insurgency at any moment. "I'm fine," I assured her through the slats. "I'll enjoy the day." After all, I was in favor of radicalism; I was in favor of this event. I always had been.

"Stockholm syndrome," said Greg as he handed me a Styrofoam cup of coffee through the slats. "Captive sympathizes with the captor. Want a bagel?" He was holding a paper plate of tiny bagels; I thought they should be called silver-dollar-sized, although I hadn't seen a silver dollar since I was a child, but they were about the diameter of the pancakes that are called "Silver Dollar Hot Cakes" on menus in truck stops.

I took the coffee and left the bagels. "I don't want her to worry," I said. "She's a good student."

"Already you're identifying with the oppressor."

Greg shook his head and pointed at two broken slats in the back of the cage. "You could shoulder your way out, and still you don't leave."

"I'm not against the students learning the rudiments of rebellion," I said.

"Isn't the real revolution to be accomplished in the stacks where we left the great thinkers of the Western World?"

John, the handyman, was standing outside the cell, and he took one of Greg's bagels. "They'll get a decent ransom for her, famous poet like her, she's gonna draw a big price and be out in no time."

They were asking two dollars a page for me (five if you couldn't show a valid student ID). In return, I was supposed to sign blank pages. Prudence had a table set up with a ream of paper and a handful of pens and pencils, but I refused. What if somebody wrote something above my signature and pretended it was mine? It was too risky.

"Nada," said Prudence.

"What?"

"Write the letters N-A-D-A—*nada, nothing*—across the paper, and sign that."

"I think it's someone else's line."

"You can't copyright *nothing*."

I looked around for Greg, thinking he'd help me with this point, help clarify the nuances of plagiarism and copyright law for Prudence, but he was gone. So, I said I'd write *nothing*, not *nada*. And I tried it. But one *nothing* didn't fill the page. I wrote another *nothing*, and another.

"*Nothing . . . nothing . . . nothing.* Nin Creed"—two dollars and I was signing *nothing* for graduation cards, *nothing* for birthdays, *nothing* for anniversary limericks. Prudence and the mimes even decided *nothing* lyrics could be inserted instead of grunts and moans for the songs the RUBS-U band performed. It was 10:30 a.m. The mimes had made one small step from preverbal to verbal, and I had earned them $180 by writing nothing.

"I knew you'd be a good one," John told me when he brought me a hot dog with mustard.

"Tofu?" I asked. Andrew and I had been avoiding meat lately, at least in some forms, like hot dogs.

"'Fraid not," John said, as he reached through the fence and took back the hot dog. "But you can have these tortilla chips instead." He gave me a paper basket of corn chips with yellow cheese melted over the top.

It seemed early in the day for nachos, even though I'd already lost two hours and felt that my volunteer stint ought to be over. "I've got work to do," I called to Prudence, pointing at my wristwatch, "time for me to go."

"What work, Professor?" Prudence asked.

"Like I said, a poem for my father in honor of his new translation of Thomas Aquinas."

"Pornography," Prudence said. "He's antifemale, and on top of that, he's obsolete. Anybody ever hear of Aquinas?"

"Nothing . . . nothing . . . nothing . . . ," chanted the mimes.

"How can you perpetrate this pornography?" Prudence asked. "Nothing you or your father or your poems or nature itself can do to perfect something that's less than perfect . . . "

I had never thought of Prudence as a Thomist, but there was a ring to her argument that reminded me of my father's translation.

"Philosophy kills," she shouted.

The president of the university was walking up the library steps toward me. He went to the microphone next to the drum set, stood quietly for a moment, then reached into his back trouser pocket, tugged until his billfold came free, removed a single bill, turned to me and nodded, then turned to the crowd and spoke. "I personally pledge fifty dollars for the release of Nin Creed if you're willing to let her write just one poem, right here, while we watch. Fifty dollars toward the poem on Aquinas for her father!" The president grinned and held the fifty-dollar bill high, so everyone could see it. "All in good fun!" he said and waved the bill at me while RUBS-U rolled the drums.

"Another fifty dollars," said a man standing there, in front of my crate. He had a small, black leather case, maybe a checkbook, in his left hand. He was a balding man, with a rim of red-sand hair just above his ears. He slid a set of black plastic half-glasses from the pocket of his pinstriped shirt and perched them on his nose. When he tilted his fountain pen to sign his name at the bottom edge of his check, I saw the blue-stoned Lake U class ring on his third finger. "I'll contribute an additional fifty dollars for the opportunity to watch Ms. Nin Creed, aerobic poet, give her father his poem on demand." It was Stone, alumnus and book editor. "Getting a chance to do your calisthenics today?" he inquired, smiling.

Stone was a problem. Even if he was an alum, he shouldn't have been there, shouldn't have mixed in a student event. It was annoying.

"Wordmonger," the sound came without a face from the crowd of mimes.

"Poetry is graffiti," again out of the crowd of mimes.

"Philosophy is pornography," more words without a face. The mimes were breaking their silence.

I went back to my seat at the picnic table, roped off from the rest of the supposedly silent world, set apart from nonword-mongers. My snow-fence graffiti booth reminded me of the section behind plastic slats where they kept blue movies in the unsavory news-tobacco-and-bookstore downtown.

When I looked up, Stone was pointing at the red-and-white-checked cardboard tray next to me on the bench. "I believe I saw you jotting something on the back of that nachos basket. Did you start your father's poem on that?" The question sounded like my sister Annie's, but it was Stone's.

Stone was right. I had started a poem on the nachos plate, but only one line before I began to worry that if I wrote it down on paper, it would become accessible to this circus. There, in my head, my poem was pure, unblemished, sheltered. But was a poem a poem if it never mixed with physical stuff? "No ideas but in things," William Carlos Williams had written, and I believed him. But did that make poems material rather than spiritual or intellectual? Was the poem the thing before it was a thing? Before

45

it was mixed with words or only after? And what were words to a writer if they were never written down?

"I think she's already done," Stone said.

"Where?"

"In her head," he said.

Prudence began to clap and chant "RUBS-U, RUBS-U," and they all began to stamp their feet and join in the chant. My father wouldn't understand this. They didn't do things like this at Stella Maris. There were rules at Stella Maris, and rules were kept. Rules and order. On the other hand, if I told Annie about having to compose the poem under pressure, Annie would have said, "You do that all the time. That's what God gave you a facility for."

Prudence handed me a piece of white bond; it was empty—no "nothings" written across this one. I went back to my bench and sat. It was a moral dilemma. To write or to maintain silence. Was this atmosphere safe for the poem? Was this why cultures resisted writing? To keep the sacred out of the hands of the oppressor? Was this a reason to cling to the oral tradition?

"Shhh," Prudence hushed the mimes, who had begun to mumble among themselves.

"Not exactly instant verse," Stone said.

I had never said my poems were instant. I simply said I wrote on demand. And Stone was demanding too much. No, I couldn't. I decided to compose the poem in my head only, nothing on paper. I'd recite this poem, and they'd let me go, but I wouldn't give Stone a copy.

"Stand and deliver," Prudence yelled.

"All right," I said, and I stood and pressed my left hand along my spine and stretched. My back hurt, low, just above my hips. I had turned to concrete, sitting there, debating the use of words. I stepped slowly out of the cage and stood by the microphone. "It's called, 'On the Soul.'"

There was a drumroll from RUBS-U.

"It's a rhyme, just this side of a limerick." I didn't usually do rhyme, but rhyme helped me remember my poem, stanza by stanza. Another drumroll, and I recited.

On the Soul

Now here's something
Really rotten.
Aquinas thinks
I'm misbegotten.

Thomas sits at his
Great round desk,
Hole cut out for
Stomach and chest,

Pondering what
The philosopher wrote,
Here and there
Jotting down a quote.

Wondering aloud
What nature would do
If it had to recreate
Me . . . and you.

Nature, it seems,
Has a predilection
For producing souls
Of Great Perfection.

But when the best
Is not achievable
It goes ahead with
What's conceivable.

This "dynamis" breathes on,
Just for sport,
And generates a creature
Of a lesser sort.

What do you get then?
Flowers? Trees?
Rocks? Moss?
Earthworms? Fleas?

Here's where Thomas'
Good sense fails:
It's women, he says. They're
Misbegotten males.

He claims The Philosopher
Took the first shot
And called a woman
Misbegot.

But Thomas, tell me,
Tête à tête,
Whose fault is it
To misbeget?

And why not let the
Syllogism thicken?
Which came first,
The sperm or the chicken?

Look at God's wonder
From my toes to my hat . . .
You really think
She misbegat?

"Is she a good poet?" Prudence asked Roger Stone.

"She's an aerobic poet," Stone said and handed her a check for fifty dollars.

"But is she a radical feminist poet?" Prudence asked.

"I'll go back to my office. I'll study the poem. I'll write my column, and then you'll know."

"Give him a copy," Prudence said. "He'll need a copy of the poem."

"There are no copies," I announced. "I've composed it in the oral tradition."

Stone opened the small, black, leather case he'd been fiddling with while I read. "This," he said, "is the new oral tradition."

"What is it?" Prudence asked.

"Might be a computer pad," said one of the mimes who had finally decided to speak, but I didn't think a computer could be that small. It was his checkbook, I was sure, unless the man was emptier than I'd originally guessed.

"Watch for his column," Prudence announced over the P.A. "Remember, RUBS-U was in charge."

RUBS-U was still playing as I walked back to my office in Lewis Hall to pick up my satchelful of books. Win or lose, my joust with Stone was over, and my forced volunteer stint for RUBS-U was finished. School was done for another year. I had answered Annie's challenge; I had written a poem for my father. It wasn't celebratory, but it was sort of playful. Annie wouldn't like it; my father would find it oddly endearing, like he found everything I did; and there was a chance it might start a discussion that was long overdue. Annoying as the day had been, it would have been a good one to ruminate over with Andrew, but he was on his way to the nature camp in the Boundary Waters to photograph the roots of five hundred flowers, and I was going home to pack for a trip to Vermont.

I walked across campus to the registrar's office and turned in my grades. It was summer. I was free to do nothing.

Oral Tradition

g began to notice I was missing things the next day. I missed my connection in Newark, so when I did catch another flight, and the plane glided down between the Adirondacks and the round Green Mountains, I was three hours later than I expected. I had not only missed tea, I had missed dinner, I had missed Annie, and I had missed my father. His habit of going to bed every night at ten was ingrained and unalterable. The last Greyhound snorted and pulled away from Lake Champlain minutes before I reached the station, so I hailed a cab back to the airport to rent a car. The cabby drove me through Burlington, past the downtown mall, where I could see chairs tilted against small round tables at Timothy's, my favorite sidewalk café; it was late for dinner in Vermont. At the airport, the only car left was a small yellow Escort. I tossed my things in the trunk and drove out of town, onto the interstate, and up into the hills. Then I headed north on 100, edging along the dark road through Stowe. I was almost home. My shoulders dropped, relaxing my neck and my arms. Tension left the bridge of my nose and the muscles under my eyes. I always felt release when I was in these hills, near mountain towns where houses pushed their back doors up against grey granite walls and gardens settled in on natural stone steps, where the largest town was still not big enough to be classified a city. Vermont was a chain of small towns, at the top or at the bottom or in between the hills, like my hometown, Johanna's Cape, named for the woman who took off her cape in the middle of a winter storm and spread it between the hills to protect and heal the Green Mountain Boys.

"Was there really a Johanna?" I asked one day when I was a child.

"Certainly was, Nin," Aurelia said. She claimed she knew Johanna—or somebody who was a lot like her.

"When did she die?"

"People like Johanna don't die," Aurelia had insisted. "They melt into the hills, but they always come back when it gets warm and the blue flowers start crawling out of the granite in the mountains."

Two and a half hours later, I turned north at Newport, where the highway makes a Y with the county road, and left where the Dairy Dream stands alone at the end of a peninsula of grass. I worked there during high school, pouring frozen custard from the slick aluminum machine, twisting the cone in my hand so the ice cream wound in soft curves to a curl at the top. I headed into the pines that stretched along the edge of Lake Memphremagog, up the hill to shops and houses and churches and the college. "Johanna's Cape," the sign said.

The town was silent. I drove to the dark brick bungalow with the brown wooden porch. Vines were beginning to climb up the front of the house. A few tendrils twisted up the pillar at one corner. The lamp in my father's sunroom library cast a golden pink warmth through the windows, and I wondered if he'd actually waited up for me. I was anxious to talk to him about Thomas. But it was Aurelia who opened the front door and came running down the walk. She seemed ageless in her cotton robe and furry pink slippers. She scooped me into her arms and squeezed. "You are the latest thing . . .," she said and took my backpack.

Aurelia led me straight upstairs to my room. She brought Port wine and Vermont cheddar and told me Andrew had called to say he was off to live in a tent and wouldn't be near a phone again for quite a while. Then she said, "You're busy with your thoughts," and went to her own bed.

Aurelia didn't invade a person's mind. So, my first poem and my second, the one I wrote late at night sipping the wine and nibbling cheese in my father's house, were still there, clear and easy to recall in the morning when I woke up and discovered my father had gone over to the convent to attend Mass with Annie. I was disappointed that I didn't see him. Still, not seeing anyone but Aurelia made it easy for me to keep my poetry clear in my head. Reciting poetry orally would not be difficult. Once I got the hang of it, I might add more "body English"—like the Russian poets— or was it "body Russian" when they unfolded their arms, unwrapped their words, and tossed them out to the audience?

I uttered the new poem to myself, still self-conscious and cautious in comparison to my image of a Russian wandering back and forth across a stage, taunting the audience. I spoke my poem quietly, one more time before walking to the Dominican priory where Annie, my father, and the rest were already inside, behind the closed French doors, behind Thomas, whose marble statue stood in the garden courtyard in front of the pale yellow stone colonial. I knew Thomas would be staring at me when I walked the gravel pathway to the Aquinas Center.

Was that path gravel or cinders? The rough, stony bits seemed to be pieces of coal or ash; they had sharp irregularities here and there, even though most had been evened by wear, pushed flat and shiny into the dry hard ground by people like me, walking up the long path through tall pines at the front of the property. The Dominicans who ran this place had planted slim pines that were different from the bold, fat-trunked northern evergreens I was used to in Minnesota. The pines in Thomas' yard were thin-armed and feathery like ferns, but they were tall, and their needles were delicate, frayed, long, and dry. The small woods in front of the Aquinas Center looked like a place where old women hung their lace mantillas, mantilla after mantilla draped over thin branches, suspended there in the breeze, drying there until the old ones came back to claim them.

I breathed deeply, and dusty pine entered my nose and mouth, rolled over my tongue to the back of my throat, and made me cough. I coughed again and stopped. I was halfway up the path, and I could still see the statue of Thomas watching me approach—Thomas standing on a pedestal, ferns at his feet, holly bushes beside him, ivy trailing down to the ground and following the cinder path all the way to where I had decided to stop by the grey granite bench. Annie must be busy setting out food, straightening chairs, stacking up piles of the book—the book I had carried around in my limbo bag and finally read cover to cover the day before on the plane.

I had never paid that kind of attention to my father's books before, and that was troubling; we were close; we were friends. Two academics, two colleagues, as close as father and daughter could be. Had I rejected his ideas out of hand, or had I accepted them without question? Both? Could I do both? Wasn't it an infraction of a rule? It felt contrary to one of those laws that rested in the back of my life: no one can swim within an hour after lunch; something cannot be affirmed and denied at the same time; the whole is greater than its parts; two things equal to the same thing are equal to each other; everyone must keep baking soda in the refrigerator; women must not walk alone after dark; and we can't have our cake and eat it, too. Who questioned rules like those?

But there I was, reading Aquinas and wanting very much to swim right after lunch, to toss out the soda, to refuse to take two dimes and a nickel instead of a quarter regardless of whether they were both twenty-five cents, to accept my father's beliefs and reject them at the same time. There was a fly on my leg as I stood on the cinder path, and I stamped my feet to scare the creature away and slapped at it with my open hand. It flew off into the green webs of lace hanging from the trees. Lace mantillas. The illusion was satisfying. The only relics left of women who were sacrificed to ideas philosophers had conjured up and I was beginning to question.

I walked toward the marble Thomas, who was grasping a book to his chest, the words toward his heart. I wanted to see what Thomas was reading, what author's intent he had been considering at the moment he was cast into stone. What made him point the forefinger of his left hand down, toward the bottom of his page as though he wanted the reader to consider footnotes? Maybe they were the same footnotes about Aristotle, Augustine, or Gregory that I had read at the bottom of the pages in my father's translation. Augustine. Thank God Annie'd changed her name. That guy was afraid to look at women; he didn't think women were made in the image of God. And Gregory? Gregory said woman was slow and unstable and suited only for animal sex and motherhood.

And Aristotle? The old father of them all? The one they called "The Philosopher," as though there really was only one philosopher? His footnotes were on almost every page of Aquinas' thoughts. Aristotle was intrusive. Here was a man fooling around with a woman's biology as well as her metaphysics and mixing the two together, alchemy tainted with calumny. At least it was obvious that he was wrong. At least nobody called Aristotle "The Gynecologist," and I could see why, but Aristotle was persuasive even when he was wrong, and Aquinas was certainly swayed by his nonsense. And my father? Why was he perpetuating it? Did a translator have any responsibility at all? He translated Thomas, who interpreted Aristotle, who claimed to understand God. Was his work invisible? Or was he coauthor? If he had a part, and it wasn't a part in blasphemy, what was it he had a part in? Something subliminal? Hardly. This stuff was hardly subliminal. It was in-your-face, obvious, and blatant. Certainly offensive enough to women to merit red and white stickers. Barbara and Prudence were right. Good thing this stuff was cordoned off in the corner of campus, in the Aquinas Center, behind leaded-glass French doors, separated from *decent* ideas by this curtain of pine-webbed mantillas.

"Philosophy kills," I repeated Prudence's words, and I was surprised how I sounded. After all, I wasn't a firebrand like Prudence. I was a poet, a poet who stood for absolute artistic freedom. Suggesting the defacement of the written word left images in my mind of crowds dancing around bonfires of burning books, and my face was there in the crowd, not the face of a vandal but a nice face, burning books out of principle the way the Christians burned the works of Sappho. Okay, so I wouldn't paint a purdah over Thomas. I'd let him pose a question; even Aquinas had a right to pose a question, no matter how offensive. But I had a right to be offended, a right to react, a right to beat his pornographic philosophy into poems.

I plucked a shiny green leaf from one of Thomas' holly bushes and turned toward the door. It was open, and my father was standing there. He was smiling, and he looked like he was still wearing that gloss of frothy humanity I had taken for Andrew's photographic trick when I saw his picture. He had on a new suit. He never dressed up in anything other than his tweed professor's jackets or his navy wool pinstriped, and now he was wearing a suit that was halfway between khaki and Casablanca white, and it made him look tan. He was holding branches of palms in his right hand, and there was a black garment of some kind draped over his left arm.

"Nina," he said, stretching his arms enough to touch the edges of the door frame, "Nina, you've made it to our party. Come, help me dress up Thomas." He told me it was Sister Hildegard's idea to put an academic gown on Thomas to spruce him up a bit, and the palms were Hildegard's idea, too. He was to tape them so it looked like Thomas was holding them. She'd had a dream about Thomas, waving palms at a college football game. "Hildegard has dreams," he said. "They're extremely entertaining. You'll help, won't you? Even if you're angry at Thomas and me?"

So, he'd heard me scolding Thomas, scolding philosophers in general.

"It was on the Internet," he said and winked.

"What was on the Internet?"

"Your surprise poem. I found it by chance; the *Duluth Journal* has a home page, and I check it from time to time. It makes me feel like I'm there with you and Andrew."

"You're on the Internet? *You* check the Web?"

"Every day," my father responded.

"There was something on there about me? I was angry at Thomas Aquinas on the World Wide Web?" That couldn't be. It couldn't happen.

"Annie's the one who explained that your poem was to be a surprise," he said.

"My poem was on the Internet? It's not supposed to be in print," I said. My voice was quiet, almost gone.

"It has a ring to it," he said. "*Now here's something really rotten . . .*"

"I never wrote it down. He must have taken notes on that little thing, Stone's black leather checkbook; it must have been some kind of computer."

"Seeing your face and hearing your voice, even that little bit. It was a veritable journey into the collective unconscious!"

"My face? My voice? He videotaped me?"

"Isn't that the sort of thing Andrew's doing out there with the roots? Of course, the roots won't talk, certainly won't recite verse."

I made him tell me exactly what he'd seen, what he'd heard the night before on his computer. How did he know my students had me in a cage?

"QuickTime," my father had turned digital. "It's like a little movie. What's happening, Nina, is that this world is about to be freed of paper. We'll become more verbal again. Soon, there'll be no need for hard copy. No need to chop down trees. Our thoughts—yours, mine—will travel to one another electronically, and we'll be able to download each other's ideas by virtue of a simple keystroke. Jung couldn't have imagined it better."

Stone was an eavesdropper, a spy. "He captured my poem, my voice, my image, and sent it all around the world through that little computer? No wonder he said it was a new oral tradition."

"That's always been the problem with ideas."

"A poem is more than an idea," I said. "It's image. It's cadence. It's the poet's swing through life."

"Like a dream?"

"Very much like a dream," I agreed, but a poem was a dream distilled, in words.

"Dreams have a way of running away, a life of their own, Nin. Just because *you* don't write them down doesn't mean somebody like this fellow Stone won't get the message anyway. This isn't a preverbal society," he said. Then he told me Annie had been upset, too.

"Really? She was on my side?"

"Seemed angry at the Internet message and you as well."

So, there was no surprise from Annie; she hadn't been on my side.

"She said something about a cow in a bookshop, but I don't think it works," my father said.

Once again, she thought I'd intruded, made noise, destroyed the hush.

"Annie's use of the metaphor—she was trying to reinvigorate it—but I don't think it works, do you?"

"What the metaphor tells you is that Annie's upset with me again."

Even so, my father didn't seem to be upset at all. He went ahead and draped the Ph.D. gown around Thomas' shoulders. "Generally speaking, I found the message intriguing, although this Stone fellow's use of the phrase 'patricidal poem' is a little overblown. I'm presuming there's no patricidal intent; I'm only sorry he shanghaied your surprise, Nina."

"Patricide? Stone says I want to kill you?"

He took my hand and pulled me toward him. Then, he folded his long arms around my shoulders and hugged me. It was an uncharacteristically strong hug, I thought, a hug that signaled that my father had been strengthening himself in the last year, not just his arms but the fiber of emotion that runs through a man's muscles like electricity runs through nerve cells.

I pulled away to look at this father of mine who had begun to learn to hug. There were smile lines around his deep grey eyes. Kill him? He was my only parent. My intellectual guide. My personal family philosopher. My father's only flaw was that all his life he had hung around people with crazy ideas and had become famous as an expert on the thoughts of a busybody man who wrote about everything as intrusively as his philosophical godfather before him, a fellow with opinions on everything—beauty and pleasure, law and the telling of lies, women's bodies and whether or not they should even exist—a fifty year old who died on his way to a church council in the thirteenth century, an icon with a marble circle of hair ringing the perimeter of his balding head, a statue draped with academic robes and holding palms like pom-poms. Thomas, this old scholastic who looked now like he was finally going to graduate from school. I had no murderous intent against my father; it was at least partially because of him and his bad companions that I had this new poetic quest. I squeezed his hand and kissed his left cheek, which was dry despite the dew of humanity I had noticed, dry and smooth-shaven and smelling of lemons and nutmeg. I patted him on the back of his new Bogart suit.

He kissed me on the forehead, gently. His lower lip was the only scratchy thing about him that morning. "This Stone fellow says you're out to do away with Scholasticism. It's made me think we better hurry up and get the complete works of Thomas into the digital library." That was his next project, he said, storing Aquinas electronically. He won a grant and had selected five student interns who were ready to start the project as soon as he came to a definition of the term "complete works," over which there seemed to be some controversy. Nonetheless, he expected to have it figured out soon so they could get the job done "before you and those feminist academics Annie worries about manage to rid the canon of the classics."

It seemed that everyone had a different definition of my respect for intellectual freedom. "It's a question of more, not less," I said. "It's always that sort of question. Look at the *whole* story, read the text, listen to the audience, look at the stuff he says about women through *women's* eyes. If I call some of this stuff obscene, the Supreme Court says the test of obscenity is found in community standards; so, let's find out what the community thought about his work, now, yes, but also in his own time, and not the male community, the female community. How on earth was this received by women intellectuals in the thirteenth century? There must have been women writing back then, too. What did they say? They must have been outraged. Let's hear the dialogue."

"Well thought out," said my father, "but it borders on anachronism. Taking a concept like community standards from the twentieth century and applying it six or seven centuries earlier."

"And what about taking a concept of philosophy from an ancient Greek and applying it fifteen hundred years later? Or keying medieval thought into cyberspace, bit by bit?"

"Both gentlemen, both Aristotle and Aquinas, were held in high esteem."

"Have you compared Thomas' comments to the comments of women back then? What about their work? Who's keying them in?" When my father didn't say anything, I thought it was like the other times I'd talked him into corners, that his silence meant he wasn't ready to answer a question yet.

He changed the subject. "Chance travels with you, Nina. I told Annie that when I came upon you on the Web."

"More Aquinas?"

"Aristotle. I told Annie, when you come home, things happen, sometimes, but not always, not necessarily, and not even usually. You're like a cold spell in the dog days."

"That's your example?" I could feel another poem coming on.

"Aristotle's again. You don't like it?" He chuckled and headed back through the door.

The allusion brought memories of Dame Fortune, the scruffy fairy in a dark blue dress, carrying money, a crown, and a rope. Her icon was hanging in the city library in Duluth. "You mean I travel with Dame Fortune?"

My father didn't respond to my iconography; he was thinking about women challenging Aquinas. "Coming? Let's get this party out of the way so you can tell me exactly what women thought about Scholasticism six or seven hundred years ago."

"Me? I'm not a historian or a philosopher. I'm a poet."

"Our friend Dante had plenty to say, none of it critical of Aquinas."

"Well, I am critical, and I'll have plenty to say, even if that makes me an anachronism." I knew, however, I was defining myself to myself. My father had already gone into the Center, and I'd missed his exit. Annie, who preferred not to become engaged in that sort of talk directly with me, was sticking her head out the door.

"Come in. *Vite*, Nin, *vite*. Three people have already asked me why you're missing." Then she extended her hand to me as though I needed to be pulled into the Aquinas Center through the French doors. "I told them you were out running, but both Sister Vera and I are hoping you've been working on another poem. Do you have one?"

Yes, I said, I had. One especially designed for Aristotle. One that had not been entered, stored, accessed, or transmitted any-where except in my mind.

Criticism

Seersucker suits, sundresses, straw hats, khaki slacks, Sunday afternoon, two hundred people on beige folding chairs lined up—row by row by row—there to hear about Thomas. For an obsolete, out-of-date philosophy, Thomism certainly drew a crowd. If there was an undertow of anachronism here, I couldn't feel it. I was swimming in the "time issue" again; the swell, the current that was supposed to buckle between "now" and "then" simply did not exist. How were these people any different from the souls who crowded around Thomas in Paris more than seven hundred years before? My father's new translation brought Aquinas back to life, and the Internet would make Aquinas as alive as a call-in talk show guest. Post a question to him on his bulletin board, some doppelgänging scholar will get back to you with the answer. Time was no barrier, so why not apply community standards—ours, theirs, then, now?

Annie pulled me into the great room set with chairs facing the faux-marble podium where my father stood, back-to-back with the true-marble Thomas outside in the garden. Places had been saved for us in the front row, next to Sister Vera, who was next to Sister Fides, who was next to two Dominican priests in white hooded robes, hoods neatly folded down on their shoulders, of course. I had met them on my last visit home, Father Marcus and Father James. Where was this new person in my father's life, this Sister Hildegard who had dreams? She was a historian, a medieval scholar, someone I could ask about women and Aquinas. She must know about women back then, enough women to fill a salon like this. I looked up and down the rows of folding chairs, all of them full now, and saw no one who fit my idea of this new nun who Aurelia said swam fifty-nine laps every morning in the college pool and skipped rope every night in her room in the convent.

"Old enough to be your mother," Aurelia said that morning, "strong and limber enough to beat you in a footrace."

I wanted to quiz this woman. Instead, I sat, uncomfortable in my beige metal chair, crossing my left canvas boot over my right, then my right over my left. The canvas boots went with my gabardine-trousered safari suit, which was wrinkling from humidity or closeness of metal chairs or crossing of legs. I put my feet flat on the floor and looked around again. Aurelia, who had been laying out the food in the next room, was leaning against the door frame, listening as my father welcomed the audience before he read pieces from his translation. Behind him, heavy brown velvet drapes had been pulled over the French doors so I couldn't see the black-robed stone Thomas in the garden anymore.

My father was beginning with a dialogue on theft and robbery.

His interrogation of the text began with a question posed to Thomas. "Is the possession of external goods natural to man?" When my father pronounced the word "man," I thought I heard something out in the garden, a low whine, a country sound like wind whirring over electrical wires. The buzz was momentary, though, and there was no sound as my father talked about private property and its legitimacy. And theft. And necessity.

Then, when he went on to the Psychic Powers of Man, I heard the groan again—no, more than one groan, a set of muffled groans. I looked back at Aurelia to see if anyone was with her, but there was no one, no one behind her, only tables set with opulent trays of food. Throughout the discussion of man's powers, I kept hearing muffled sounds like unhappy souls moaning until, finally, my father began a reading of Aquinas' theory of beauty, and the noise of human sadness rattled windowpanes and shook brass door handles, and women pushed the French doors open. Thirty, maybe more, forced their entries, erupting into my father's definitions of *integritas sive perfectio, debita proportio sive consonantia,* and *claritas*—integrity, proportion, and brilliance.

"*Reduxio ad absurdem,*" called out a woman with white hair tucked up into a fedora. She had left the group and was pacing up and down the center aisle, leaning down and talking to the men and women seated along the aisle. "You cannot talk aesthetics without talking ethics," she said, moving on, "and you cannot talk ethics without talking politics." Then she turned to my father and said, "And you know, Michael, as well as you knew when we were at St. Dominic's in kindergarten, you cannot talk politics without talking sex."

So, this was the famous Gala Stark, the founding mother of the feminist movement who'd gone all through grade school in Burlington with my father. Gala Stark, there to answer my prayers.

Annie left her seat and went over to Stark. The two of them went behind the podium to talk to the others, and everyone was watching. I couldn't catch every word, but I heard someone ask Annie something about me, and was I or wasn't I?

My father, who was trying to talk through the interruption, had turned and was facing his critics instead of facing his seated audience, but he kept on explaining beauty, talking about pleasures of various kinds, and how if you really love organ music, it's impossible to pay attention to a preacher reading his sermon while the organ music is playing because what you really enjoy is sound rolling over organ pipes, not sound rolling out of the preacher's mouth. And just then, he seemed to realize what he was saying, and he stopped talking about Thomas altogether and stood mute, listening, like everyone in the audience, to the women speaking with Annie.

Gala Stark's voice carried, partially because she addressed my father's audience as she spoke. "The aesthetic issue masks the issue of patriarchal political power that undergirds every relationship, literary or philosophical, between women and men." She left Annie and paced toward Aurelia. "Let us hear Nin, the poet who uses language like an Irish angel and sends it forth on the World Wide Web."

A woman with milk-white bobbed hair took one step forward and said calmly, "What we would like is to hear Nin Creed recite. We have heard men speak for many years, for many centuries. So, now we have no more questions for Dr. Creed, and we don't want to hear any more answers. We have come to hear Nin." Her voice was resonant, but even in the big room it was spare; it gave off no echo, no repeating of her request. "This is all we want," she said and took one step back again.

My father turned back to his audience and bowed and said his distinguished guest was right, he had been talking for over half an hour, and he was ready to stop and let the women have the day. "Let us listen as Nina's poems roll!" he said and bowed again.

Sister Fides looked at me and nodded.

My father walked over to me and clasped my hand. With his assent, I went to the podium to speak my two poems, but even before I could begin, a woman standing behind the podium began to cry. She was just inside the French windows, weeping. Several women went to her and huddled around her, then there were deep breath-snatches and the huddle opened and the crying one stood silent. The woman who had requested my poem nodded at me, a sign that I was to begin.

I spoke only the first line, "Now here's something really rotten," and the women shouted back the next line, "Aquinas thinks I'm misbegotten."

They must have all read my "unwritten" poem on the Internet. I waited a moment, turned and grinned at this appreciative audience of women who were standing in a semicircle behind the podium, and then I began the poem again. They liked the poem apparently; they applauded enthusiastically, so I began my second poem, "The Law of Contraries."

Too bad the Philosopher
didn't think twice
before he said a thing cannot be
and not be
at the same time.
Aristotle says it's absurd
to claim something can be its own negative,
but I don't find it strange at all.
Hasn't he met the woman who holds her opinion back,
and still feels pushy,
scours her world,

and still feels messy,
starves herself,
and still believes she's fat?
Dumb, they say,
and a know-it-all, too.
Tough-talking broad
and a sissy.
Prude and adulteress,
virgin and whore
all at once.
And the woman who shaves clean the curve under her arm,
smoothes her calves and tugs the brows from above her eye,
she knows what it is
to be hairy and sleek
at the same time.
She's been called equal, yet been underpaid,
she's been poor when she felt rich,
she's been famous when she didn't know herself at all.
And she's been loved and abused
by the same man,
under the same circumstances,
at the same time.

When words have no meaning, the Philosopher says,
conversation, even with yourself, must stop.
Too bad the Philosopher didn't have second thoughts.
He could have kept the dialogue alive.

I was reciting the last stanza when I noticed my sister copying
down my words, and a very big man in a loose, wrinkled khaki
suit standing to the left of Aurelia in the doorway, taking notes.
They unnerved me, those two, shuffling writing instruments

across paper as I recited from memory so that I could keep this poem unpublished until I found a safe medium for my words.

When I finished, the man raised his hand. He was wearing a curiously large pin on his lapel, a radiant figure that resembled the statue of Thomas in the garden. He asked when the poems would be published, and I said I didn't know. I was confused by the Internet, and I wasn't going to publish anything until I understood what that strange electronic contrivance could do with a writer's work. And then Annie, of all people, asked again when the poems would really be in print, and I said, "Maybe never."

Annie, who always thought she knew better, showed the group the notes she'd taken on my poem and assured them I was kidding about not publishing.

Then the woman who seemed to be leading Gala and the group vigorously shook my hand and strode back out through the open French doors into the garden, her white head moving down the cinder path alongside a salt-and-pepper head and other grey heads and black heads and brown heads and blonde heads, all of them, toward the gate, leaving as suddenly as they had arrived. I was trying to remember her face; I was sure I had witnessed a scene like this before.

My father declared it time for refreshments, and Sister Vera led the guests into the dining room, where Aurelia had tables full of fruits and meats and vegetables and huge round breads. As Sister Fides passed me, she leaned over and said, "This is going to be an eventful summer. When *they* come to town, the Holy Father's never far behind."

"Who?" I asked.

"Divany Schulman and Gala Stark."

Of course. Divany Schulman, that was Divany Schulman with Gala Stark. They were primary sources, pillars of feminist thought. But what was Sister Fides saying about the pope?

"Not himself in person but his scouts. I've been told they've been following Divany Schulman since she declared her work 'post-papist,' keeping track of what she says, reporting back, I suppose."

"Reporting back to whom?"

"The Vatican."

I thought of the Vatican as a place, not a person, the birthplace of my sister Annie, a place populated by a bunch of people, mostly men, of course, almost all of whom wore wide-brimmed hats of the kind that I had always coveted. Sister Fides was acting as though they were members of a religious secret service, out in the world in advance of the pope. I wondered about the big man in the ill-fitting suit. Was he one of them, listening to my poems? I turned to point him out to Sister Fides, but he was gone.

"The man taking notes, is he from the Vatican?"

"Which man?" Sister Fides asked.

"The one who was curious about the poem."

That man was my father's friend, Sister Fides said, an expert on Thomas.

I glanced around the room again, hoping to get a longer look at someone my father would consider an Aquinas expert, but the man had vanished.

"Sister Hildegard calls him the specter, always flying in from Paris. But your father thinks he's quite the authority."

I left Sister Fides and went out after the women, hoping for a chance to talk to Stark and Schulman. No wonder Schulman looked familiar; I'd met her years before. She'd published a book using Aquinas' proofs for the existence of God to prove the existence of a nonmale god. It was clever, using Aquinas' stuff to show him up. I bought the book when she was in Duluth on tour, and I've still got the copy she signed for me. But today, she was saying women had heard enough from men. Did that mean she wouldn't have used Thomas' proofs if she had it to do over again? I wanted to know. I used Aristotle's rule of being and nonbeing in my poem. I wondered what she thought of that. Should I have waited to write the poem until I found a woman's model?

The crowd of women stopped at the edge of the grounds, where the path turned to blue mosaics around a patch of fern before it hit the gate and the public sidewalk. Through the trees, I could see them, their faces turned toward the low branch of a willow tree, the branch I used to sit on when I'd come to meet my father. There was a figure there, a figure moving its arm over a large tablet of paper. I took the figure for a man, a monk—wearing what looked like the traditional robe of the Order of Preachers—but this robe was dark green like the foliage, rather than white like the robes they were wearing inside. The figure's cowl collar was pulled up in the back, over hair, over forehead, stopping just at the eyes. I moved closer. I could see the back of the dark green gown. I moved between the trees, around the flowers. Was this another Vatican guy? I stepped carefully through pink violets and white lilies of the valley. I didn't want to crush them, the flowers were drooping as it was. They needed watering.

Finally, I was facing the stranger who had been staring into the empty sky and then filling the page of a drawing book. The mysterious figure was a woman, a woman with women's legs, legs with faint blonde, nearly invisible hair on them, strong, tan women's legs angling out from the long green gown. Her feet were remarkably well-tended, as though she'd had a pedicure and left her nails unpainted. They were clad in simple brown sandals. She wore no makeup; her cheeks were high and pink, and the hair that was visible was like white sand. Was this woman old? She had crow's-feet at the corners of her eyes, but her lips were smooth, free of the small wrinkles I try to ignore. I squeezed into a spot next to Divany Schulman, and both of us watched as the green-vested woman looked up into the sky again and then back at her tablet, up at the sky and back, silent, the only sound the rubbing of colored chalks against paper. After ten minutes of this, Divany Schulman touched my shoulder and whispered, "Tomorrow you must ask Sister Hildegard to put words to her vision."

So, this was Sister Hildegard. Exceptional. Finding Sister Hildegard and Divany Schulman and Gala Stark at the same time. I agreed. I'd ask her, of course, I would. My voice came loud over the rubbing of Hildegard's chalk. "Of course," I said again, and my talking set the weeping woman to crying again. She screamed and wailed, and this time, she continued her lament even when women huddled around her.

I don't think I was being insensitive, but I'd never heard anything like this woman's crying, and it didn't seem to be related to anything I was actually saying so I tried to use the moment to ask Schulman about Aquinas and Aristotle. How I noticed that she'd used their theories a few years ago but now what was she saying? Was she saying something different? When she said men had spoken long enough, did she mean something more? In fact, I wondered if she'd uncovered women's texts like the ones I was seeking. Did she mean to get that point across? Should I read between the lines?

But Divany Schulman raised a forefinger to her lips and whispered "Shh . . . " and turned toward the gate and left, she and the women who had come with her. Gone. Out through the gate as easily as they had come in. All of them—Gala Stark helping the weeping woman—up the steps of a small bus that had been waiting. I was left at the gate, alone, confused, staring at the strange woman in the green habit.

"There is a time for everything," said the figure, who, I realized, was no longer casting glances back and forth between sky and paper but was staring directly at me.

"Can you read my thoughts?" I was ready for just about anything from this woman.

"Of course not, but I've been sitting here for quite a while. I know you must be Nin, come for your father's book signing, and you stole the show, and he doesn't mind at all because you allow him to remember your mother. Divany Schulman and Gala Stark came for your poems; they brought a whole group of women who seem to be on an organized tour. One of them is a bit mystical, but now they're gone, and you and I can go inside and enjoy the party, and you can talk to your father whom you haven't had much time to see yet."

I wasn't sure I liked this woman. She was different from the nuns I'd grown up around; and, for somebody I'd never met, she knew too much about me. I pointed at her now-closed tablet. "When will you put words to your drawing?"

"Oh, I don't know. I don't know if it's ready yet."

"May I see?" I was checking on protocol, if there was one, for visionaries, if that's what this nun was, this nun who had dreams, day dreams as well as night dreams, apparently.

Sister Hildegard opened the tablet and showed me a mandala of roses the size of poppies surrounding flowers blooming on apple trees. I had seen this picture before. In fact, I had seen it twice. The first time, I realized, was in my dream the night before, only it had been a rose window at the back of a church somewhere. And the red fruit, were they apples? In my dream, I couldn't tell if they were apples or stained glass red peppers hanging from mossy branches, but everything else was there: ice-green asparagus spears standing upright like candles on a Victorian Christmas tree and a net of sparks holding tree after tree in a circular web and the blue flowers crawling out of granite stones. She handed the tablet to me.

"I saw this in my dream last night. There was a late afternoon sun—dripping in from the west, drizzling through the mandala of roses, flushing me in light as I tried to walk through some sort of cathedral."

"Where were you going?" Hildegard asked.

I didn't know. In the dream, I stopped and looked back over my shoulder into light pouring from the Christmas-apple-tree-rose window. I didn't see my father or anyone else I knew, but I felt myself growing anxious.

"Your father's always been your guide," Hildegard said simply.

He wasn't there. Instead, there was a woman in a dark gown, in my dream, a woman with a dark scarf over her hair, carrying a tray in her right hand, holding the tray high like a waiter would, walking out of the light. "Actually, she looked more like the Borghesi perfume lady," I told Hildegard, "You know that kind of person—women who give away perfume samples in department stores?"

Hildegard smiled and said she knew about perfume women in department stores.

"Well, one followed me all over last week," I explained. In Duluth, when I had a couple of free hours, I went looking for clothes for the trip, and the Borghesi perfume lady kept showing up. First, I was next to cosmetics on the main floor, and as I walked by, the Borghesi lady bent into my space until she was uncomfortably close and asked if she could spray my wrist. And then two floors up and twenty minutes later, the Borghesi lady loomed out from behind a rack of soft silk slacks, still carrying her tray of samples. "She was like that chess player in the Bergman film," I said. "You know who I mean?"

She knew. "You said you saw my vision twice . . . ," Hildegard tapped the back of her tablet.

"This morning," I said. "I saw the edible version on a tray of fruits and vegetables. Aurelia was arranging them when I woke up." Broccoli spears—trimmed back into slim branches to form dark green trees, tree after tree, on a net of silver paper lace doilies. There was parsley twined tightly around the trees, clinging like moss. And between the branches—peaches, pears, and apples, cut into generous florets so they resembled abundant roses. Shiny red cherries drooped from the branches, and young tender asparagus extended above. "They're probably eating it right now," I tucked the tablet under my arm and pointed toward the Aquinas Center.

"'Visu . . . auditu . . . gustu . . . odoratu . . . tactu . . .,'" Hildegard said.

"What's it mean?" I asked.

"Sight, hearing, taste, smell, touch . . . words Marguerite d'Oingt saw in her vision of a tree in the wasteland."

I often write that sentiment on student papers, in English, but I never knew I was quoting the tree vision of someone named Marguerite d'Oingt. And what about this recent tree vision, what did it mean?

"I've been drawing it for days now, and Aurelia thought your father would enjoy having it as a fruit plate."

"But what does it mean?" I asked.

"To me or to you?" Hildegard asked. "Mine, yours, or Aurelia's? Before we eat it? Or after it has become a part of us?"

I was thinking the fruit plate was a bit rococo, not that Aurelia would be put off by that, but the physicality of Sister Hildegard's dream represented in fruits and vegetables seemed overdone for my father, at least for his reading at the Aquinas Center. Wasn't it sort of pagan?

"Medieval. My meditations have been termed distinctly medieval," Hildegard said. Sister Hildegard stepped away from the willow. She bent at the waist and plucked small pink flowers. They were like lilies of the valley but smaller, growing wild around the trunk. "Dogbane, sweet dogbane. And look here," she was behind the willow now, "wild raspberries. Will you have a taste?" She came back toward me talking of mystics and the senses and her feminine medieval heritage, and her distress that this garden had been left to fend for itself.

Medieval men I could list. I had their arguments at my fingertips, but I couldn't think of a handful of women.

"There's more than a handful," said Sister Hildegard. "All of them very different, as different as your Divany Schulman and that woman with her who reminds me of Margery Kempe. Unusual. Not many women today take on Margery Kempe."

"Margery Kempe?"

"She wept her way through Europe. Actually, I think it all started in Jerusalem."

"Around the time of Aquinas?"

"Later by a bit, I suppose, by a hundred years or maybe more. But her tears, they were eternal. And Schulman, doesn't she remind you of Christine de Pizan?"

She was one of the women I knew of, though not well. Christine de Pizan was the only one I thought I had a chance to find before I talked to my father about community standards again. At least I'd heard of her work. She was later than Aquinas, but to the point anyway—a woman, a poet, fatigued by overworked stereotypes of women, tired of misogyny disguised as romance, fed up with schools that were teaching young boys to despise women.

"Is that who you're looking for? Someone like Christine de Pizan?"

"She got in that public argument about literature," I said. "I figure maybe she knew what men were saying in their philosophical tracts, too."

"Clerics kept their writings on women to themselves."

I imagined them passing metaphysical slanders from bishop to bishop, interoffice memos marked "confidential." Weren't there some women who read those memos? I was hoping Christine de Pizan knew about that stuff. I'd read a few chapters of her work in grad school with a professor who was displeased that she'd written a line in which she wished she were a man. I wondered how Hildegard read that line. "Do you think she wanted to be a man?"

"No more so than George Sand," Sister Hildegard said and pointed at my trousers, "Or you yourself, come dressed like that. Is your outfit a matter of convenience? Are trousers the most comfortable attire to wear when one wrestles with the texts of Aquinas, or are they an issue of sexual politics?"

She reminded me of Gala Stark's words when she told my father he couldn't talk aesthetics without talking politics without talking ethics without talking sex.

Hildegard reached deeply into a pocket of her green gown and handed me a piece of blue chalk. "Perhaps you should make a list, starting with Christine. Then we can go backward and forward."

I was annoyed that there wasn't already a good list, available in the bookstores.

"The big problem is that even when the women were there—standing right in front of your list makers—they would not all have been seen, and they certainly would not have been counted, not by the men. Observation wasn't highly valued in the Middle Ages, not even in science. They didn't use empirical methods. Authority's what they believed in. Who had the authority? Men, of course. And they didn't notice a lot of things."

We were walking toward the French doors. She was telling me what the authorities had missed. Women's bodies, for one thing. Around Thomas' time, they began to dissect human bodies, but when they looked at a woman, they only saw what some authority told them to see. I imagined robed physicians opening a woman's body and fairies flying out—some on winged horses, some floating with colored paper umbrellas. I could hear whispers and giggles and saw light dancing on the wind.

Hildegard said it was simple veterinary medicine. Somewhere

in Italy, some authority cut a pig open and thought he counted seven cells in the sow's womb. From that time on, men were convinced women were just like pigs. "Seven cells, they insisted, even after they dissected a woman."

"Why seven? Why a pig?"

"It may be the only truth they had, although I doubt they knew the noble origins of the pig." Sister Hildegard said I should read Christine de Pizan. She wrote about women. "She took on the boys in regard to the whole misbegotten issue."

I wanted Hildegard to go to the library with me and find Christine's quote, right then; we could get back before the reception was over, and show it to my father, immediately. "I knew there had to be debate."

"Language as argument leading us to an end . . .," Hildegard smiled at me. "Is that the language of the poet? Did your father talk about *claritas* this afternoon?"

"This is exactly what I wanted to talk to Schulman about," I said. "What's the difference between this and the pigs? Why do we keep using men's ideas to do women's work?" I was making an observation; I didn't mean it as a question, but Hildegard answered anyway.

"Women are bilingual," she said. We can argue like men, but we can also sing and dance and cry. She wanted to sit there in a grassy spot to the left of the robed marble Thomas and make a list of women who argued and women who sang and women who danced and women who cried. "Turn your ear, set your glance, accept what your senses descern, and write what is unveiled before you." She was quoting her patron, Hildegard of Bingen. "Will you make a list, with this uncertainty of yours about writing? Will you write down something that isn't a poem?"

Of course, I made the list; list making is different from poetry making. I was anxious about getting to a library, finding the quote from Christine de Pizan, but why go to a library without this list? I started to write.

Her mind was full of women who had experienced fame in the Middle Ages. Fame came easily, she said. It was power, land, virginity, and the right to be alone that women had trouble holding onto. When a woman did hold onto one of those, her fame came easily. In those days, being alone meant abandoning husbands, children, sick mothers, and going off into the woods to wander around in rags. "If you make this list, you'll find the names of women who had all sorts of impulses you might not recognize as leadership qualities today," she said.

As she talked, I wrote their names in blue chalk. Some of the names were hard to spell, like Gunhild and Euphrosine and Mechthild; it was even more surprising to me that Hildegard knew more than one woman named Mechthild.

"Did I tell you about Radegunde?" Hildegard asked, "or Adele de Blois? How about Hrotswitha?"

Hrotswitha was a poet who defined writing as wandering around—freezing in snow—alone. She wrote during the tenth century, poems and epics and plays and legends—one about a cleric who made a deal with the devil and was trying to get out of it. "A long time before Faust," Hildegard said.

Funny we never heard about her. More writers, I told her. I wanted the names of more writers, women whose work I could set side by side with Aquinas, women I could look for in the library.

She kept naming: woman after woman after woman. Some names were vaguely familiar; most I'd never heard. Margarethe Ebner, Beatrice of Nazareth, Hadewijch. Sister Hildegard smiled as though she were paging through an album of old photographs.

"Hadewijch would enjoy Aurelia's fruit plate. She was really into food metaphors almost as much as Beatrice d'Ornacieux, maybe more. Beatrice is the one who got the piece of the host stuck in her throat, and it kept growing. Don't forget Marguerite Porète. She was a beguine and a free thinker in the fourteenth century; when she got her ideas, she felt drunk on something she never drank. Then there's Mechthild of Magdeburg—don't miss her—she was afraid her books would be burned, but God told her nobody could burn the truth. Sadly, nobody told that to Marguerite Porète."

"Why not?" I asked.

The look on Sister Hildegard's face told me I was about to get bad news, the way people get bad news about a classmate they haven't heard of since long before the last reunion. "You don't know?" Sister Hildegard asked. Then she was quiet for a while, and I couldn't tell whether she was calming herself, soothing her own sadness over the memory of a medieval writer's fate, or if she thought I needed time before the catharsis.

Finally, I interrupted her silence. "It's okay," I said "I never heard of your friend Marguerite. I didn't know she existed, but I do know bad things happened back then."

"You never heard of Marguerite?"

"Never."

"They burned her at the stake," Sister Hildegard said and shook her head. The memory seemed to make her disinclined to go inside. She took off her sandals and rearranged her body so she could sit cross-legged. She leaned forward, stretching the way she might to warm up. When she sat erect again, she was reciting from one of the visions of Hildegard of Bingen. "Turn your ear, set your glance, accept what your senses discern, and write what is unveiled before you. Give the people memory."

I wrote the last few words at the top of the first page. "Give the people memory . . .," and I kept building on Sister Hildegard's inventory of names. Each time I started a new page, I wrote Hildegard of Bingen's exhortation again: Give the people memory. I wasn't sure how long we were there, but I know people came out of the Center, paused for a moment, peered at the words I was scribbling, and then continued down the path toward the gate. A few more and then a few more, all of them pausing, none of them speaking, all of them leaving. "Give the people memory" going at the top of page after page of women's stories. Some of the women were midwives; some were soldiers; some were troubadours; some were screamers; some were silent; some were walled into small rooms at the edge of town.

"The problem is that these women all seem to exhibit the qualities of the literary stereotype," I remarked. "They're crazy or pious or religious nuts; they're hysterical or witches burned at the stake. If they're not invisible, they're men-women, shrews." I was hesitant to use the word *bitch*. "Where's the whole woman, the complete person, the well-rounded character?"

"One can be still and one can dance," said Sister Hildegard, and she stood and shook her legs, bent down, touched the grass, and pirouetted twice, her toes making circles in the grass.

I had a list, but it was a quixotic bunch of names, so many of them mystics, with such unusual tastes in religious metaphors. I wasn't sure they were going to supply me with the kind of pure logic my father would demand before he'd admit defeat for Aquinas and his old friend Aristotle—and, by association, for all the male philosophers of western civilization. Aquinas and Aristotle would use this sort of evidence to argue in favor of misogyny. Look what men had done to these women in the first place! Perhaps I could get help from Margarethe Ebner, if only she hadn't levitated. Or Heloise, if only . . . Sure, there was Christine de Pizan. She seemed to have substantial arguments my father could test and analyze, but there was that passage where she toyed with the notion of writing like a man. Bilingual or not—pinning too much on her seemed risky. And even Sister Hildegard, I'd

81

certainly enjoyed the afternoon in the garden with her, but look at her—making drawings and dancing alone on the grass, like Aurelia said my grandmother danced in Haifa. I couldn't help but notice she was having an effect on my father, but not enough for him to give up his insistence that knowledge be based on ideas, not dreams. So far, I didn't have much faith in my ability to muster a community to challenge Scholasticism. I brushed off my trousers and picked up the drawing tablet and turned toward the French doors, and there was Aurelia, in the door frame, watching.

"Quite the pair, you and Sister Hildegard," Aurelia said. "Everyone's been looking for both of you, but how they could lose two such flamboyant people is beyond me. I've never had any trouble finding either one of you. Come in. Come in."

Aurelia ushered us to the corner where the two Dominican priests, Sister Fides, Sister Vera, and Annie were sitting with my father. Annie was nibbling on a slice of turkey, and one of the Dominicans was sipping orange punch. Aurelia insisted that Sister Hildegard and I eat. She brought us plates of cold salmon and pasta salad, which I couldn't resist after all that talk about food. My father smiled and suggested we each have a cold glass of Pinot Gris. He uncorked a bottle of a smoky Alsacian variety and poured the light amber wine into two green-stemmed crystal glasses for us.

"You were talking about the inevitability of truth in debate," said Sister Hildegard, "don't let us interrupt."

"Sounds like Milton to me," I said and sipped my wine. It was a little sooty for my taste.

"Or Abelard," said Sister Hildegard.

Any dichotomy among the views of Milton and Aquinas and Abelard would have to be exaggerated, my father insisted. He was just as convinced that Thomas was extremely open-minded as he was that Abelard never meant to outlaw wine. "Abelard would have enjoyed the Pinot Gris, and Aquinas would have enjoyed the disputation you and Sister Hildegard seem to have been mounting in the garden."

"Nin has sought the help of a medievalist," Sister Fides said.

"And they've come armed with pages of notes." Sister Vera pointed at the drawing book in my hand.

Annie was the youngest of the sisters. She and I were still children in this crowd. She leaned over my shoulder. "Nope. Nin's been writing a poem. Thank God, Nin is over this silliness about not writing. Nin, I knew you would write again, I mean on paper, like before. I knew you were only kidding. It's the skill God gave you."

"I haven't actually decided about writing," I said and handed the drawing book to Annie. "See, this isn't a poem. It's just a list. And even if it were a poem, it wouldn't be mine. It's Sister Hildegard's. I was only taking notes for her. It's not my work."

"Who's to decide whether you wrote only Sister Hildegard's words or added your own?" said Annie, her eyes scanning the list.

"I was merely a recorder or an editor. A translator at most," I insisted.

"Sister Hildegard, what do you say? Have you seen this? Whose ideas are they, yours or Nin's?"

Sister Hildegard sat, slightly apart from us. "You must ask Nin."

"Read it," said Father Marcus. "Read the words, and we will be able to establish authorship by analyzing style."

Father James liked that idea. "As St. Jerome would advise. Words, expressions . . . are they part of the author's style?"

"I think *I* can say it's not my style," I said, dryly.

Annie began to read. "The note at the top says, 'Give the people memory . . .'"

"Of what?" my father asked.

"It's a quote from Sister Hildegard," I said, "actually from her namesake."

Annie read quickly and silently down the first page and then the next and the next. She looked at me and said, "All right, I see how it goes now. It's an antiphonal piece. I think a good editor would add the word 'of' at the start of each line so that the antiphonal phrase flows from one line to the next instead of falling only once on each page, which the author must have done for simple convenience, not for content or style. I'll read it at the start of each new stanza, as it was obviously intended. All right, Nin?"

It wasn't the debate I'd been preparing for, but—ready or not—I was knee-deep in this dispute, and I'd apparently brought Sister Hildegard's dead writer friends with me. "It's not my work," I repeated my denial. "Nor is it a poem."

Annie ignored me and began reading.

Give the people memory . . .
  Of Catherine of Siena
    whose feet lifted above tile floors,
    who was suspended in thoughts of god,
    who smelled evil and who saw beauty,
    who lectured popes and who ate the flesh of lepers,
    who drank milk from the breast of Christ.

Give the people memory . . .
  Of Joan of Arc
    who crouched at the top of the pile,
    who waited for fire,
    who wore words of blame,
    who burned slowly like moist wood,
    who was still there in the ashes of morning.

Give the people memory . . .
  Of Beatrice of Nazareth
    who found frenzy in the quiet of her well-kept house,
    whose veins opened, whose bones cracked,
    whose chest exploded in the rage of love.

Give the people memory . . .
  Of Margery Kempe
    who journeyed around the world,
    who screamed in Jerusalem,
    who cried for her own sins,
    who cried for the sins of others,
    who cried to scare the devil,
    who was found to be mad, who was taken away.

Give the people memory . . .
  Of Marguerite d'Oingt
    who dreamed the wasteland,
    who saw a tree washed away,
    who tasted and smelled the tree replanted,
    who heard and touched the tree when it reached the sky.

Give the people memory . . .
  Of Margarethe Ebner
    who published her visions,
    who told of her misfortunes,
    who lectured on politics,
    who knew herself,
    who knew the written word,
    who knew her freedom came through writing.

Give the people memory . . .
  Of Dhuoda
    who wrote a handbook for her son
  Of nuns in convents
    who wrote the lives of the saints
  Of Marie de France
    who wrote the Lais and Fables
  Of Héloïse
    who wrote at 17
    who wrote to Abelard
    who wrote history into myth
  Of Bieiris of Roman
    who wrote to Maria, the woman she loved.

Give the people memory . . .
  Of Julian of Norwich
    who stared, who fainted, who forgot;
    whose illness was etched into walls of her spiritual world.

Give the people memory . . .
  Of Marguerite Porète
    who mirrored the invisible
    who wrote the inexpressible,
    who drank what she had never drunk
    who lay in ashes at the end.

Give the people memory . . .
  Of Christine de Pizan
    who heard sibyls,
    who challenged philosophers,
    who jousted with poets,
    who founded the city
    where good ladies spring from the earth in plenty.

Give the people memory . . .
  Of Hildegard of Bingen
    who felt the radiance of the sun,
    who listened as winds passed through her,
    who sang in a new voice,
    who did not relinquish her pen.

Give the people memory . . .

When Annie was finished, she looked up and asked, "Whose voice is it that you hear?"

Sister Vera had been studying a new theory of voice and wanted to test the idea that not only do male authors build female characters who really think like men, but often female authors construct male narrators who speak in female tones. On the other hand, she said she was now becoming aware of women who construct women's voices but who are only impersonating women and speak, really, from the point of view of men.

"First," she said, "we must establish if the author is writing in a male or female voice and whether the voice is female-male, male-female, female-female, male-male, or some other possibility."

"But we're simply trying to settle a dispute between two women," objected Father James.

"There is no dispute," I insisted again. "If you find my style here, it has nothing to do with me. I am not here."

"Nin is playing the dead author," Father Marcus observed. "Although it is done in her handwriting, she insists that she is absent from the text."

"When I looked outside, I thought Nin was playing the journalist," Aurelia said. "Just listening and taking notes."

"Suppose," Sister Fides said, "that we agree Nin was simply transcriber or translator. You were interviewing Sister Hildegard for over an hour, and yet your list took only moments for Sister Anne to read. That means you selected among thoughts that passed between Sister Hildegard and you—some to write down, and some to leave in the garden . . . "

"Journalists distort all the time, Aurelia," Annie said. "The very act of taking notes means making choices . . . creating a funnel through which information must be twisted and squeezed."

"That doesn't make me an author," I said. "Nor does it make this list a poem. A list is different from a poem. Notes, a list, ideas taped to a door. Someone wrote this, but no one is the author."

My father asked, "Will no one claim this discourse?"

"If it is a poem, it belongs to Sister Hildegard," I said and looked at Sister Hildegard, who was busy drawing again.

"But how do we know where Sister Hildegard got the ideas?" asked the young Dominican. "Suppose that she simply repeated things that she had heard from someone else."

"Or read in a book . . . "

"Or in several books . . . "

"'A trumpet only brings forth sounds, but does not cause them.'" Was Sister Hildegard reciting again?

"Exactly," said the young Dominican, "the poem—or the list—may not be Nin's, but it may not be Sister Hildegard's either. In fact, because we do not know where Sister Hildegard gained her information, if indeed the information came from Sister Hildegard, this poem need not have originated with any woman at all, and the original question posed by Sister Vera comes back to the center of the discussion. Was this poem written by a writer whose voice was female or male? At this point, I would suggest that we must recognize the possibility that this poem is not the work of either one of these two ladies but is the work of an unknown writer, and in all likelihood, because of the predominance of men in the field of writing, the bulk of the information came from a writer who is a male."

"How could you come to that absurd conclusion?" Annie dismissed his argument. "There were only two of them outside, both women, and when I read this poem, I hear the voice of Nin Creed. Doesn't everyone?" She turned to my father for arbitration of the contest.

"If this belongs to Nin, she informs us this is a simple list, plain everyday speech, and therefore not a text that can have an author," he said. "If, on the other hand, this text belongs to Hildegard, we must ask which Hildegard, Sister Hildegard or some other Hildegard?"

"And if it were some other Hildegard?" inquired Sister Hildegard, who was back in the conversation now.

"Hildegard of Bingen suggested harm would befall anyone who changed her writing," my father said. "Her integrity as author was not to be tampered with."

"But she always maintained she was collaborating with God," Sister Hildegard said and then looked directly at me. "That very fact may have kept her safe from the harm that came, eventually, to Marguerite, who claimed she was writing quite of her own accord."

Sister Fides wanted Annie to read the poem again, poem or list or whatever it was. "It's put me on alert," she said. "Listen again: role models, sisterhood."

But the day had grown far too long for us. Annie was tired and could not participate any further in this interrogation of the authenticity of authorship, even if she had instigated it herself. My father had a litany running in his head, one he intended, as Sister Fides suggested, to repeat to himself as he headed home. Everyone went home. Annie back to the convent, and Aurelia, my father, and I back to my father's house.

Aurelia went straight to the kitchen with the spare fruits and vegetables, and I could hear her talking to herself, marveling that it was easy for all of us to agree that one kind of something was of value and another kind of the same something was not. I was going to talk with her about value, when Annie called to say the sisters had found a couple of volumes on their bookshelves that might interest me—a Christine de Pizan and a Marguerite Porète. Annie said Sister Hildegard suggested I come over right away.

"Tell Sister Hildegard I'll be there," I said and put on my shorts and running shoes and headed for the convent. It was only seven minutes down the boulevard. I turned at the old mulberry tree and went up the back way to the garden, my NIKES thumping on the wooden planks of the footbridge that crossed the creek. I pulled open the cedar gate and took the stairs two at a time, first the stone steps, then the wooden ones. The keys were in the iron gate at the edge of the granite balcony. There was just enough room behind the convent to make the sisters' French garden, stairs and gates and a place in the granite cliff chipped out for the tall thin marble Madonna. I used to sit on that ledge between the shrine and the hollyhocks, drinking lemonade with the sisters and Andrew. I went through the garden to the back door. When Annie opened the screen, I pulled the earphones off and let them hang around my neck and pointed at the birdbath where Andrew and I used to burn incense. I could smell it in the evening air.

"You were silly children," Annie said.

Sister Fides came to the door holding four books in her arms. "Will this be enough for tonight?" she asked.

"Are there more?"

"There are more," said Sister Fides.

"Many?"

"Many."

I took the large leather bound one and opened it. It was old, its pages chamois-soft and yellowed. "Where was this when I was studying here?"

"These are all very rare books, " Sister Fides said. "All but the new one, of course."

"Were they on the Index?" I was fond of books that had been on the Index. I checked the card in the back cover to see who else had read the book. "Sister Fides. You read this one, Christine de Pizan. You read it thirty years ago, and Sister Immaculata long before that."

"Yes," she agreed. "I know you'll enjoy reading it now."

"Sister Hildegard didn't check out this book until six months ago."

"That's when she joined us."

"But why didn't any students read this in-between?" I looked at the other two old books. They had the same cloistered history. "You've had these books checked out of the library, you or one of the other sisters, for almost forty years." I was ashamed of my desire to interrogate this holy woman, ashamed of my desire to interrogate all of them, even Sister Immaculata if she were alive. How could they have had these books, read these books, and not shared them, not passed them along?

"We always kept them renewed."

"But Sister Fides, weren't you the one talking about role models, sisterhood . . . "

Annie interrupted, saying it was late for Sister Fides. It was almost time for evening prayers.

I had forgotten nuns still did things like pray. "Annie," I said, getting ready to ask why she was participating in this cover-up, but Annie said good night and went inside.

Sister Fides was right behind Annie, but before she shut the door, she told me that Sister Hildegard wanted me to read *The City of Ladies,* chapter one, question nine. "Sit down, here, like when you were young. Sister Hildegard will come down and join you after prayers."

"Maybe you and I can talk about it tomorrow," I said, leaving the "it" vague where I wanted to put "hiding women's work." At least Annie's name was absent from the card in the back of the book.

I sat down at the ice cream table and sorted the books. The old one was called *Commentary on The Boke of the Cyte of Ladyes*, an annotated discussion of the sixteenth-century translation into English. I paged through quickly. This was going to be rough, even though some of Christine's passages were repeated in modern English. The smaller blue volume was in French: *Epistres du débat sur le Roman de la Rose*. That was the literary squabble, one of the first times a woman took on the literature boys for the way they were toying with women. And there was a slick-jacketed book, a new edition, in thank-god-readable English all the way through, a fresh-off-the-press anthology of selections of Christine's work. I checked for pieces of the *City of Ladies*; chapter one was included.

The last was a book I had never heard of, not before that afternoon when Sister Hildegard put its author on the list. *Le Mirouer de simples ames*, written by Marguerite Porète between 1285 and 1295. The book, so the foreward said, was condemned by the church and all but a few copies burned, as was Marguerite herself.

Illumination

Pages in a new book are crisp and have sharp corners, yet they're still pliant in my hand. They let me bend them, fold them, turn them quickly. Old books are soft and dull on all sides, but sometimes when you page through them, small angles of paper chip from the edges. I am still learning not to break the smoothness; I am still discovering the right pace. That night in the garden, I started with the new, with the pliant pages, the one in easy English, the one with segments from Christine De Pizan, *The Book of the City of Ladies*. I was looking for chapter one, question nine, but the notion was there right from the start— Christine de Pizan, sitting in her library, asking why men say such horrible things about women. There, the questions, the answers, the engagement of community standards, what I knew somebody had to have asked, there in expanded *Paris Review* style. They used to write that way, back in the Middle Ages, set up conversations with scholars out of the past, dialogues with spirits and virtues. Like Scrooge's visits from the ghosts, only all on the same night. Like Steve Allen used to do on TV.

In Christine de Pizan's version, she was sitting in her library reading and brooding because whenever she read a book written by a man, it included a chapter attacking women. "Like a gushing fountain, a series of authorities, whom I recalled one after another, came to mind, along with their opinions," she wrote. Of course, she knew she didn't suffer from all the flaws these famous men claimed women were stricken with, but she wished God had let her be born a man so she could be perfect—like all those scholars said men were.

It was good to read that passage again. It was obviously a joke, a setup, irony. My poor professor who'd been put off by that line hadn't been very good at irony.

So, Christine was sitting there in her library, and she was visited by three ghosts—women named Reason and Rectitude and Justice—who helped her construct this revisionist view of history. It was a utopia she was building. A city for women. They took her out to a place called "the field of letters," where Christine asked questions and the three Women Virtues answered until they'd re-told stories of women going back to ancient times, and—story by story, brick by brick—they built a city in which it was safe to be a woman.

The part Sister Hildegard told me about was where Christine asked Lady Reason about a book called the *Secrets of Women*, which some people were saying Albertus Magnus wrote. So, Reason said some people thought Aristotle was responsible for the book, but she couldn't believe he'd come up with lies like that. Lies about the formation of the female in the womb of the mother. Lies about Nature being ashamed of creating a female.

Eureka! It sounded an awful lot like Aristotle and his friend Thomas Aquinas to me. Christine didn't say it exactly; in fact, she seemed to keep her distance on purpose, knocking the blasphemy without naming the blasphemers. There were plenty of blasphemers. Christine de Pizan certainly engaged my question. Bull's-eye. It *couldn't* have been Aristotle—more irony. What's more, she said that men wrote about these things to each other and that women probably didn't even know the argument was going on. Isn't that what Sister Hildegard said? Misogyny was tucked into intra-masculinia memos from bishop to bishop, scholar to scholar? Well, here in Christine's work was the cause—the pope had threatened to excommunicate anybody who let women read this stuff. So there was an actual conspiracy to keep women out of the loop.

"You know why?" Reason said to Christine. "Because women would laugh that kind of nonsense right off the page."

Community standards! If only they could have been applied!

I was anxious to tell Sister Hildegard, who hadn't surfaced yet, even though I'd been there at the ice cream table for over an hour. I walked over to the garden shed where Andrew used to hide when Sister Immaculata wanted him to help her weed the flower beds. The door was unlocked. Inside, it smelled like earth, moist and dark. In the corner, there was a bag of cedar chips, and there were baskets of bulbs hanging from the ceiling. Sister Immaculata's garden tools were still there, with her gloves, in the wooden box on the small table. The nuns had been good friends for me and Andrew, two adolescents in khaki shorts with bony knees who liked to dress alike. When we were young, before high school, we told strangers we were twins, not many strangers, a few deliverymen who believed us easily. We ran up and down the stone steps as though the convent were a tree house connected to the rest of the college, down to the bookshop where we bought holy cards and red crystal rosaries and water and oils from exotic shrines in France. We reviewed the lives of saints and sang the responses to litanies in Latin and drank skimmed milk from the convent's restaurant-style stainless steel milk dispenser, blue-white foam, liquid ice.

I closed the door to the shed, went back to the table, and opened Marguerite Porète; the foreword said the book had been considered anonymous until a few decades before. On the first page, there was a poem. My French was only passable, and this was not modern French:

Vous qui en ce livre lirez,
Se bien le voulez entendre,
Pensez ad ce que vous direz,
Car il est fort a comprendre:
Humilite vous fault prendre,
Qui de science est tresoriere
Et des aultres vertuz la mere.

I struggled it into English. My version went like this: You who in this book read, if well you want to understand, think to that what you say . . . it is strong to understand . . . humility you will need.

She was right about that. The further I went in old French the more rapidly my humility was compounding. I paged through the notes at the end of each chapter; a tiny brown triangle chipped from the page and dropped through the grillwork of the table. Finally, I found a translation:

You who would read this book,
If you indeed wish to grasp it,
Think about what you say,
For it is very difficult to comprehend;
Humility, who is keeper of the treasury of
Knowledge
And mother of other Virtues,
Must overtake you.

I skimmed through the book, reading pieces here and there—
poetry, prose, a lyric. Was this a list? A list poem? Marguerite's
writing was difficult, even when the editor gave me translations,
but I could tell she was talking about a journey of some kind. And
a dream, but it could have been costumes or something about an
abyss. The confusion came from an argument in the notes about
the meaning of a word: *abbit*. Marguerite's writing survived in
Old French and in Latin, and now the notes were giving me a
choice of which language I wanted to follow. If I took the old
French *abbire*, I ended up with a dream, or the word might have
something to do with a costume, a habit, an outfit. If I chose
Latin, I opted for *abyssus* and the notion of an abyss. What if I
didn't choose? I liked them together, clothing herself in a dream,
journeying to the abyss. Or dropping her costume piece by piece
in a dream, clothing herself in the abyss. She has this mountain,
maybe that's the abyss, inverted abyss (does an abyss have to be a
cave?) where the soul was "totally dissolved, melted and drawn,
joined and united to the most high Trinity . . . " Spiritual stuff.
Stuff this woman died for.

I wondered who she was. The details of her life were scant. She
was one of those women who never married and lived on their
own, not in convents, but moving from town to town in
northern France. They called them beguines. It was the end of the

thirteenth century when they told Marguerite to quit publishing her ideas, and they burned all her books, all they could find. But Marguerite kept her book in circulation, "As if it were good," the church authorities had said. As if it were okay for common people to be reading her work. She kept it out there, the equivalent of an airport book. I wondered what she looked like, who I knew who was like her. Who had the confidence to go through what she went through—prison, trials, the threat of burning? This Marguerite Porète refused to answer anybody's questions. Right to the end. Then, according to the notes kept by the inquisitors, she went to the stake calmly. How many women could I name who would do this? Would Steinem? Would Daly? Divany Schulman? Gala Stark? Maybe. Kate Millett almost did, in Iran.

Witnesses said Marguerite looked good when she walked out of the prison that morning in May 1310. She looked good when they killed her. But what exactly did *good* look like? Did she have shoes? Did she have on the same dress she was wearing when they arrested her a year and a half before? How bad had it been? Was death preferable? Was she angry? Did she curse them all as she died? Did she know what was coming when she wrote these lines?

> Thinking is no more use to me,
> nor work, nor verbal skill.
> Love draws me up so loftily—
> Thinking is no more use to me—
> with her godlike glances,
> that I've no other goal.
> Thinking is no more use to me,
> nor work, nor verbal skill.

I closed Marguerite's book and went back to the anthology of Christine's work, to the very last selection—the eulogy Christine wrote to Joan of Arc in 1429. I was looking for clues about the kind of woman who braves burning, the kind who knows she's going to be annihilated and still follows dreams into the abyss. I thought maybe there were characteristics Marguerite and Joan of Arc shared. But Christine's eulogy for Joan was written in the time when Joan was still a hero—predicted by Sybil, by my old friend Bede, even by Merlin. There was talk of questioning, but no mention of witches or burning, only tribute. Christine called her brave, strong. Braver and stronger than Achilles.

The editor says the eulogy to Joan of Arc came at the end of Christine's career, a writing career completed in glory, but no one knows for sure, not exactly. The editor thinks Christine died shortly after writing the Joan poem, because it was the last piece of her writing that anyone ever found. No more of Christine de Pizan. Nothing other than her daughter-in-law's applying for permission to move back into Paris, after Joan was burned.

What happened to Christine? Did she die, or did she go into hiding? I liked the idea that she went underground, that they moved her the night Joan died, packed her things into a cart, and headed toward Alsace in the dark. Her household goods would have been simple: her books, her writing things, two hatboxes, maybe a pair of boots, two pairs of slippers, and those slashed-sleeved dresses—one black, one taupe—as well as the purple silk she wore when she was writing.

It was quiet on the sisters' patio. I stood, stretched, slipped out of my running shoes, and sat down again in the wrought iron chair. The flat iron chair wasn't a comfortable surface for my body, but I pulled out a second chair and propped up my feet. Finally, I found a position that let me read more comfortably in the dusk.

⌛ ⌛ ⌛

Christine sat on the book crate and rested her feet on the small trunk where she kept her papers and pens and inks and water-colors. She smoothed the skirt of her silk dress and straightened her sleeves. She had always maintained that a woman should be able to wear beautiful clothes without being accused of impropri-ety. People were always asking her that question, "Why do women wear beautiful clothes?" And she always said women wore beautiful clothes because it pleased them, not because they wanted to stir up hostile instincts in men. Try to tell that to people nowadays, Christine thought as she wrapped her cloak with the lapis tapestry lining around her shoulders.

Her family had been worried when Joan got into trouble, con-vinced that Christine wouldn't be able to maintain the kind of silence necessary for survival. The last piece of Christine's writing to reach the public had been her poem to Joan, and when Joan was executed, the family thought the authorities would come looking for Christine. So they bundled her out of the convent and carted her off to live in an apartment above a winery in a walled village called St. Hippolyte. After Christine was safe, her daugh-ter-in-law moved back to Paris, and Christine had been in St. Hippolyte ever since.

She herself never felt danger. She had not been concerned. She'd been quarreling with authorities all her life. In fact, she'd managed to make a living by writing about her quarrels. When her husband died—and she was left with three children and a mother and a niece to support—she'd become a writer, and she'd done well at it, the free-lance stuff in the publishing house: the how-to book on education, the manual on war that the publisher put out under a man's name so it would sell, the biography and the autobiography, her writings on the woman question, and her women's utopia. The women's stuff, that was what the new feminists were interested in, that and the advice books for widows and single mothers. The poems she meant to write only for herself, but they caught on, too. She'd always been able to make a living off her ideas and her words. She built a reputation. By the time she wrote that poem praising Joan, she'd been working in the trade for forty years.

So, when her family decided she wasn't safe—not near Paris, not if she spoke out, not if she made statements—when they pretended to all the world she was dead, life became oppressive for Christine. She felt truly dead. And she felt alone. At sixty-five, she was unharmed, cared for, and safe. Still, she had never felt so alone. Not even when her husband died, and she was left with the children and her mother and her niece to care for. Then, she had been left with responsibility; now, she hadn't even that. She had only long empty afternoons of quiet. She was living like one of those consecrated widows in a separate sanctuary in the church constructed by Hippolytus of Rome.

Every afternoon, Christine sat in the garden below her apartment, behind the winery fence, behind the town wall, veiled by grapevines and trellised roses. On clear days, she could see the Black Forest. Once, she hiked the mountain behind St. Hyppolyte until she could see the other way, down the edge of the Vosges along the road to the tips of church spires in Kaysersberg, to the castle there on the hill, and beyond. She might as well have been imprisoned. Townspeople said the village was named for Hippolytus, who thought widows belonged in separate sanctuaries, but Christine had decided it was named for the Amazon warrior Hippolyta. Dear Hippolyta.

Christine's stay in the country was tolerable only if she thought of herself as a guest of Hippolyta, who had knocked Theseus off his horse and nearly killed him before she was taken prisoner.

Hippolyta's Amazon queen would have ransomed her with every penny from the treasury of the Amazons, but there was no need. The Greeks were so impressed by the fighting skill of this woman, they asked to keep only her armor. Then, Hyppolyta stayed in Greece and married Theseus and gave birth to her son Hippolytus. And like Hyppolyta, Christine stayed in this new country, but she gave birth to nothing; she had written nothing, nothing since her poem to Joan. Most afternoons she took her pens and her paper to the garden, and she simply sat in the sun, trying to decide whether to continue her silence, trying to understand whether she was alive or dead.

Over the years, things had changed. Paris was not the only place for a scholar to be anymore. People studied everywhere—in England, even in that place they called America. Her work, like most of the work of women who'd written back when she was young, had been set aside and forgotten. Hers. Hildegard's. Marguerite's. Marguerite traveled constantly and always sent news. In one message, Marguerite said she found a copy of her *Mirror* in a bookstore, and it had been attributed to "Anonymous." What they did to Marguerite because of that book, and now they claimed they didn't know who wrote it! Of course, the fact that Marguerite didn't believe in fame or in any worldly honor or virtue made it easier for her to tolerate the slight, to enjoy the irony of it all, a famous nihilist now known for nothing.

And Hildegard's work had never even been translated into English, except for a page or two, until 1982, when they finally did a whole book. Christine had never achieved that level of self-lessness. She saw to it that her work was translated a long time ago, some of it when she was still a young woman. The translations had been declared inaccessible, but she heard the publishers were coming out with new ones.

So, the message she received that day in St. Hyppolyte was more than she could resist. It came from a scholar at one of the new American universities, and it asked what she thought of the work of the Scholastics at the University of Paris. It was a call for a fresh discussion of her *Book of the City of Ladies*, chapter one, question nine. Christine left the garden and began to pace the inner hallway. She walked up and down, all afternoon, as she normally did only when she had a restless night.

This hall was Christine's side court, running from the front door to the back bedroom, a corridor onto which every room in her apartment opened—a library, a dining room, a kitchen. On the other side of the hall was the window, one floor-to-ceiling window. As she walked, sun came through the window in beams five to six inches across, coating the planks with a dusty, grey-brown appearance. Her slippers touched the dry wood, no varnish, no wax, but cold and smooth, no slivers. Outside were the wine makers' assistants, washing down oak barrels in the patio below; they were the only people she'd seen in years, and she had never spoken to any of them. What a change it was going to be. She had decided to go to this place called America to discuss chapter one, question nine. She was anxious to meet the scholar who sent the question. She wondered if any of the other women writers had been queried. She was convinced Marguerite would be there; Marguerite so enjoyed travel. Christine made a mental note to contact Marguerite about making the trip to America.

Marguerite had nowhere to go when her plane touched down, so she sat on a hard plastic chair up against the wall in the international terminal, watching these Americans, who seemed comfortable being shuttled through the air on huge airwagons. They traveled a good deal, Marguerite thought, perhaps even more than she—who really had no home at all in France in the last years.

Some of them had luggage that was very different from hers—square containers with wheels built right onto them or folding sacks with handles sewn on. Marguerite's luggage was manageable. One black cotton duffel bag, one dark wool blanket rolled tight with leather braces, and a bulging tapestry sack—once blue, yellow, and red threads faded to varying shades of grey but still strong enough at the seams to hold her books: three Old French, four Latin, two Italian, three Middle English, all that she could rescue when she had to leave Paris so quickly, and under such painful circumstances. She didn't need the luggage cart the friendly woman in the airport wanted to give her. She had no needs, really, none at all. She traveled light, her duffel bag something like the packs that young people carried in New York, her blanket and tapestry bag like the blanket and plastic pouch that belonged to the woman who sat beside Marguerite most of the night, another woman who had no apparent need to go anywhere.

Not until the next morning, when the woman suggested Marguerite go with her on a bus that took them to another building, still there at the airport, where there was the smell of coffee in the air. Her new friend seemed to be on good terms with people, and they were invited to sit at a table, given coffee and sweet-tasting rolls by a baker woman who pushed a cart full of the sweet rolls into the café. Marguerite was impressed by her friend's style. She had not asked anyone for anything, and yet they were all giving her what they had. Marguerite didn't need food or drink, however, and she gave her coffee and the roll to the woman, who tucked the roll quickly into her bag.

"You need a luggage cart," she told Marguerite. "With a cart, you blend in." She said she had one tucked under a pew in the airport chapel where they let her keep things, and she left Marguerite there, guarding their luggage and the coffee in two paper cups. When the woman came back, she gave the rack to Marguerite.

"You need this. If they tell you to leave the airport, you'll have to take a bus to another terminal, and this will make it easier." The woman took a gulp of coffee. "You'll be okay as long as you stay around the airport. If you need money, go into Manhattan, go downtown, spend an hour or two on a good corner; for you, maybe St. John the Divine—but come back here to sleep. It's safe. It's a good place. Just don't beg inside the airport. They'll throw you out for good."

The woman reminded Marguerite of people she'd known years ago. "Are you a mendicant?" Marguerite asked her.

The woman grinned. She was missing one tooth, the central tooth at the bottom. "Like Francis of Assisi," she said.

Marguerite was surprised. She wasn't aware of this movement of itinerant mendicant women in the United States. "Are there many like you here?"

"Just a few. Nobody bothers us here."

"Are you religious?" Marguerite asked her.

The woman leaned over the table. "I don't tell everyone, but I'll tell you. Jesus sent me here. He wants me to stay here, at this airport." The woman looked at Marguerite, from her old brown sandals to her bare head. "You dress like a nun. Like nuns used to dress, except your hair, but you can see nuns' hair now. You're a nun, aren't ya?"

Marguerite wasn't pleased to be mistaken for a nun. It had happened several times before, and the result was always bad. There were rules against impersonating nuns. On top of that, she just plain didn't like being questioned. She folded her hands in the black serge of her skirt and sat, quiet.

"You act like being a nun is against the law," the woman said. "Are you one?"

Marguerite had never been one to answer questions. This talk about law was discomforting. People were always concerned about law, using intellect to line up a ruler of right and wrong, measuring all those gradations in between, wasting brilliance. Humility was what was needed. Love and faith and humility. Succumb to their energy and rise above the need for law. Marguerite stood, so straight-spined that she seemed buoyant.

"Okay. You don't have to answer. I don't like it when people try to make me talk, either."

"I must keep going," Marguerite said.

"Take the cart."

"I have no need of it." Marguerite picked up her rolled blanket and duffel and her tapestry bag full of books. She didn't wish to be unkind to this woman; she understood kindness, but she had no intention of staying in that airport, and she had never been patient with questioning. She had to be on her way. She lifted a book from the tapestry bag and gave it to the puzzled woman. "Put your trust in love."

The woman leapt to her feet and took Marguerite by the hand. "I've been told to read this book," she said. "I can't remember who told me, but I know I have been told to read this book."

"It's not easy to understand," Marguerite said. "And you may get in trouble for having it. There are people who don't like this book, and I've been warned not to hand it out."

"You on the run like that fellow Rushdie?"

Marguerite heard about a man named Rushdie when she was in London. She'd stopped awhile in a cappuccino bar at Gatwick, and three people on the stools next to her were talking about this fellow, how he was there, somewhere in London, hiding.

"Sort of," Marguerite said. Then she left her new friend and walked out of the airport, to a large yellow and red bus marked, "Grand Central Station."

It was inside the train station that she noticed how many itinerant mendicants this city had. Perhaps this was the

Franciscan group the woman at the airport belonged to. Yet, they all were wearing different dress, one carried a sign that spoke again of Jesus, but few seemed to be related to one another. She boarded the train to Vermont and looked for a seat close to the door so she could get off easily that evening when she arrived at Johanna's Cape, the town where she'd been told to stop.

It was dark by the time the trained pulled in, but Marguerite knew how to find her way. When she came to the convent, she crossed the footbridge over the creek that looked like a little moat and unlocked the great wooden gate. Then, she climbed the stairs in the dark, three stone steps first, four worn wooden steps next, to the balcony where she unlocked two locks—a small one with a small key, a large one with a six-inch skeleton key, turning the small key on top two times around to the right. She banged her hand against the bottom key hard, pushed it in, slammed it one more time, and turned it twice to the left. Inside finally, inside the French garden. She walked across the polished stones, sat on the granite ledge next to the thin marble statue in the recess and gently removed the old books from her tapestry bag, one by one. She was humming.

Christine had been standing, silent on the dark side of the patio. She listened to the soft hum and watched the woman she knew so well from stories and writings. Marguerite was heavier and taller than she had imagined. Her dark skin pulled taut over her strong jaw, but it relaxed when she smiled, which she was doing now. In the years the two had been sending each other ideas, Christine had never thought of Marguerite-the-free-spirit as having a body, or anything material at all, nothing except her book, the *Mirror.*

"You still have a few of your books," Christine said finally.

Marguerite looked up. She'd received Christine's message so she knew Christine would arrive, but she hadn't expected her to arrive first. "I should have come before you," Marguerite said and smiled again.

"Chronology can be annoying," Christine answered, "especially when the story's just beginning."

"The story of the journey of the soul," Marguerite said, "an ongoing process. The evolution of stasis."

Stasis indeed, Christine had become bored by her St. Hyppolyte stasis. "I enjoy the constructing. And reconstructing. I have always loved the response."

Marguerite said responding to existential crisis, necessary though response may be, would take some getting used to. She was more accustomed to breathing in, breathing out, and going on her way.

Christine mentioned all the messages she had received from Marguerite over the years. The ideas, so many ideas, passing between them.

"Like rivers from the sea and back into the sea," Marguerite said and breathed deeply, in and out. "But this, confronting reality in a granite garden, this is a long way from my annihilated life."

⧗ ⧗ ⧗

I was hearing sounds again, like earlier that afternoon at my father's reading, but these sounds were more puzzling. I listened as the sounds tumbled around the garden. First there was a hum. Then the hum separated into smooth bits of speech, with breaths between the sounds. The bits were falling out of two voices, one light and airy, one deep and grounded. Two women's voices. Perhaps the sounds were words. Yes, words. "Book" and "idea" and "sea" and "life." And what was that with life? "Nihil," it sounded like "nihil." *Nothing* in Latin. Were the voices speaking in Latin? Did I have the first words wrong? Or was my problem simply the word "nihil," because the other words could go together, in a sentence, could carry meaning. But what did the sea have to do with nothing? It wasn't Prudence Rodney, was it? Prudence following me to Vermont, again demanding nothing?

"I myself like to start with the vision, rather than the sound," said Sister Hildegard. She had changed from her green outfit into a long simple cotton dress, dark blue, very dark blue. She opened a box of oil pastels that had been on the table and began to draw on her tablet with an oil stick the color of her dress. "Midnight blue," she said.

I hadn't noticed Sister Hildegard come out onto the patio.

"You were listening to other sounds," she told me.

Was she reading my thoughts again?

She said she'd talk about it later. She wanted to concentrate on the vision.

I watched as Sister Hildegard switched from color to color, making circles, ovals, flowers. Then lines, boxes, books. Rivers circling into a dark sea, a sea of rivers circling. Or was it faces and hair circling breasts and shoulders? Arms pouring out of bodies, hands flowing from arms, fingers, toes? Now I heard laughter, soft laughter coming from the ledge next to the statue of the virgin.

"There," said Sister Hildegard. "Personally, at this point, I see nothing. It's too long a process for me. I will have to float in the river, lie still in the sea before I understand. Perhaps you can ignite fire from this kindling. If you were to put word to vision quickly, how would you respond?"

She was asking me to do a Rorschach. "Woman," I said. "Women. Talking. Hands. Writing." I was also hearing laughter. "Don't you hear laughter?"

"Don't you see it, the laughter, on the page?" Sister Hildegard asked.

No, I didn't see laughter. Not yet. "I'm definitely beginning to see the women," I said and pointed at two forms who had decided to step out of the shadow. One was wearing a long gown—dark purple—with sleeves split like the sleeves of the academic garb worn by holders of a master's degree. The other looked like a nun without a veil. She was tall. Her dress was plain, dark, serge. She wore sandals, Birkenstocks, I thought.

"You see us because we are here," said the academic woman in purple.

"Here at someone's invitation," said the other, who had a lower voice. "I think it was yours, wasn't it, Hildegard?"

"On behalf of Nin Creed," Sister Hildegard responded, and she kissed the one called Marguerite first on the right cheek, then on the left. "How good of you to come, Christine," she said and repeated the greeting, kissing the one in purple twice, on the left cheek, then the right.

"And who is Nin Creed?" Marguerite asked.

I was looking into eyes that were staring directly at me. The woman wasn't smiling, but she didn't appear stern either. Firm is how she appeared. Her square jaw was set firm. When she asked about me, her voice was full of breath, but her tones were deep and strong.

"Nin is a poet," Sister Hildegard said, "brooding over the question."

"Chapter one, question nine," Christine said and nodded. "You said she wanted to discuss my use of that question in my *Book of the City of Ladies.*"

They were talking about me, but I wasn't sure I was in this conversation. I motioned toward the copy on the table in front of me. "I've been reading it."

"I was speaking with Reason about Ovid," the woman was saying, "how Ovid slandered women, and about Cecco d'Ascoli, who also slandered women, and about the book called *Women's Secrets*

—a horrid tract written by a man who claimed Nature was ashamed when she made woman."

"Exactly!" I shouted and looked to Sister Hildegard for help.

"This is what you wanted, isn't it, Nin?"

"Are they really here?" I whispered.

"Can you see them?"

"Of course, can't you?"

"Yes," Sister Hildegard said, "but you know I have visions."

"Is this a vision?"

"It certainly could be," Sister Hildegard assured me.

"Then, whose vision is it, yours or mine?"

"Attribution is very important to you," Sister Hildegard remarked.

She was right. I did think attribution was important. How else could we know where an idea came from, where it was last? For instance, if Christine wrote of talking with Reason about slanders against women that were published in a book she called a vicious little tract, and she challenged the author, I wanted to know who it was she was challenging. I wanted to follow the chain of custody.

"Some said it was Albertus Magnus," Christine said.

"I don't think so," said Hildegard. "I really don't think so."

"It was 'written carelessly and colored by hypocrisy.'" Christine said she was quoting Lady Reason.

"Didn't you ask Lady Reason if it was Aristotle?" Hildegard said. "He applied such odd notions to a woman's body. I preferred the ideas of Trotula."

"Trotula's work was important," Christine agreed.

"Trotula?"

"The midwife," Sister Hildegard explained. "She wrote a book about sex that ended up in an anthology, a sort of medieval *Joy of Sex.*"

"*Mirror of Making Love,*" Marguerite had used the word

"mirror" in her own book. "But I think Hildegard's discussions of sex are more joyous."

So, women were writing about bodies, sex, and love. "Do we have science writers on the list?" I asked Sister Hildegard. I wanted to be sure that women were represented in science. "The boys are always willing to grant us success in trivial work like tapestry making, but now we're talking science."

Marguerite was displeased with my reference to tapestries. "What's wrong with tapestries?"

"I only meant that women have always been regarded as good at certain things—domestic things, the arts, the crafts—but those are not the pursuits by which men judge power and excellence."

"So, who made the rules?" Marguerite asked.

"What?"

"Who decided which skill is significant and which one is not?"

Hildegard and Christine pointed out the obvious—it was men who had decided.

"Then why keep their rules?" Marguerite had never liked rules; she didn't think any rules were necessary. "When you have a system of rules like this, you can't argue around at the bottom of the syllogism. You have to go right to the top and ask who decided this in the first place? Who put everything in categories?"

"Who sorted the threads," Christine agreed. She meant it as a statement, not a question.

But I still wanted to know who sorted the threads. She did mean to challenge Aquinas and the boys, didn't she? "This *is* a challenge to Aristotle and therefore to his disciple Aquinas, isn't it?"

"It is an unending challenge," Christine asserted.

"Specifically, when your character Reason says it's a 'treatise composed of lies' and then later when she says that to say a woman is less than perfect is 'overweening madness . . . '"

Christine interrupted, "Not to mention 'irrational blindness.'"

She had taken a seat at the table. "Oh, how I enjoyed putting those words together," she said and smiled. She was resting her elbows on the table, and her chin on her hands, so that the split sleeves dropped off and lay on the table top revealing the deep violet inner sleeves that touched her wrists.

"Exactly who were you talking about?" I asked.

"Whom," corrected Hildegard. *"Whom* is a word that is falling into such disuse that if we—in discussions such as this one—neglect to tend to its grammatical roots, it will whither and die."

"The language is still alive," Marguerite countered. "This is the nature of a vernacular. It will grow as it grows, wither whither it withers."

Hildegard was saddened by the notion. "Isn't it hard? This dying into living?"

"Not at all," Marguerite responded. "No more difficult than the river becoming the sea."

I was distracted again. Was this the comment I thought I heard a while ago before I saw these women? Had I had this bizarre conversation before? This entire conversation? Was this a recurring dream? Was I going to recognize additional polished sounds, more and more? I tried to recall the other pieces of speech that had come tumbling to me, but the effort made me feel faint, and I wanted to get back to my question. "Whom then?" I asked. "Whom were you talking about?"

"All of them."

"All of whom?"

"Any author who carries the flag of misogyny."

"But not specifically any one?"

"Yes," Christine said. "Specifically every one who created a similar 'treatise composed of lies.'"

"All of them afflicted with 'overweening madness' resulting in 'irrational blindness.'"

"Precisely."

"But how are we to find them all, how are we to know what they've all said?"

"By reading them, of course," said Christine. "You read Latin, don't you? All women should read old languages as well as the new ones that Marguerite champions."

"But why read slanders?"

"Because they are the classics," Christine said. "Erudition comes from knowing the classics."

"Aren't you simply giving attention to ideas that ought to be disregarded?"

"No one with any sense disregards ideas they haven't regarded yet," Christine said.

"But they do," I reminded her. "Men do it all the time."

"It never occurred to me to remove the men from the required reading list," Christine said.

"Or to toss their work onto a bonfire of indifference?" Hildegard asked.

"Burn the canon?" Marguerite had taken a spot in the middle of the patio and was half sitting, half kneeling. Now she breathed in deeply and exhaled, a long slow breath. "Is it beginning again?"

"Of course not. We read their works. We become fluent with their works," Christine said.

"It's *our* work they have always removed from the canon," Marguerite said, breathing deeply between her words.

"And you see what that has done to them," Christine said. "They've boycotted women's work for so long that they don't even remember the real canon anymore. I think they actually believe that they were the only ones who wrote."

"They burned my books," Marguerite said. "Hildegard's were left untended. Christine has had some success, but how often does she show up on the list? It's a lesson in humility. They helped the soul annihilate herself, to become nothing, which is all she needs to be."

I thought I recognized the law of contraries. "Can something be and not be?"

"Depends on what thing you mean. My fluency is in regard to the soul. And I know that there is no boundary around her. When she is joined to love, she is no more. She is love."

Was Marguerite saying a thing could not both be and not be? "You're not, are you, agreeing with Aristotle?" I asked.

"The soul knows nothing and wills nothing. How can I agree or disagree with something?"

"You say the soul becomes love, yet she is the soul, and she is the body as well, isn't she?" I asked, aware of the odd feeling it gave me to have slipped, like Marguerite, into the use of female pronouns when I talked about the metaphysics of the soul, something I had always heard referenced with words like "he" or "it." Never "she."

"Love draws matter as fire draws wood, and there is no difference. The soul is joined to love, and she feels no antagonism."

"She is, and she is not?"

"She is not. And she is."

"But how do we know?" I asked.

"The soul has no need to know. Not when she is at this level."

But I was nowhere near that level. I had been floating, momentarily, with Marguerite, and now I had fallen hard, back onto the granite patio.

"Humility," Marguerite said and smiled. "What you are feeling now is humility. Let it overtake you, and none of these questions will bother you so much."

"Questions are her guides, now," Hildegard said. "They have brought her the two of you."

Christine said she liked the questions I asked in that poem I sent them, "The one about the eggs and the chicken."

I was wondering how spirits got hold of a poem I wrote on earth, but I ignored my skepticism. I was learning not to argue with visions.

Christine said it was easy for her to get my poem; she gets messages almost every day, now that all the scholars are talking to each other on the Web.

"You're on the Internet?" I asked the woman who died in 1429.

She corrected my thought pattern. It wasn't that she died. It's just that she hadn't written since then. And the Internet, she wasn't on it, she didn't own a computer, but it was impossible for her not to pick up the messages. Bits of imagery were flying all around. She couldn't resist the impulses.

I told her my poem was transmitted without my permission. "This is dangerous," I said. "How can I keep my ideas safe from the misinterpretation of men?"

"We went through all this with Gutenberg," she said. "It's just another challenge."

I told them this challenge was unsettling to me, that I thought I'd just keep my poems to myself. "I'll memorize them and tell them to the outside world when it's safe," I said.

"She means like Osip Mendelstam's family," said Sister Hildegard, "memorizing the poems he wrote in Siberia and telling them after his death."

Marguerite uncurled her body from the S-curve of its half-kneeling, half-sitting position and stood. "There might not have been any other way for Mendelstam," she said, "but this not writing things down is too big a risk for every day. You must write, and you must publish, and you must remind other women to write; how easy it's been for men to remove women's works from the canon, to claim their ideas as their own, to label them the works of anonymous authors, but we women know, anonymous women always know who they are. And one day we find our works on dusty shelves and bring out new editions. But what if we never wrote anything down? Intelligence reposes, and speaking labors," she intoned, explaining that the idea was from her own writing.

I wasn't sure I understood. What was she talking about? Memory, orality, virtual publication, books?

She turned away from me and Christine and Sister Hildegard and went back to the ledge by the statue of the virgin and put her books back into her tapestry sack. She was shaking her head. "Even when the soul achieved nothingness," she said. "I still held onto my book." She seemed to be packing, but she said she was simply making sure she was ready for the journey.

"Journey where?"

"To the sea. To the plain. To the mountain," said Marguerite. "To the farnear."

I did not understand a word of what Marguerite was saying.

"She is saying you must start with what you know," said Sister Hildegard. "Pick up your life and look at every side, rotate it, better yet, rotate with it. Spin backward on your own path."

"Where are your roots?" Christine asked.

"Here," I said.

But Christine wanted to know where I was born and where my mother came from.

"England, and somewhere else, beyond the mountains," I said, remembering Aurelia's words. "But she died in Israel, where I was born."

"The Holy Land," Christine said. "I always wished that Joan had gone to the Holy Land." Christine stood and pushed the chair back into the table. She wasn't ready to return to St. Hippolyte. She had decided to stay in the convent with Hildegard for a few more days, and she convinced Marguerite to stay, too. Hildegard suggested they all get some sleep and continue the discussion later.

I pointed to the books on the table. "Will you keep these here for me?" I asked. I was running home, and it was tough to run and carry books at the same time.

"Tell me about it," said Marguerite.

I bent over to tie my running shoes, and when I straightened up, the three women were gone. Sister Hildegard had taken the books and left the box of oil pastels on top of a slice of her drawing paper where she had written a note saying, "Nin, if you have a pocket, take these." The box was just over a quarter inch thick and not more than four inches long. I folded the note and slipped it into the pastels and then tucked them into my waistband. I unlatched the gate and went back down the steps, crossed the footbridge, and reached the street. The night was still warm, and the air was overwhelmingly blue, full of the scent of plum blossoms on grassy edges of black-tarred streets. I ran in the middle of the street—toward home. I usually ran to music, but I didn't seem to need any that night. My feet fell directly beneath my body. I shook my arms—first, one at a time, then both, then I let them dangle. They flopped as though I were a rag doll. I felt aligned. Even my nose was aligned with my navel, just like the Japanese monks who run up and down mountains for meditation. Yes. Everything was in place. I was straight. I was going forward. I emptied my mind and paid attention only to my breathing, the pace of my feet on the path, the swing of my relaxed arms, the coolness of the air as it touched the perspiration on my neck. Once in a while, the street turned from black to blue to violet at the edge, a ribbon, as a mixture of red moistures in the clouds passed by the moon.

I saw circles now on a pale horizon, blue and purple circles like Sister Hildegard's, but bigger. Spiraling out of the circle was an oval, white and black and purple and blue and sheets of blue-black. Around the circle-spiral-oval were folds of midnight. And, once again it looked to me like a woman rising with the moon. When I reached the house, I ran up the stairs to my room and sat on my bed and pulled the oil pastels from my belt. I unfolded Sister Hildegard's note and turned it over and began to draw images on the back of the page.

The next morning, when I woke, I looked again at the page I had colored with oil pastels—violet, purple, and blue pushing out at the top and on the sides beyond the bounds of the page. When words came, I wrote a poem in the space at the bottom.

Blues

Woman
slides to the rim
of the moon
like blues
to the edge of a trumpet.

She has no eyes
to veil the incense
of her gaze,
and yet she stares.

She has no mouth
to ease the twilight
of her voice,
and yet she sings.

She has no mute
to dampen the belly
of her prayer,
and still her words sound like rain.

Forensics: I

The pine box in my father's attic was a perfect cube, half-inch planks of pine held together with two-by-fours. It was sturdy; the lid fit down into the sides rather than resting on top. It was where Aurelia stored off-season clothes. When I was a girl, my swimsuit always smelled of mothballs on the first hot day because, even though the box was lined with black paper of a sort believed in the fifties to have preservative qualities, Aurelia kept a box of mothballs at the bottom. It was in the room upstairs where we kept things that we didn't need yet or were already done with or hadn't ever found a use for. I placed my blue poem in an empty stationery folder and went up the wooden stairs to tuck my writing in the black box for safekeeping. There were two rooms up there, the box room and the extra room where Andrew used to sleep when he stayed summers at our house. The extra room was finished, carpeted, and paneled with knotty pine. It had a bank of windows across the front of the house, so you could see down the hill over the trees to the college and beyond to Lake Memphremagog.

The door to the extra room was open, a light was on. Sound. Bach. Single-hand piano trills and light plucks of the violin. It was 7 a.m. My father was there, amidst wires and thin grey boxes, red and green pinpoints of light, black speakers three inches high, a telephone, and a small computer that had come out of a briefcase. There were color photos of old sheet music on the screen; Bach was coming from the laptop.

"You look like a spy," I said, "abandoned here during the war, unaware that it's over, still sending messages from the front."

He turned around slowly, a smile on his face. He'd made the room his second office, he said, where he did electronic work. "I've just disconnected from a philosophy web site, answering a few queries on Thomas. People are excited about this Nin, about Thomas coming on the Web."

So this is how he knew about my poem.

"You'll never be the same once you indulge," he said. "Andrew's into it, capturing his vegetation for data transfer; I think he's into it head over heels. But I am sad that Stone fellow shanghaied you; it's not part of the protocol."

He opened a slick magazine that was all pictures of computers and printers, and there were photos of Michael Jordan and Hillary Clinton and Bette Midler, as though they all used the small checkbook-sized black cases like the one Stone had in his hand. "Maybe he was running some kind of Newton on a PCMCA card, or he had an air communicator. What I don't know is how he did the video, although he may have had a ring cam."

"Ring cam?"

"A small camera, like my FlexCam here but one size down."
He reached for a Ping-Pong ball mounted on a thin goosenecked
stand and rotated the eye of the lens toward me. "This is my
multimedia setup. If Andrew has a communications system up
there, we'll get him on the wire and have a video conference for
the two of you."

I told him Andrew didn't even have a phone.

"Still at the data collection point with the project then," he
said. He had turned off Bach and was going through a set of files
in his computer mailbox. He was looking for one in particular, he
said, one he found just an hour ago, one he saved for me because
it seemed to have something to do with the women Sister
Hildegard and I had listed in our discourse yesterday. He clicked
a pointer at a line that said http://spirit.satelnet.org/Spirit/mys-
teries.html. A file opened. "They call this Bartlett's for mystics,"
he said. "We're going to go much deeper with Thomas. But look,
here, read the message someone posted. Isn't that one of your people, Marguerite Porète? And this next line is mystical."

I leaned over his shoulder to read the screen. "Intelligence
reposes and speaking labors." I'd heard that line the night before.
"This came to you on e-mail?"

"The original recipient claims to have picked it up from someone using Porète@farnear.nil as an address. It's someone having a
run at us, I suspect, perhaps Sister Hildegard."

"She's got all these gizmos, this much stuff, over in the convent?"

He said the college had a complete computer laboratory for
the students and faculty, and all Sister Hildegard had was a small
computer, air-linked to the college system. She didn't even need a
modem like his, he said, because she was on campus. I imagined
the two of them, sending messages across the trees at night, the

way Andrew and I used to communicate by pinning notes to a string we had running round the end of our bedposts, through the hallway, up the stairs, and back again. My father was turning into Abelard.

"Come to present me with your readings from Christine de Pizan?" he asked and held out his hand. He thought the folder with the poem in it was for him.

I told him I was going to put something in the black box, for safekeeping, for a while. "I'll see you downstairs." I kissed him on the forehead and went into the other room, the warm, unfinished room with bare ceiling boards. The box was where it always stood, next to the small round "ship's window" under the eve. As I lifted the lid, I noticed my father had followed me into the room.

"There's a folder of papers I've been keeping in there," he said, "one I didn't know if you were ready for yet."

On top of Aurelia's Christmas table linens was an old black ring binder, yellowed graph paper too big for the binder sticking out the edges. Inside, hand-penciled notes, printed, the letters no bigger than a typewriter font.

"Aurelia's wanted to send them to you since you were in graduate school." There was a trace of apology in his voice.

"My mother's writing?"

"I didn't think you were ready for this," he looked down at his feet because he knew he had waited too long.

"How old do I have to be to read my mother's writing?"

"It's not writing, really, just notes, assorted notes, things she was working on when we went to Haifa."

She was working in Haifa? This was news to me. I had always pictured her as a dutiful wife who accompanied my father, caring for her mother, both women tending his daughter, all of them aware, like Aurelia was, of every physical need, so he wouldn't have to notice any needs at all. That's why it never added up, her stepping in front of traffic. It never made sense to me because I thought her only work in Israel was to take care of physical issues, and whether or not a car is coming around the curve on Mount Carmel is a physical issue. On the other hand, if she was as separated from the exigencies of daily life as my father was, and if her mother was, too, then Aurelia's stories made sense. They were looking at the sky. They were sifting through stones at the curb. They were tasting cool mist from the sea. Perhaps my mother wasn't like Aurelia at all; perhaps she was like Sister Hildegard.

"I've been through that set of notes," my father said, "I read them again the other day. She had such a strong desire to go to Israel."

"Mother wanted to go to Israel?"

"It was she who asked Father Louis to invite me. I was quite satisfied to stay in Rome."

"Didn't she tell you why?"

"She was always looking for patterns, gestures, repetitions. She had what she called her 'steaming notions.' She had been playing with them all her life, even before she studied antiquities at Cambridge, back in Glastonbury when she was with her mother."

I opened the black binder. There were lists and lists and lists. And then there were unreadable pages. Strange scratchings, some penciled in orderly fashion, as though there was a proper way to write these darts and arrows, as though there was a proper way to read them. I looked at my father; he looked away. I thought that meant he didn't know what these doodads were. He never ignored something he knew enough to talk about. "The answer must be in here," I said.

"What answer?"

"What she was looking for, why she had to go to Haifa."

He looked back at the folder. "I'm afraid not. Certainly not the whole answer. Certainly not in this set of notes."

"This set?" I knew, immediately, why he kept the folder from me. Not because he was afraid of my reading what it contained, but because he knew I would want to find what was missing. There must be more notes. Other binders like this one. The meanings of the signs and symbols that were less intelligible than hieroglyphics. Left in Haifa. The rest of her ideas. I pictured my father, as I had always pictured him, getting off the train in Johanna's Cape: a sad young philosopher, a small girl clutching one hand, his other arm holding an infant in a laundry basket. What I had never before considered was his luggage. Where was luggage in all the stories? Aurelia never talked about settling this bedraggled family into a car and slipping quarters to the porter who had been tending to the kind of luggage they must have had after years of travel from Cambridge to Rome to Israel. In all the years she described the scene, Aurelia said nothing of luggage.

"Was this all she had?"

He said this was what she'd been working on the week before she died; it was on the bedside table in their room. When he packed a travel bag for himself and Annie and me, he tucked the folder in. The plan was for Father Louis to send the rest.

"There were more papers; she had so many papers. Most of her things were improperly bound, even reference pieces, all hand-written in notebooks and on graph paper in folders or bound with plain grey cardboard she'd taken from the ends of tablets. She kept them all in a bag, like that bag you carry with you," he said referring to the limbo bag I had lugged his book around in for weeks before I read it. "But hers was a raffia sort of thing, a bit like a Mediterranean shopping bag."

The image of my mother was shifting, from Aurelia to Sister Hildegard to Marguerite Porète. I slid the paper folder with my blue poem into the back of my mother's notes and placed them on the rough wooden windowsill, then my father and I replaced the lid on the box. I kissed him on the cheek. He walked back into his extra room. I heard seven little beeps, a faint ringing, a short screech, and his fingers tapping keys. It was getting stuffy in the box room. I grabbed my folder and went downstairs for coffee.

Aurelia added heavy cream. "Father Louis had all the clothing packed and sent it straight here to Johanna's Cape. Your father had his hands full enough, without steamer trunks and boxes. He came with one suitcase. I didn't mention it because it didn't seem important to me."

So everything else was sent, everything came here?

"Not everything. You know how it's always been. He looks for a book he thinks he has, and then he remembers he hasn't opened it since he left Haifa."

"My mother's books?"

"Those too. Perhaps those especially." Aurelia said my father was next to ruin after my mother's death. Father Louis may have felt it better not to remind him.

I told her that was a hideous assumption for Father Louis to make. What right had he to edit my father's life, our lives, like that?

Aurelia said it was a right Father Louis and all spiritual counselors used to have, like the rights parents had. "It was thought that emptying the brain would lessen the pain," she said. "And apparently, some things were lost in the fire, when Father Louis' office burned—or wherever it was he stored her work."

Fire. The ultimate editor of history. Aurelia was carrying my coffee and a plate of her fresh cinnamon rolls toward the round oak table on the front porch. I followed her out and sat down. Sun was there as a feeling at first, warm on my ears, then its heat moved to my face, the bridge of my nose, my eyes, and finally there was a glare, and I had to squint. Red and yellow water sparkled in beads on the pines in the front yard. Someone coughed across the street. Sounds carried in the morning, like the sounds of my father on the computer; either that or my ears were getting better.

I opened my mother's notes. They smelled of mothballs. My father called this her Glastonbury folder. It wasn't immediately obvious why. Apparently, she liked to write on graph paper; all her pages had small squares instead of lines, and her printed letters were controlled and carefully fitted into the boxes, just as the odd marks had been. There was no talk of mother and mother's mother and mother's aunts. On one page, there was a collection of what she called "gestures and phenomena," columns of verbs, actions like wandering, jumping, dressing, undressing, questioning, dying, eating, drinking, giving birth, and weeping. Another page contained bundles of things: castle, sky, lapis, cave, cup, gate, silence, fire, a howling face in a scarlet cloth, and birds, bats, and "winged things." Her lists were getting grim. I began to scan the pages of neatly penciled notes. Eventually, I found the words *ritual, journey, woman,* and *grail.* So that's why this was the Glastonbury folder. Her work had something to do with the quest for the holy grail.

I knew the story of Joseph of Arimathea bringing the grail to Glastonbury and throwing it into the well and the water running red like blood ever since. I guessed if you grew up walking by that well on the way to school, you might come up with lists that were like my mother's, but her lists didn't seem to be part of the standard legend. She was doing something of her own, and it wasn't until the last three pages that her notes mentioned anything resembling purpose. There was a quote she dated "Paris 1919." "Mysterious Border-land," it said, "Chain of Evolution from Pagan Mystery to Christian Ceremonial—J. Weston." My mother had crossed through "Chain of Evolution" and underneath had written, "Chain of Custody FMDLC."

My father came out onto the porch and sat down next to me. He was sipping on a mug of coffee. He wanted to know if I was ready for the debate between Thomas and the women of the Middle Ages. I told him I wasn't close to ready. We both knew that I was no longer interested in anything other than the black ring binder open in front of me, amber pages exposed, contents still indecipherable.

"What's the reference to FMDLC?" I presumed it was a scholarly device, the annoying kind that forced me back to the foreword and foreword to the index, instead of letting me read.

"Her initials," he said, "Faith Morgan DeLacey Creed. She forgot the stop. Custody. Period. Faith Morgan DeLacey Creed. Period. It means that's *her* idea. She does that in her notes. Always puts quotes around other people's ideas and initials her own."

She was as picky about attribution as I was. So, this was her idea, this was her question: what is the chain of custody? Custody what?

"The grail, but not just the grail. Others. There were other folders like this. Ulysses."

"Greek or Irish?" I asked.

He cocked his head a bit to the left as he looked at me. "The difference? Isn't one the heir to the other?"

I agreed, and he went on. "In each, she makes lists of people and things and places and what she calls their 'gestures.'"

"You think she thought people used these gestures in Haifa?" I asked.

He answered as though he hadn't heard my question. "She was busy all the time. And she kept your grandmother busy. They were reading and talking and watching, all the time."

"Watching for what?" A gesture, like people waving? I imagined my mother waving at Guinevere waving at Molly Bloom waving at Circe.

"It seemed she was looking for rituals," he answered. "Rather powerful rituals."

"Religious rituals?"

"Some religious, some profane, some both. It didn't matter. She seemed to find them everywhere."

"You never asked what she thought she found?" I thought about Andrew's interrogations while we cooked, the interest we had at the end of every day in each other's stories, and I realized my father had let the key to my mother's work slip by because it hadn't occurred to him to ask what on earth she was doing with all those lists. "You didn't ask her exactly what Israel had to do with her chain of custody?"

"I was busy with my own work," he said. "She was doing hers." He looked away. He knew I was displeased with his answer, but he had no intention of giving me another. He stood. He pushed his chair into the table and picked up his coffee cup. "Sister Hildegard would like you to call her when you get a moment." It was Sister Hildegard he had dialed up on his modem upstairs in the attic. "She insists she did not post the message from Marguerite Porète. She seems to think you'll believe her."

Of course, I believed her. I still had the illumination and the poem I had written the night before with me on the table. When my father had gone back inside, I took the stationery folder from my mother's binder and read the poem tucked at the bottom of my blue drawing. From its brief stay in my mother's folder, it already had a scent.

"A bit like William Blake," said Aurelia as she leaned over my shoulder and poured fresh coffee into my cup.

I looked at my small poem. "Songs of Innocence," I said. "Or is it Experience?" I confused the two. One was the other and the other was the one, and I forgot which poem came from which. What Aurelia meant, however, was that I had made a drawing with a handwritten poem inset. It didn't matter to her whether it was innocence or experience. To her, the circumstances were interchangeable.

"Sister Hildegard seems to want to talk to you, soon," Aurelia said. "She phoned."

"I know. She sent an e-mail, too."

"It seems urgent," Aurelia said and went back in the house, leaving a small white pitcher of cream next to my cup on the table.

My green pearl pen was clipped at the open neck of my shirt. I kept my pen there and my glasses when I wasn't wearing them, looped over the second button, handy. I unclipped both and made a note to myself on the outside of the folder. "Gestures— Grail, Ulysses, Other." I clipped the pen back on the neck of my shirt and looped my glasses over it again.

Carefully balancing the black ring binder in one hand and my full coffee cup in the other, I pried the screen door open and slipped into the house. The phone was on a small round table next to the love seat on top of a piece of Bulgarian lace Father Louis had sent us for Christmas when I was a child. Before I lifted the receiver, I realized that of all the college phone numbers I had stored in my memory, Sister Hildegard's was not one. She had never been there when I was student. Just then the phone rang. I picked it up, and there she was, Sister Hildegard, calling me.

"What do you think of the proposal?" she asked.

"What proposal?" I didn't know what she was talking about.

"Haven't they explained the opportunity to you?"

"Who?"

"Well, Sister Anne, for one. And your father. And Aurelia."

I hadn't spoken to Annie since the night before at the convent. My father and I had talked, but nothing he said had the ring of a proposal to it. "All I know is that both Aurelia and my father said

I was supposed to call you, and I was going to, but here you are calling me."

"Sister Anne said nothing?"

"I haven't talked to her today. What proposal?"

"Sister Anne was very negative about it; she thinks you'll get too involved. Your father, although he knows it's a good thing, was hesitant. Aurelia said she'd go along with you if she could, and she was sure Andrew would, too, but of course, they can't."

"Go along where?"

"To Israel. To Haifa."

"Haifa?" I could hear the echo of Andrew's words. *Haifa, in the summer this year, don't go.* I wasn't so sure Aurelia knew how Andrew would react. "What's the proposal?" I asked again and untied my tennis shoes and rubbed my bare feet on the red oriental rug. "Whose proposal? When?"

Aside from the message that Marguerite had apparently accidentally posted last night, Sister Hildegard had several other e-mail messages waiting for her when she woke up that morning. One was from Divany Schulman. It was about a traveling seminar she was supposed to accompany to Israel—a women writers' conference on imagination and the soul. The writers were a mixed group, at "different points in the process," Divany had told Sister Hildegard. It was a tour her friend Veronica Joyce had put together, students who knew one another from Divany's night school course down in SoHo on the metaphysics of soul. They'd been encouraged to consider writing the story of their souls.

In the end, they decided the group should go on a pilgrimage, to a place where major soul stories had happened, to consider soul while standing in the shadows of famous souls. Divany was well known for her book, *Soul as Archetype/Body as Stereotype*, and she had asked Veronica, a professor of religious anthropology at Schulman's university, to put together the pilgrimage. When

Divany arrived home in New York after Nin's father's reading, however, she had received an urgent request to come immediately to Moscow to help women organize the aftermath.

"Which aftermath?" I asked. There had been several.

Sister Hildegard said Divany had reminded her that women were in a fragile state there. Think of what history would say if she didn't go. She couldn't pass up Moscow, but she had promised this study tour that she would accompany them, and she needed a substitute. In any event, she'd made some inquiries, and the group was perfectly happy to travel with a substitute scholar, or two substitutes, if they could get them for the price of Schulman's expenses and stipend. She had suggested to them that she replace herself with Gala Stark—Gala filling in as a philosopher of politics—and also with me, filling in as a literary type who understands the soul. Most of the students were in the group at my father's reading, and they admired my work on the soul.

I protested, pointing out it was only one poem.

Sister Hildegard said one was apparently sufficient under the circumstances. There was money enough to pay both passages if neither Gala nor I insisted on a stipend. Without Divany, the group had lost its philosopher, but they thought Veronica the anthropologist, Gala the political scientist, and I the poet added up to more or less the same thing.

"Divany wants you to know some of the students are better at soul than they are at writing, but she hopes that won't put you off. If you can make the decision this morning," Sister Hildegard said, "actually, within the next half hour, all your expenses will be covered. Do you have your passport with you? Can you go?"

For some reason, I always traveled with my passport, in my Filofax, behind my credit cards. I had no reason to carry it. I hadn't left the country in years, other than to go to Canada, which was no reason because I didn't need a passport for that. From

133

Duluth, I drove between blackened-red cliffs and Lake Superior. In Vermont, I skirted alongside Memphremagog to the border. No one asked for papers when I went from the U.S. to Canada and back. I simply carried mine.

"When is this trip?" I asked.

"The sixteenth. A Sunday. Leaving from Kennedy."

"What did Annie say? Why did she think I'd get 'too involved?'"

"She said Haifa was no place for you to go on some quest. She said you had your own life now, and it wasn't in Haifa. She said there was nothing for you in Haifa. Nothing you don't already have. I don't think I've ever seen her pout like that."

"And my father?"

"Your father is discreet, but I think he worries about your going there, what with the history. He's hesitant."

"The family history?"

"And the tensions," she said—obliquely referring to shootings, millennial fears, apocalyptic frenzies, worries in the Golan, worries in the West Bank, talk of peace in Jerusalem. Peace never comes easily. Precautions were essential. Annie and my father had read the State Department warnings, travel advisories on the Internet. There was always the possibility of danger.

"He thinks I won't come back?"

"We came to the conclusion you'll be fine if you stay with your group and don't go off on your own."

If that was his conclusion, he hadn't offered it. And what about Andrew? I would have to reach Andrew. How? I tried calling the Ag station again, but no one answered. They had all left the base camp and gone deep into the woods. They didn't have a recording device on the phone. State troopers? Rangers?

"He's bound to call before you leave," Aurelia said.

Sister Hildegard said the pilgrimage would be brief; we'd be back in late July. Andrew would be out in the Boundary Waters almost that long, at least another two or three weeks. She said Annie's biggest concern was the accommodations and the date. "Your father expressed worry in that regard, too. Staying at the convent of Stella Maris, for the Dog Days."

"Stella Maris? Where they lived? Where I was born?" Where my mother's notes might still be. Where she still was? For my birthday?

Sister Hildegard said yes, that very place. She wanted to know if I knew anything about Dog Days in Israel.

I thought they came later, when the lakes turned green, in August.

Sister Hildegard said the real Dog Days were marked on the old calendars in Israel and Egypt, and they could come in July, in a month called Tammuz in Israel—or later. It all depended on the coincidence of stars. She said they often came on my birthday, July 19.

I didn't know that, but my father obviously did. I remembered what he said the day before: when I come, things happen, sometimes—but not always, not necessarily, and not even usually— like a "cold spell in the Dog Days." He was quoting Aristotle when he called me a cold spell in Dog Days, and now I saw that he was probably talking about my birthday, too.

"Dog Days," I said and unclipped my pen from my shirt. I removed the stationery folder from my mother's binder, turned it to the side where it said "Gestures—Grail, Ulysses, Other." Under "Other," I added "Dog Days."

"It's the opportunity of a lifetime, Nin."

"Yes," I said. I had decided to go to Haifa.

Andrew called twice before I left, once when I was out running and again when I was over in Burlington buying the luggage Veronica, the weeping woman, had recommended. It turned out that anthropologist Veronica Joyce was the woman who wept at my father's book signing. Veronica, who had regained composure and was not crying at all when she called me on the phone, said each of us could have one small suitcase and a backpack, small enough to be stowed underfoot in the van she hired to take us around Israel. I had a backpack, but I went to Burlington because I saw a roller suitcase advertised in the paper, the kind flight crews use, and I had a few other things to buy, like the clothes Veronica Joyce said would be required—cool trousers for places where pants were allowed, skirts for where they weren't, easy-wash shirts, a vest with pockets for money and passport and anything else you need when you leave the van, underwear that dries overnight, sturdy but comfortable shoes for hiking to pilgrimage sites, a water bottle, a good outfit for celebratory dinners, and a large scarf to cover my head in places where my head was not allowed to show. So, while I was shopping, I missed Andrew's second call.

He talked to Aurelia and told her he was going back up to the Boundary Waters for another week, perhaps two, because the ground had thawed late and roots weren't easily attainable in the cold earth.

Aurelia told him I was going to Haifa.

He said he knew I would go eventually.

She said I'd been trying to reach him.

He said his group was leaving late in the afternoon, and then they'd be without a phone again, and would she please tell me to try to reach him before it was too late?

She said she would tell me.

Aurelia told me when I drove back into the driveway at twilight. I called him, but of course, it was too late. Sunday morning, my father suggested we use the FlexCam and send him a message on the Web. I put on my new pilgrimage clothes and wrapped my dull scarf around my shoulders to give him a sense of my journey. I tried to explain the series of events that had aroused me, and I told him to ask Aurelia because she knew the whole story. I told him I thought my father was afraid I wouldn't come back, so if I didn't, somebody better come over and get me, but then I thought he'd be upset by that, once I was gone, so I told him the last part was a joke. I had a return ticket, and my father said if I stayed with my group I'd be fine, so he wasn't to worry. I promised to stay with the group. Talking into something the size of an eyeball was odd. I told him I would write and said good-bye. I said my plane left soon, I was all ready to go, I was driving to Burlington in my rental car and flying down to New York, and I said good-bye again. I explained the group was meeting in the international terminal, and we'd land in Tel Aviv around noon. I said good-bye. And I told him I'd miss him. And I said good-bye, once more.

My father said that was a typical Morgan farewell because none of those Morgan girls—not my mother or grandmother or her mother or her aunts—none of them could get their good-byes out of the way quickly. They were always waving, going, returning, going, always returning. "They stood around on porches a good deal," he said.

"In Glastonbury?"

"Apparently."

I was still transmitting a signal into the little camera. I told Andrew my father said this was a Morgan good-bye. I told him to think of me singing and dancing on the porch. I said good-bye.

Annie and Aurelia and Sister Hildegard were outside in the driveway, next to the open trunk of my car. My father set my suitcase gingerly into the trunk and said he doubted anyone in Haifa would remember him but to give his regards to anyone who did. Aurelia hugged me and kissed me on my right cheek, then my left, as though we had suddenly become Europeans. Annie said she wanted to let me know one more time that I really had no reason to go. Our lives were here; there was nothing there, not even memories. Sister Hildegard handed me two books, the old Christine de Pizan and the Marguerite Porète. I protested I didn't have room, but she insisted, opening the cover to show me the initials—FMDLC. These were my mother's books. The night I read them at the convent, I hadn't deciphered the initials.

"How could you not tell me that you had my mother's books?" I was accusing them all.

Annie said she presumed I knew. "Isn't that why you fussed at Sister Fides?"

I couldn't stay to argue with Annie. Airline schedules were keeping me from being angry over my mother's books, forcing me to push the Pizan and Porète into my backpack—there with my mother's notes and the clean tablet of graph paper I bought for my own notes. Time was compressing me, preventing me from talking to Andrew, insisting I hurry up and kiss everyone twice, once on each cheek, except Aurelia who broke through the schedule and kissed me twice again and then I kissed her twice and then she kissed me twice more.

I waved good-bye, drove to Burlington, and flew to New York.

The 1950s international terminal at JFK is hard-edged. Floors are linoleum; walls are mortar; the roof is a concrete tent top bolted down with steel cables. This is, I believe, to tether the passengers, to prevent us from flying away before our journeys are supposed to begin. The terminal is sealed against the caprice Annie was accusing me of. I went to the café to wait for the proper hour. Under my table were crumbs and a piece of foil ketchup packet, what might have been a slice of strawberry or the peel of a very dark orange, and a morsel of chicken that had dried grey, petrified. There was a woman who reminded me of Marguerite Porète at the next table drinking coffee. I thought for a moment I saw a copy of Marguerite's book, *The Mirror of Simple Souls*, in one of her bags, an old duffel bag there in her luggage cart. When

138

she saw me looking at the book, she looked alarmed and left her table and walked out of the restaurant quickly. I went to the bar for a bottle of mineral water and noticed a sign above the bartender's head that said, "Double-Dog Days—all beef wiener, an inch of extra beef."

"That," said the woman I now knew as Veronica Joyce, "is what Jung would call synchronicity." She seemed to be having a fine day—no tears, no moans. She smiled and said my presence on the trip was a good thing.

When I asked what all this Dog Day business was about, she said it had to do with the eye of Canis Majores and festivals in many cultures in which holy people and feral people alike released their numinosity during times of intense heat. Divany and she had come up with the idea of taking a pilgrimage now, to a place where souls were alive and had always been alive. "Going during Dog Days, to be pilgrims in places where myth steams up from the very heat of the season and ignites our souls, what an adventure in these post-post-post days. What a time to consider soul and its stories!"

I asked about the places we were going—places with history, places where we could touch rough walls of rooms where gods and prophets had lived, smell the scents, hear the sounds. "I think my mother used to make lists of such places."

Veronica said, "I understand you have a personal quest."

I admitted I did have a quest. I felt I could use a word like "quest" in her presence; after all, she was an anthropologist, and she had organized this journey for the soul. Her very act of noticing my quest made it apparent she understood its importance to me.

"You sound like you're searching for the Holy Grail," she said and laughed. "Just don't be disappointed. No one ever finds the grail." She looked at her watch. The hour that kept us locked in the restaurant had passed. It was time to board the plane.

Veronica rushed off to find the others. She still appeared quite happy.

I was sitting in a blue tweed seat, blue with lines of yellow and dark red running through. The seat to my left was all red, and the seat on the aisle was bright yellow.

A woman's voice came over the loudspeaker telling us there were spare seats, so we could sit near friends, but the aircraft would not move until everyone was seated and buckled in.

As the plane taxied away from the gate, I saw the twin towers of the World Trade Center out the right window. On the left, there was water. A small girl in the seat behind me was complaining. She had been unhappy since she boarded the plane. "I, too, would like that," she said, but I couldn't see what it was that she wanted. Then, I felt pain; the little girl was gripping the back of my seat and a handful of my hair at the same time. Suddenly, she broke loose and was out of her seat and running toward the front of the plane.

"The girl must be seated," a voice came from a seat next to the emergency door. "The girl must be strapped in while we're taking off."

Hands reached out from the seat backs and caught the child. She was trapped, stopped in the web of adult arms until her mother could reach her and take her back with her. "You must, must, must come with me," the mother said. "You must come with me."

I was very tired. I opened my backpack and removed the things I wanted to read before I slept: my mother's Glastonbury notes and the two books I had started so feverishly at the convent and then abandoned when I found my mother's work. Now I realized they were connected, and I hoped reading them together would clarify things. It would be helpful to see some connection before I arrived in Israel. Annie had asked what I expected to find over there. How could I go halfway around the world in search of secrets when I didn't even know what secrets I was after?

"You're not going to find her," Annie had said.

"Who?"

"Mother. You won't end up knowing her any better than you do now."

We were traveling into the sun, flying toward morning. The flight attendant was walking down the aisle, leaning across, drawing the beige plastic shades closed.

"I'd like to watch for the dawn," I said, and he left my shade up.

"Few will see the brightness," said a woman in the red seat next to me where no one had been sitting when we took off. There hadn't been anyone in the yellow seat on the aisle either. Now, both were taken.

"She said it was all right to sit with friends," said the woman on the aisle. "So, we waited until you were situated, and we've come to talk to you again."

It was Marguerite Porète and Christine de Pizan, still in their travel clothes. What were they doing there? How did they get there? "Do you have tickets?" I asked. Did it matter?

"We're on our way to the Holy Land," said Christine. "I want to see if Canaan is a land where all the fruits and freshwater rivers are found and where the earth abounds in all good things."

I thought she was quoting the Bible. Christine said it was her own, *Cite des Dames*, chapter one, question eight, the "Field of Letters," where she built her city of women.

"Hildegard says you're going to a dead writers' festival," said Marguerite. "Actually, I'm surprised we weren't personally invited."

I explained to Marguerite that this was not a dead writers' festival but a conference, a study tour, a writers' pilgrimage to find the story of the soul.

Christine asked what we expected to do.

"Write the stories of our own souls while standing in the shadows of famous souls," I said, trying to remember how Sister Hildegard had described the agenda.

"Sounds like a dead writers' festival to me," Marguerite repeated.

"The famous souls aren't all writers," I pointed out.

"Don't worry," she said. "Some will be. I invited a few friends."

There was a tug at my hair again. The small girl behind me was standing now, looking over my shoulder. "There is no one there," she said and pointed at the two seats next to me. I looked back and saw that her mother was leaning against the window, eyes closed.

Marguerite unbuckled her seat belt and stood.

The little girl said, "Now there is a lady."

Marguerite went around to the child's seat and took her hand. "Would you like to run up and down the aisle with me?" she asked. "I, too, am not good at being buckled in."

Hours later, when I thought we should have been in Israel, the plane stopped in Rome, even though it wasn't on the schedule. The pilot's voice said it was a routine maintenance check. Christine and Marguerite disappeared, and I imagined them off on a holiday. I closed my eyes and fell asleep. When I woke, Marguerite was sitting next to me again, reading a book in Latin, hers, she said; two copies of the *Mirror* had been preserved in Latin.

There were two American teenagers coming toward us, wandering in search of new seats. The boy was husky, fourteen or so, wearing a baseball cap; the girl was older, maybe sixteen. She had black hair pulled into a ponytail. Both were wearing T-shirts. The boy's shirt bore the words *in utero*; the girl's had the opening lines from the *Aeneid*. Same story as the *Odyssey*, it seemed to me, when I read it in high school, in Latin, slowly. Funny how the story got repeated, again and again. That's what my father was getting at

142

when he said the Irish Ulysses is the same as the Greek Ulysses; Joyce's story is the same as Homer's. And of course Virgil's; he'd add Virgil. I read Virgil on the teenager's shirt: *Arma virumque cano, Troiaie qui primus ab oris, ad Italiam fato profugus . . .* "I sing of arms and a man who left the shores of Troy and was driven toward Italy by fate." I wondered if they were traveling with a group from Latin camp.

Christine came back and slipped around the teenagers to reclaim her seat. "An apparent revival of the classics. The *vita classica* is good, as long as it's not an unquestioned *vita classica*," she said. For all her willingness to study the writings of men, she informed me, she was particularly critical of Ovid. "The affronts that man makes to women."

The teenaged girl asked in English if the seats next to me were taken. The child behind me answered in a shout, "Yes, they are!" The teenagers moved on. On the back of the girl's shirt was a green square with the brand name "Benetton."

"The old, the old, it never really grows old," said Veronica, and she shrugged as she passed toward the rest rooms.

We had been sitting on the tarmac in Rome for hours. Outside, the afternoon sun was fading. I wanted to leave the airport, take a cab quickly to Vatican City, see if I could catch a glimpse of the fates that drove my mother and father from Italy to Israel, but no one was permitted to get off the plane. A representative of the duty-free shop was allowed on board with a cart full of perfumes, liquor, jewelry, and miniature copies of antiquities and art objects. I was attracted to a small statue—actually, it was only a head, a copy of a woman's head, and I bought it. It was made of a roseate stone, dusty pink beige with a salmon tinge, and the woman had the crown of her hair braided and curls rolled, skimming her neck in back and touching her jawbones. Two locks fell toward her chin. They ended in wiry coils leaving only her earlobes uncovered.

143

Gala Stark came by as I was handing the saleswoman my Visa card. Gala had gathered up her hip-length white hair under a straw fedora she'd been wearing since New York. "Her nose is broken. Her eyes are gone. Her mouth is torn off. And of course, her body is missing altogether." She pointed toward the head the woman was wrapping in tissue. "Even idols suffer from politics." She was pacing the aisles, for exercise, she said. She had gone around forty-eight times; I'd been counting. I needed fresh air. I had lost faith in the wings that had held me above the ocean and kept me away from the sun, but the pilot's voice came on again and said we were about to climb back into the sky; the fuel gauge had been replaced. Gala came by, the forty-ninth time, and said we had actually started the flight without enough fuel and now the tank had been filled so we could make it to Israel. She did not seem worried. She smiled. I remembered she had gone to kindergarten with my father. I was among friends.

Marguerite tore a page from my tablet of graph paper, and on it she wrote a series of names: the naditu, the beguines, the nuns in convents, the Shikibus, the Catherines, the Mechthilds, the Beatrices, Sappho, ninshatapada, enheduanna, et al. There were maybe a hundred names, including the two at the end that weren't capitalized because Marguerite said that's just the way it was, or sort of the way it was.

"I'm afraid it's only partial," Christine apologized.

"Partial what?" I asked.

"A partial listing of members of the dead women writers' group," said Marguerite.

Christine noticed the arch in my left eyebrow. "It's not as though we do workshops," she said. "None of us can revise our work anymore, so we don't have to worry about anything tedious like that."

"It's a large group," I said.

"It's not the half of it," said Marguerite, who was picking up vernacular. "Somehow we missed all the contemporaries and moderns and Victorians."

"Not to mention the seventeenth and eighteenth centuries," Christine pointed out.

"Everyone between them and us."

"And Juana Inez de la Cruz."

"We've called Hildegard; she says she'll send something out."

Veronica passed by my seat. Her light complexion seemed lighter now. She leaned across Christine and Marguerite, put her mouth close to my ear and whispered intimately, in a clipped cadence that canceled her native southern drone, "We've noticed your spells. It's good. Don't worry. Have talks. Make lists. It's Israel. It's a blessing."

"This used to happen to Margery, too," said Christine. "Such empathy for the torments of others. The skin pales from the tears she holds inside. She may soon begin to weep."

The flight attendant asked that we all return to our seats, have our papers ready, buckle up, and prepare for landing. The air between me and Israel was the color of dusk.

Forensics: II

We walked off the plane, passed through customs and into Israel effortlessly. People were friendly, especially the woman who changed the tire on our van after it blew, just past Herzliyya. The tire didn't blow, really, it split and hissed and flapped its rubber against the road, which was both new and old, unfinished as though older roads had been torn up and cast aside, leaving pieces of a crumbling but indissoluble rock—cement-grey, both permeable as sand and solid as granite. Everything was in the process of being built and rebuilt. Gala was driving because the chauffeur who'd been hired to take us on the seminar pilgrimage went home when our plane was eight hours late.

"It was possible you wouldn't come today," said the man behind the counter. He suggested we hire several taxis to Haifa and make arrangements with a new chauffeur there in the morning, but Gala insisted on a rental van without a driver.

So it was Gala who was driving when the stone shards tore into the tire, and she piloted our Dodge Ram across three lanes of traffic. A woman was sitting—resting or thinking or waiting—in her Citroen by the side of the road. The Citroen was brown-red, the shade of rust-proofing primer my father brushed over all his outdoor tools.

When Gala stopped the van on the gravel shoulder, the woman stepped out of her car and came back toward us. She was older than Gala, perhaps seventy-five, perhaps older. The floppy brim of her yellow sun hat touched the short white edge of her hair, curling around her ears. She was wearing baggy-legged striped trousers, a navy polo shirt, and a washed-out denim jacket that was almost white but still carried a cast of lavender. On her hat was a lavender fish. She leaned on Gala's door and smiled and gestured so that everyone would get out; then she removed the tools from the box under the last seat. She operated the jack easily, and the only time she asked for help was when it was time to swing off the old tire and lift on the new.

Before she pulled the old tire off, she looked at me, screwed her lips together, and used them to point at the new tire that she had taken off the back door and left resting on the earth behind the van. I understood the message and rolled the tire into her grasp. She took the new tire as though she were handling nothing heavier than air. She hadn't said a word, so we thought she must not speak English. She put the toolbox back in the van; Gala shook her hand, and we all smiled and waved good-bye. She stretched and said, "Now the problem's done, we can have a social moment. I'm Hannah Pales. Who are all of you?"

We introduced ourselves. She knew Gala's name and mine as well. "You're a free thinker," she said to me, and to Gala she said, "And you, you're one of the originals, a superb delineator of political issues. I've heard of you." She looked at Veronica, squinted, and then apologized, saying Veronica reminded her of someone, but it wasn't possible. She was always mistaking one person for another. It was a habit that came from forever living in the Middle East. She was traveling now, she said; she had been traveling for a number of years, and she intended to continue traveling. She was enjoying this part of life. We had pulled up behind her as she was deciding whether to go north to Galilee or south to the Dead Sea.

Veronica said we were in Israel on a pilgrimage. "We've come to examine the stuff that the story of the soul is made of."

"There's a lot of that here," Hannah responded.

Gala explained we were staying in the pilgrimage hall of the sisters at Stella Maris and asked directions to Haifa. The woman looked at her watch, shook her head, and said we'd better hurry. They didn't keep the gates open much after dark.

So, we left quickly and drove north along the Mediterranean. In the time it took to change the tire, the sun had disappeared. The sky was darkening. I couldn't figure out the landscape. Gala couldn't figure out the route.

"You've come to Akko," Marguerite was back with us, "the crusader city. The Templars used to have a place here. Could you stop?"

"You need us to stop?" I asked.

"No, but you need to stop. You've gone on past Haifa and have to turn around and go back."

Christine said that she and Marguerite were going to leave us for a while. They wanted to check on the Templars, and there was also a woman Christine wanted to find in Nazareth.

"Mary?" I asked.

149

"Beatrice," Christine answered.

"Beatrice of the *Vita Nuova* and the *Divine Comedy*?" Christina had been reading Virgil after all, and it was Virgil who Dante said called Beatrice "the light between truth and the intellect."

"Beatrice of Nazareth," she said. "She's in our writers' group. She wrote *Seven Degrees of Love*."

I was recalling what Sister Hildegard had dictated about Beatrice of Nazareth that afternoon in the garden, there was a house and frenzy and veins. Suddenly I heard Veronica begin to murmur.

"It's your spells," whispered Kathryn Deere, the woman sitting next to me in the van. Kathryn was a nurse, and she wanted to write a book about how to comfort hospital patients and their families. She seemed to have volunteered to help Veronica with her moods. "Veronica is affected by your spells."

It was midnight when I first saw the lighthouse. The light was flashing in steady time, flash-two-three-four, flash-two-three-four, flash-two-three-four. A smaller strobe was beating counterpoint beneath it, flash-flash-flash-flash, flash-flash-flash-flash, flash-flash-flash-flash. It was Stella Maris, Star of the Sea. We had arrived. Gala saw the sign this time; perhaps it was easier to see coming from the Akko side. She turned left up Allenby, and I knew this must have been the route the ambulance took (my grandmother dead, my mother giving birth) screeching back down toward the hospital we'd passed at the bottom of the hill. We snaked back up Stella Maris Street where we seemed to be heading straight into the sky until Gala abruptly rounded a corner. Traffic seemed heavy for midnight. It must have been heavy the day I was born. Gala pulled the van into the beginnings of a driveway and stopped. The wrought iron gate I could see through the front windshield was closed.

I saw a smaller gate for pedestrians about fifteen feet down; I wondered if they'd come out that way to cross the street. We left the van and walked through the small gate onto the convent grounds, but the closest we could get was the steps of the little basilica. I found a path that led around the side, under mimosa trees at the edge of the church, to the driveway we hadn't been able to enter. Our Ram crouched on the other side of the gate in the night. There was another walkway, covered in vines on the right; on the left was a wall, waist high, where the cliff drooped into dark space. Across the dark, on another hill, houses cut black figures against the sky. Below, lights flickered on boats in the harbor. The walkway led to the side of the convent and to a large oak door studded with iron, shut, firmly locked. I was about to knock when Veronica touched my arm. The sisters had warned we must arrive by 10 p.m., or we couldn't enter until morning. "I suggest we get coats, blankets, jackets, what have you, and camp out here on the church steps," she said.

I couldn't believe anyone would bar the door because the sun went down, not nuns, not nuns who knew people were coming from another country to stay. Surely, if I knocked, someone would come to the door.

"This is a convent, not a hotel," Veronica said. There was a stern note in her voice. "You can't knock on a convent door as though it were any other door."

"Of course you can," I objected. "I've done it all my life." I knocked and I waited. No one came. Perhaps no one heard. "I was born here. Don't worry, nuns don't mind, really. They're people." The sisters at Stella Maris College had always been available, especially to someone in need. I knocked again. Nothing happened.

"These are Carmelites," Veronica said, "contemplatives. They live in cloister. They're not the same as your nuns in the United States."

It was true. We were too late; we were not going to get inside before morning.

The nuns who ran the college where my father taught and I studied and Andrew and I played were a different order, French originally, but not Carmelite, and though they contemplated a good deal, they were not contemplative. Not so contemplative that they'd leave expected guests to sleep outside on the ground. In all my life, this was the first time it occurred to me that the Stella Maris where I was born and the Stella Maris where I was raised were connected only by name. Father Louis was the only other person I knew with links to the Stella in Vermont and the Stella in Haifa, although his link was actually to my father's school—established and dissolved in the forties. And he had fastened Aurelia to both places by fastening her to us.

I suggested a hotel, but a woman named Rose Aldin said she was there on a shoestring. She was an acupressurist in private practice and didn't have extra money to spend on unnecessary hotel rooms when we could just as well camp right there by the wall or back around the front by the church. Her friend Nancy reminded us that adversity was good for the soul and asked for a show of souls who wanted to sleep on marble steps. They outnumbered the soul who wanted to go find a hotel and have a shower and a glass of Israeli wine before bed. Veronica said schnapps would be better and more customary anyway because people leave sacred schnapps and cookies at religious sites for pilgrims. I looked around. Either someone had forgotten to leave the schnapps in the Stella Maris parking lot, or other pilgrims had been there before us.

When we went back to the van to search for bags and blankets and jackets to soften our sleep on the church stairs, I noticed people sitting at tables across the street, behind the pay phones, in a space that looked like the rest area just above Duluth. I wasn't ready to sleep there on the ground, so close to my mother's grave, which had to be somewhere nearby. On a hill, my father had said, and we were on a hill; of course, all of Haifa was on one hill or another.

The night was quiet, and the air was warm and heavy. The back of my neck was damp from the thin film of perspiration glazing my skin and giving me an odd chill. Perhaps Annie was right about the place and the time being wrong for me. I took my backpack and left my traveling companions, whom I hardly knew, and went to sit in the light with people I didn't know at all, but who smiled as I walked between their tables. It was an outdoor café. People had plates and glasses and silverware, and there was a young woman bringing their bills and taking their money. She came to my table and spoke English. "Good evening. We are closed now."

I told her I would simply like something to drink—wine, Coca-Cola, coffee, schnapps.

"Ancra?" she said, smiling.

Whatever she could give me at this hour, I said.

"Water. I will bring you water."

I sat there, sipping water until all the strangers had left and the young woman had taken my glass. I gave her an Israeli note with the number ten and a picture of Golda Meir on the face. "You've given me four dollars for a glass of water," she said. I told her that was fine, if only she would allow me to stay there for a while. The tables were outside, and there was nothing to lock up so she let me stay in the café. Then I was alone, watching the lights on the Mediterranean. In the quiet, I could hear waves washing up on shore at the bottom of the hill. At first, waves hit the land below me one at a time, rhythmically, one long lap and then silence, another long lap and silence. Then I began to hear another wave beating against the count, washing into the silent space, and then fainter, further away, yet another. Waves and counterwaves starting at different points in the rhythm and then recurring, hitting

153

the shore on the pulse of the lighthouse strobe, until, without warning, they all suspended their meters and rolled in together.

It was two in the morning. In Vermont it would be 7 p.m. I went to the pay phones to call Aurelia. The phone would not accept either a shekel or five-shekel coin. There was a slot, the size of a credit card or a phone card like my "phone home" card, but that wouldn't help because it would call directly to Andrew in Duluth, and he wasn't there. I tried dialing zero, no tone. I hung up and went back to where my companions were sleeping on the steps.

Gala had taken off her fedora, and her long white hair cascaded down the steps. Veronica was curled up under the mimosa. Rose and Nancy were leaning against the church doors. Kathryn Deere, the nurse, was stretched out, flat on her back, on the third step from the top. Her hands were folded on her stomach. There were four more I hadn't spoken to other than to nod and smile when introduced and shrug as the journey had grown longer and longer: a woman in a yellow shirtdress named Astrid who wanted to enter a Catholic seminary, but of course she couldn't, and so she'd taken Divany's night course on the soul instead; an auburn-haired woman named BeeBee Dock, who had trained at the Jung Institute in Zurich before she moved to New York, where she worked for the transit authority; two women who taught at NYU, Liz Town the art professor and Stephanie Douhie, who taught English. Those four had gone to the vine-covered path and were nested there. Varying stages in the writing process. Some better at soul. No one awake.

To the side of the main church doors was a smaller iron door painted ivory like the stone frame around it. I was going to try to make myself comfortable there and wait for dawn, but as I settled my back against the door, it creaked and opened. I went inside to a grotto chapel and a small altar, where a candle was burning next to a worn brown wooden statue. The air was cool and moist, like in the cellar under the French garden at the convent in Vermont where the walls were granite, the cellar hewn out of the hill. I curled up in one of the pews with my head resting on my backpack and fell asleep.

Was it morning, or had I simply adjusted to the dark? And the sound? Tapping, a hammer striking nails, my father picking at his keyboard, a woodpecker hitting a crisp, regular pace, then changing. I sat up. There was another statue in the chapel, too, the virgin. There were rose colors all around her. I lit a candle for the wooden man and another for the flushed virgin and dropped two five-shekel coins into the metal box in payment to them for my night's sleep. Outside, Rose and Nancy were doing morning exercises, each of them with a jump rope, the adult kind with polished wooden handles. Heavy white rope slapping the ground was the sound that woke me. It was morning, and I was standing in a cemetery.

"French. Napoleon's people," said Gala. "Another Waterloo."

"I'm looking for the graves of my mother and grandmother," I told her. "They're buried here somewhere."

"Probably not here. This is a monument commemorating all the wrong instincts, as most monuments do. There must be another graveyard near here."

Gala and I had walked all the way around to the back of the building, looking for another graveyard, when a nun came out the door. She indicated we should follow her, and we did, into the kitchen. She poured coffee, no cream, and handed it to us.

"Divany Schulman?" she asked.

She was disappointed when we told her neither of us was Divany and that she would not be coming. Gala explained her credentials, and I told her mine, adding that I'd been born there. She looked at me oddly. "My father was teaching here. Michael

Creed." She shook her head. "My mother used to make tea for the sisters; my family lived here, in the convent, in the cloister." She frowned, still shaking her head. "It was over forty years ago, when Father Louis was here." Then she smiled, but her smile made her look sad. Father Louis was dead, she said; he died fifteen years ago, before she came to Israel. Michael Creed? She hadn't heard of him. "My mother and grandmother were killed in traffic right here, on the street. My mother was pregnant; she died, and I was born."

"The women in the street?" She seemed to know the story.

"The women who died in the street, in 1951. Do you know where they're buried?"

"Not here," she said. "Maybe in the American cemetery. Very sad."

"They weren't American. They were British." I reminded myself of my discussion of obituaries. "And Welsh and French-Irish. Something else, something from near here. Maybe here. They were Morgans."

She looked puzzled again. "They are not here."

I asked if there was anyone who was old enough to have been there in the early fifties, anyone who would remember my family, know where the graves were, perhaps have my mother's notes. "She was studying here. Father Louis was going to send her things. He forgot to send her books and the notes she was writing. There was a fire; some of her things may have been destroyed, but some may still be here, somewhere . . . "

She said maybe Sister Pia would remember, and then she disappeared. Gala went out to find the others. It was 7 a.m. Veronica wanted to start our pilgrimage by eight. I was pouring myself a second cup of coffee when Sister Pia walked in. She was a round-shaped woman—her face, her body, her hands. She was older than the nun who had been talking to us, but much younger

156

than my father. I didn't think she'd been there in 1951.

"You're looking for the women in the street," she said and took my hand. "I am so sorry. I've heard the story many times."

"Do you know where they are buried?"

"Not here," she said.

"Not in Haifa?"

"Maybe in Haifa, not here in the convent."

"Are there records?"

"There would have been, but many papers were lost in the fire just before Father Louis' death."

"My mother's papers?"

"It could be."

"All her books, everything she had been writing?"

"I don't believe we have anyone's books. No one's writing. Except Teresa of Avila, we have copies of her *Castle*."

"Is there anyone who would know where my mother's writings would be, if there were any?"

"Maybe Brother Hugh." Brother Hugh, she told me, was a Franciscan, a scholar who lived near Tiberias, on the Sea of Galilee. He used to study with Father Louis. He was always traveling. Even to Baghdad in the old days, not now. There was no one left who knew my father, not even Sister Pia, who only knew what Father Louis had told her. But Brother Hugh came shortly after my family was there. He might know something. When Brother Hugh was in Israel, he usually lived at the Church of St. Peter in Tabgha or at the Franciscan monastery in Capernaum. He usually came for the festival, and that would be soon, so he probably was in Israel already. She took my hand again. "You're the infant from the street?" she asked.

I said I was.

She smiled and patted me on the shoulder. "Welcome home." The younger sister was standing there now with Gala,

Veronica, and all the others. Veronica said if we hurried, we could put our things in our rooms and still leave for Tiberias by eight o'clock. She said it was important for us as pilgrims to keep to our schedule. I commented that I thought we were writers. She said yes, that too; everyone was to remember to bring a notebook and a pen.

Later, I found out that shortly after I left for Israel, my father and Sister Hildegard found messages on the Internet, posted to the newly established Thomas Aquinas Users' Group; he said the group was a text-based society, an assembly of philosophers who met electronically, in something he called a Multi-User Dungeon, or a MUD. After my father read the messages, he sent a message to Sister Hildegard, who replied, and he replied to her reply, and she to his, and he to hers, and she to his.

Date: Seventh Month, '00
X-Sender: christine@pizan.cite
To: thomaquin@paris.summa
Subject: Summa Theologiae (on the body and soul)

I know of a small book in Latin . . . which discusses the constitution of women's natural bodies and especially their great defects.

You can see for yourself without further proof, this book was written carelessly and colored by hypocrisy, for if you have looked at it, you know that it is obviously a treatise composed of lies. God created the soul and placed wholly similar souls, equally good and noble in the feminine and in the masculine bodies. (Citè des Dames)

Date: Seventh Month, '00
X-Sender: porète@farnear.nil
To: thomaquin@paris.summa
Subject: Summa Theologiae (on the soul)

This Soul, says Love, is the lady of the
Virtues, daughter of Deity, sister of
wisdom . . . I was, says this Soul, and
I am, and I will be always without lack,
for Love has no beginning, no end, and no
limit, and I am nothing except Love. (Le
mirouer des simples ames)

Date: Seventh Month, '00
X-Sender: christine@pizan.cite
To: thomaquin@paris.summa
Subject: Summa Theologiae (on the mind)

. . . if anyone maintained that women do
not possess enough understanding to learn
the law, the opposite is obvious from the
proof afforded by experience, which is
manifest and has been manifested in many
women . . . who have been very great
philosophers and have mastered fields far
more complicated, subtle, and lofty than
written laws and man-made institutions.
Moreover, in case anyone says that women
do not have a natural sense for politics
and government, I will give you examples
of several great women rulers who have
lived in past times. (Citè des Dames)

Date: Seventh Month, '00
X-Sender: vonbingen@mystik.illum
To: thomaquin@paris.summa
Subject: woman

O feminea forma, quam gloriosa es!

Date: July 16, '00
X-Sender: mcreed@stellamaris.edu
To: shildegard@stellamaris.edu
Subject: thomaquin@paris.summa

Sister Hildegard,
Have you read the debate entries that someone (you? Nin?) has mustered on my Aquinas line? I appreciate the humor, and scholarship. Can you verify accuracy? Don't you think the sender should own up to the messages and sign her own name? all best . . .

Date: July 16, '00
X-Sender: shildegard@stellamaris.edu
To: mcreed@stellamaris.edu
Subject: thomaquin@paris.summa

Prof. Creed:
These seem to be direct references to the works of the women cited as senders. Bingen accurate; C. de Pizan slightly paraphrased but substantially in context. Can't verify Porète; Nin has only copy.

You write >Don't you think the sender should own up to the messages and sign her own name?<

I believe they did sign their own names. all best . . .

Date: July 16, '00
X-Sender: mcreed@stellamaris.edu
To: shildegard@stellamaris.edu
Subject: thomaquin@paris.summa

Sister Hildegard,
If it's not you and Nin, who is it? It's all good fun to pretend these writers posted these messages, but your friends

should have the courtesy to identify themselves. Net etiquette may tolerate
anonymity, but scholarship can't allow it.

P.S. . . . on second reading, they don't
give much analysis, do they?
all best . . .

Date: July 16, '00
X-Sender: shildegard@stellamaris.edu
To: mcreed@stellamaris.edu
Subject: thomaquin@paris.summa

Prof. Creed:
Even Millett, who chastised Woolf for not
sufficiently explaining the source of a
character's suicidal ambitions, has said
that she would rather express female experience than analyze it. all best . . .

Date: July 16, '00
X-Sender: mcreed@stellamaris.edu
To: shildegard@stellamaris.edu
Subject: thomaquin@paris.summa

Sister Hildegard,
I insist on knowing who these authors
are. all best . . .

Date: July 16, '00
X-Sender: shildegard@stellamaris.edu
To: mcreed@stellamaris.ed
Subject: thomaquin@paris.summa

Prof. Creed:
I believe they did sign their own names.
all best . . .

Forensics: III

Vanilla and milk, dough in reheated oil, onions on a griddle—warm, sleepy scents woke me as Gala steered the Dodge Ram into a parking lot next to a lake the size of Memphremagog, but the feeling wasn't Vermont. Somehow, we'd been transported to a town in Jersey in the summer—boardwalks, the smell of pitch from tar streets in the sun, metal-fronted T-shirt shops, and fried sweet food—and a Caesar's Palace, but this one was looming over broken walls, old broken walls. Ruins. We were in Tiberias.

While Veronica ran into the tourist bureau, I stood at the edge of the Sea of Galilee and stared at the other side because it was unambiguously near. I could see across it the way I saw the opposite shore of Memphremagog. It wasn't the mysterious Sea of Galilee I recalled from childhood, not the Sea of Galilee in my memory, a memory I'd conjured from Bible stories and grade school lessons about Jesus walking on water in a storm. In my memory, the apostles had a grey and red wooden fishing boat and no life vests, and they were out on water like Lake Superior with waves up to their shoulders. It was dark and windy, and they were about to die, and you couldn't see hills on the other side at all. In fact, you couldn't see hills on your own side, and Jesus was coming on the crest of a wave, walking in the eye of the storm.

The sea I was standing next to was not the one in my memory. This sea was small and peaceful, and I could see naked hills jutting up and down all the way around. I began to count hills—twelve, thirteen, fourteen. I was still counting when Veronica came back and said the plan was to keep driving since the guest house was all the way up the sea, and we might as well go on up to the Golan Heights and come back down and have a swim and dinner and sleep and breakfast and hit Capernaum and the Mount of Beatitudes and everything else, including Tiberias, in the morning. That meant I wasn't going to get any closer to my mother's work, wasn't going to find Brother Hugh until the next day, but I was sleepy after only a couple hours' rest in the chapel with the rose lady and the wooden man, and I was drawn to this body of water and those hills. So, Gala headed up the coast of the Sea of Galilee which is called Kinneret, because in Israel, like in a Russian novel, everything has at least two names and sometimes more.

We worked through the day, which became longer and longer as though we were piling tombs on top of each other to build a tower, and building it higher and higher and higher. We went from tomb to tomb to tomb. We heard about soul after soul. We stopped at shrine after shrine. We were on a field trip through the cemeteries of the Bible, assembling a carnival for the dead, some long dead, some recently dead. We whizzed by a few memories.

"Look quickly, on the right. Migdal," Veronica called out, "the home of Mary Magdalene. We'll pass again, soon. Tomorrow. Another time." And we paused and browsed and shopped for mementos at the sites of other shadows. Veronica had the agenda, and none of the rest of us had a clue about whose sepulcher we'd haunt next. Except I knew we were getting no closer to my mother's tomb. I was calm only when I suspended my longing and agreed with Veronica that we were in Israel as simple pilgrims, which is what she now called everyone she met, and that was disconcerting for me because, although I knew full well what she meant, I was continually looking for people who were either characters in Thanksgiving illustrations or costars in a John Wayne movie, and I never saw anyone who fit in either group.

To Veronica, we were the pilgrims of the soul, now heading away from the sea. Along the edge of the road, there were chunks of cement work, grainy concrete mixed with a compound that was as smooth and white as saltwater taffy. I remember the shoulder of one hill that had been opened, its gravel spilled down its side, and at its foot were pieces of rusted transit bus and fiberglass camper and pipe of varying lengths. We stopped at the River Jordan, at Jacob's Daughter's Bridge, which was really two bridges separated by a short piece of road. The bridges were made of loose boards, and they rumbled as a truck full of soldiers rolled over them. A sign said: Do Not Leave the Pavement.

Gala gestured toward the rocky shoulder, "Land mines could still be here."

We left the Ram and walked, carefully, on the road, toward the bridge where Jacob's daughter predicted what would happen to Joseph.

"Jacob's daughter?" asked Astrid, the woman I will always think of as a priest, her desire being stronger in my mind than the church's dictates. "Dinah was his only girl, wasn't she?"

"She prophesied Joseph would be dropped in the pit," said Stephanie, the English prof.

"The crusaders called it Jacob's Ford," added BeeBee, the Jungian. "Jacob wrestled the angel here."

"The Haganah blew it up in '46," Gala informed us, "in protest against the British."

There was black electrical wire coming from under the bridge, and I stepped toward the sandbags, propped around a trench enforced with black basalt and lime-green concrete. It was a leftover gun emplacement. Concertina wire spiraled around the sandbags and through the tall grass where it joined razor wire under the bridge.

"Should we be here?"

"Of course," said Veronica, who had not been teary-eyed since we left Tiberias. "This is what we came for."

"The Bible says the whole thing happened somewhere else," said Astrid.

We were about halfway into the Golan Heights when we stopped at Qazrin and wandered through a museum where I saw a dragon who, according to the fiche, was either a serpent or a panther, but to me it was a dragon. I was sure I had seen it somewhere else, with its bulging eyes and lips turned inside-out like I used to be able to do when I was a child.

"Looks Mexican," said Liz, the art professor, "like one I saw in a museum in the Yucatán."

In the little store next to the museum, I bought a plaster figurine that looked like the Israeli-Mexican dragon. I also bought a clay head belonging to someone else, a woman long gone, this one with a nose like Charles deGaulle, heavy upper lids, and big soft buns of hair that seemed to be crowned with some ornamentation—a wreath, maybe roses, leaves. I bought her because she was

166

haunting; she looked like someone I'd met somewhere, and she was affordable compared to the expensive basalt carving Gala bought. A few miles away, there was a town called Gamla where there were small houses left from before the Romans came. One house was open to tourists, one that could have been built by the father in *Swiss Family Robinson.* We went up a ladder made of rustic wooden poles and out on a patio, across to another section and down another pole ladder on the other side. The house had a stove made of clay, dug into the ground, and a young man whose job it was to reenact the ritual of flat bread baking, just as it was done in 68 A.D. Another everyday ritual for my mother's list.

We kept driving north. The road was still, no traffic going up, except us. No vehicles coming down other than white ones bearing the letters "U.N." There was a volley of gunfire.

"Just Israelis practicing," Veronica stated.

I tapped Gala on the shoulder.

She shrugged. "Here, you never know," she said and kept driving north, past a place that was called Mas'ada, but not *the* Masada. When we reached the top of a beige, treeless hill, Gala pulled over and got out. I followed her to the edge of the hill. "I couldn't resist," she said. "The politics are riveting here. I had to stop. Look, down there. That's Syria." She was pointing toward a U.N. base at the bottom of the hill and beyond. "Imagine your boundaries shifting around you like this." Gala was lured by politics the way I was drawn by my mother's dreams.

Veronica called us back to the Ram. It was time to head for Banyas, where the Jordan River was born and where people who worshipped Greek gods had built a temple to the shepherd god Pan.

"They took up with Pan when they got rid of that fellow Baal," said Astrid.

Now, the temple was a simple recess in the mountain, a mere alcove like the niches cathedral architects afford to lesser saints. "It seems a modest little nook," I said. Perhaps because Marguerite and Christine had been gone since the night before, I was beginning to talk to my fellow travelers.

"Both Pan and St. George were men with leaves and branches. Reflections of the green man," said BeeBee.

"For thou art Pan, thou Bacchus art, and Shepherd of bright stars," Stephanie answered.

I was taken with the expertise of my fellow travelers. They had a grasp of specific sites in a country not their own where they had never traveled and in an area of that country that was certainly off the beaten track. I recited Byron in order to offer my share of culture. "The Gods of old are silent on their shore since the great Pan expired, and through the roar of the Ionian waters broke a dread voice which proclaimed—the mighty Pan is dead."

Kathryn and BeeBee had gone to the museum of culture next to the tourist office in Tiberias while I was staring at the sea and had picked up pamphlets. Kathryn offered me hers. There, on page 7, was the section on Banyas and the words Stephanie had quoted from the Great Mysteries. I thanked her.

"Pan means bread in Spanish," said Rose.

"But he was Greek," said Liz.

BeeBee didn't want to be limited. "The soul can travel from one language to another without papers," she insisted. "It's important in analysis, this freedom to associate. If Rose wants to associate Pan with the Spanish as well as the Greek, it's important not to separate her and her view of the god who is there, in the cave, where stream begins and river has not yet swelled."

I thought about my father and his concern with anachronism. Could I demand a trial by community standards in the thirteenth and fourteenth centuries, especially since I was defining the community as feminine? Why not? Why should I be devoted to chronology and geography any more than Rose?

168

In the heat of afternoon, we stopped at a campground where ancient oak trees stretched up from rocky soil. There were picnic tables and water fountains, and we sat in the shade of the ancient trees where Mohammed's men camped before there were any trees there at all. The men had to drive wooden stakes into the ground to tie up their horses for the night, and when they woke in the morning, the stakes had turned to giant oaks. Early in the day, Veronica bought tomatoes, bread, and melon; we sliced tomatoes and broke pieces from loaves of crispy bread with our hands. I dipped the broken bread into hummus and then into a seedy red sauce meant for falafel. Rose unsheathed a knife and cut into the red meat of the melon. I filled my water bottle from mineral-heavy spring water that gushed when I turned the spigot on the fountain. I was warm and sleepy and rested my head against one of the oaks, wondering if the miracle could be repeated, if sticks were driven into the ground here again, would more trees grow while we slept?

When Gala woke me, the group had cleared the grounds of any sign of picnic, and perhaps because we had pounded no stakes, there were no new trees. We drove down the hill away from the giant oaks and into a pine forest where the trees closed in behind us. There were two places where we had to get out of the van so Gala could gun the engine and spin the wheels over rocks in dried-out streambeds. We were enroute to the grave of Rabbi Jonathan Ben Uzziel who, because he never took the time to fall in love before he died, had become famous for helping the living find love. Not just love, but their beloved—the one true love, the love he never sat quietly enough to notice. It's not a sexual thing—this finding of a one true love, Veronica said, it's not a sentimental issue. It is finding a soul mate. I wasn't sure I understood the distinctions she was making. I tried to think of pruning sentimentality and sexuality out of my life with Andrew and having strong soul left over. I didn't want to weed out either.

She said she didn't mean to imply asexuality. Of course there was sexuality here, but there was something more as well.

"What?" I asked.

"Beginnings," she answered firmly and walked quickly toward the curio stand below the rabbi's tomb where there were blue stones and gold beads and hats embroidered with red and purple and yellow threads.

I selected three hats and a set of fish to bring back to my students in hopes magic here at the tomb could be transferred. The boy who sold them to me told me to put them on the tomb of the rabbi and walk around it seven times.

"It will help you find your beloved," he said.

"I have my beloved," was my answer.

"It will let you keep him then," he said, asking where my beloved was.

I told him he was in a forest, exactly like the one we were standing in, only across a sea and nearly to the top of a continent.

He said, in that case, I should definitely walk around the rabbi's tomb seven times. "One must be heedful."

"Heedful of what?"

"Heedful of chance."

So, I bought a pair of blue fishes for myself and another pair for Andrew. I walked up the slope toward the smoky fire coming from a metal box set high on a stand next to the concrete shrine. There was a woman selling candles, and people were tossing them into the fire. Paraffin was creating blue smoke. I bought a candle. Inside, young people were circling the elevated glossy blue enamel sarcophagus, reading prayers, repeating them. I placed my blue glass fishes on the tomb. The thin brown bag of hats I had purchased seemed a large burden to heap on this man's grave, but I wanted his spell, so I opened the sack and let smoke and prayer and circling seep inside, where the hats were folded, one into another. My favorite of these hats, the deep red and purple one, was for Andrew. After we had gone round and round the rabbi's tomb, we climbed back into the Ram and headed back toward the dry stream, where we had to portage its rocky bed again. The ground was warm there under the dried brown pine needles. How easy it would have been for Andrew to find his roots under those copper and turquoise mosses.

Gala drove on toward the town of Meron.

"What's the agenda for the rest of the day?" I asked her.

"There is no agenda; we go where we go."

"But you know where to drive. Sister Hildegard said Veronica drew up the itinerary. What are we to see next? What are we to learn next?"

"Veronica's plan is that we resist any specific system of travel. She has given us a day of wandering, like bar Yochai and his god."

Bar Yochai, Gala explained, was a rabbi who wandered around this very area, talking about creation, talking about god, talking about splendour. "He had no agenda, nor did his god. He wandered with his son, from cave to cave. And of course, the politics of it is that they were probably being chased because he'd been a part of a 'rising.'" With that, she pulled into a parking space off to the side of a building circled by a high wall. The roof was made of shallow domes that bulged only slightly over a mausoleum. We walked toward the building. "See," Gala pointed, "with very little effort, we have come to the tomb of Rabbi Shimon bar Yochai."

It was bar Yochai who gave me my first taste of sacred schnapps. Veronica said the way to remember this rabbi was to sing and dance in the spring and to exhibit piety at his grave—women's piety to the right, men's piety to the left, rejoined piety again on the other side of the tomb where the mood was more relaxed. I was wearing a short-sleeved shirt, and I slipped a mauve sweater over it. Then, to satisfy my own piety, as though I were about to enter a Catholic church before John XXIII when Catholic women still covered their heads, I took the scarf I usually kept tied around my waist and wound it around my head. As we walked through the tomb, I could hear men raising their voices in another room, and then I saw them push out into the garden, leaning in toward one another, shaking their hands in each other's faces.

"They are scholars; good scholars. As we all know, scholars need to argue," Veronica explained, as she passed the schnapps and buttery cookies left for us because we were pilgrims. "A gesture of respect for souls abroad."

I swallowed a shot of the clear sacred brew. It was licorice. Anisette. Ouzo. Aguardiente. Aquavit. I had tasted this sacred liqueur in nearly every country I'd ever visited. It always tasted the same, and it was always known by a different name.

We made a U-turn, back to Rosh Pinna, back down toward the shores of the Sea of Galilee. There was a cave half-covered in vines and leaves at the bottom of the hill, next to a waterfall, and I imagined bar Yochai and his son hiding there, where the river cascaded over black rocks and foamed as it hit the streambed and rushed on. They would have been dry inside. No one could have seen them behind the foam and the mist, in the wet shadow at the entrance. They could have stayed there a long while, drinking from the falls, stealing out to pick berries and wild apples, eating fish, safe except for drought or flood.

Since we hadn't used the entire day, Veronica thought we should climb the Mount of the Beatitudes to the round church at the top, where blessings were written in rose-stained glass letters: blessed are the poor in spirit; blessed are they who mourn; *beati pacifici*. There were red birds flying through the blessings. I thought they were cardinals, three of them, flying over the peacemakers, but Liz Town, the art prof, said the red glass birds were doves, not cardinals. They were ardent doves.

I went out onto the colonnade that circled around the outside of the church, hoping for a glimpse of Capernaum, somehow thinking I would be granted an aerial view of Brother Hugh, a man I'd never met and certainly would never recognize. Wind tore up from the Sea of Galilee below, pounding like waves I'd expected on the sea, not in the air above it, beating against the palm trees, crashing loudly. I held onto a pillar so the undertow whipping around my ankles wouldn't steal me away. Down below, a sailboat moved slowly, skimming the top of the water silently, three rust-red sails splashing in the wind. It was an old schooner, rounder, wider than the sailboats they build today. Its cabin was mottled green. I hoped the sailboat would dock near our guest house on the sea so I could get a closer look; I knew if it docked, it would strip its sails; but even without the blood-red sails, it would be different from the others. The wide moon of a hull was blue, and there were seven windows in the green cabin. The sun was going down quickly now, the boat heading straight toward evening. My eyes went back to the sails, wings carrying the boat into the sun, dark red doves flying through the beatitudes. The sailboat floated on, ignoring me and all the others standing on the balcony of the round black stone church.

The guest house was just down the road, at the bottom of the hill, on the sea. It wasn't a hotel, but it had two hundred rooms, with a long green yard that spread to the rocks at the edge of the sea, like lawns spread out under the feet of guests playing croquet and horseshoes at resorts on Memphremagog and Lake Superior. When dinner was over, pilgrims strolled toward wooden chairs. These people were dressed in slacks and sandals and beach shirts that kept their shoulders warm in the cool evening. The round stone beach hurt my feet, and the sea of Galilee was cold at night, but I was out there in a swimsuit in the dark doing laps to make up for spending the day in a Dodge Ram. I planned to buy something light in the snack bar and take it with me to the soul story meeting that Veronica scheduled in the guest house conference room for eight o'clock.

These story meetings were to be my responsibility. They were one of the reasons I had been invited on the trip. It was time for me to show the soul seekers how to pull living story from the tombs we had visited all day long, time to teach them to rob tales from all the graves. It wasn't going to be easy. Our day had no story line, other than bar Yochai's wandering. And too many crucial moments. And so much denouement, day unraveling into more day unraveling.

I had been swimming for twenty-five minutes, laps I invented by swimming from the willow dipping into the shore of the sea at one side of the lawn to the willow bending at the other, long enough to feel alive again, so I swam to shore and walked out of the dark sea to the chair where my yellow towel seemed to glow in the dark. I dried my hair and my face and legs, then wrapped the towel around me like a sarong before I walked toward the others gathered along the edge of the sea. I wondered if there was a difference between a pilgrim and a tourist. There didn't seem to be, except that tourists were out to capture profane places, and pilgrims needed to capture sacred ones. The Eiffel Tower could be acquired by a woman in a straw hat; she could show her friends that she'd secured it, there in the photo over her left shoulder. Just then, I was engulfed in the flash from a camera, and there I was, a strange American woman stepping out of night foam onto the beach, captured in a pilgrim's snapshot of the holy sea. I felt naked. I covered my shoulders with my second towel and scurried inside to dry off before the story session.

It had been my idea that each of us should open our notebooks and read to ourselves the notes we took during the day before we began our writing session. It would refresh us, remind us how important detail was to memory, open us to the discussion of whether story needed an itinerary. Then I told them to go ahead and write for fifteen minutes, to let the images roll through them, onto the page. To write without regard for anything except impressions, passions, details. It was quiet in the room and warm. I opened the door for air. I could hear pencils moving across paper. When the time was up, I asked for volunteers. Who wanted to read what they had sketched as memory of our first day as pilgrims of the soul?

Nancy said she'd read first. I had learned during the day that she was a noninvasive masseuse who touched her clients only with the warm glow of candlelight, exploring them as though they were eggs, moving her candles from hollow to hollow in the body, wicking away harm. When she began to read, I expected free association, flickering glimpses, pencil dancing from hollow to hollow in the day. But hers was remarkably linear, the chronology I had been yearning for before we drank schnapps with bar Yochai.

"We awoke on the steps of a beautiful church and then, driving, came to Tiberias, where we found maps and guidebooks and planned our day and then, according to that plan, we started en route to the Golan Heights, and looking over toward the sea, we saw the city of Mary Magdalene and the road through the hills to the point in the sea where we might see Jesus' fishing boat . . . " Nancy went on, spot to spot to spot to spot. And much as I wanted to believe Gala, to hold onto the notion that we could wander and find splendour whenever we were ready, I knew that if I ever made this trip again, it would be Nancy's notes I would want on the seat of the car next to me as I drove.

I asked if anyone else wanted to read. Rose said she was not able to write on a full stomach; writing was like exercise to her since she'd begun free associating, so much jumping and skipping and untying the knots of the day. She apologized. She had nothing to read. Perhaps in the morning, before breakfast.

Gala broke the silence. "High are the hills; armed are the valleys. The relics of politics and the soldiers of peace."

Kathryn joined in, "The oaks of Mohammed, the stream of Pan, the tombs of rabbis."

Astrid listed her own beatitudes, blessing everything we had seen that day, ending with "Blessed is the Mount. Blessed is the Sea."

Stephanie made lists, she said, all inspired by the discussion over the meaning of "pan," which she considered a prefix of location and distance. Therefore, she would recite a parade of places related to that prefix: the bridge where Dinah tells Jacob what's to come, the house where bread is baked, the hill where Syria waits, the stream where gods change into saints, the picnic grounds where horses wake up tied to ancient oaks, the tomb where love is hoped for, the tomb where scholars argue, the hill where Jesus preaches, the sea where a woman swims in the dark.

I remarked on the use of the present tense. Did she mean to use present tense?

Yes, she means to use it throughout the pilgrimage. She is reliving story, recreating reality, continuing myth.

Veronica was pleased at her response, so pleased that tears came to her eyes, and she asked for a tissue. Kathryn gave several to Veronica, who dabbed at her eyes and waited for the tears to stop.

Liz had drawn her journal. As an artist, she found herself unable to distinguish between language and image. She was like Sister Hildegard, I thought, only for her there was never any need for words. Design was enough. She held up her notebook and turned the pages slowly. On each page was a simple sketch, not apparently representational at all.

"What do they mean?" asked Gala.

"Each is simply what it is. Signifies what it signifies. Depicts and classifies what it depicts and classifies."

"And it prays," Veronica was once again touched. The nurse said Veronica should go to bed; in fact, she thought we should all go to bed.

I agreed. "Remember to keep your notebooks handy tomorrow," I instructed, and we went to our rooms. I stopped at the indoor kiosk where I'd bought coffee, flat bread, and jam for supper. I was hoping they'd tell me how to use the telephone so I could call my father and Aurelia and check on Andrew. The woman explained the need for a phone card and sold me one and told me how to use it, but she said the phone was out of order and wouldn't be fixed until morning. I bought another cup of coffee and took it to my room. As I fumbled for my key, I heard voices inside. I tapped my coffee cup against the wood, and Marguerite opened the door. Christine was there, too, sitting at my desk.

"Beatrice was unusually busy," Christine said. "But we had a lovely day perusing her library. She may join us yet. Or she may send friends."

"What did you think of the first day of pilgrimage?" Marguerite asked and motioned toward the chair by the window She wanted me to sit awhile and chat about the material my fellow travelers had collected in their journals. I told her it was interestingly empty of climb, climax, compulsion, necessity.

"You wanted Aristotelian tragedy?" asked Christine. "*Peripeteia*, narrative development? Why did you tell them not to concern themselves with anything but memory and passion?"

"You were there?"

Yes, they were. Over behind Veronica. Perhaps a bit too close. Veronica did seem to become emotional when they were around. She was turning pale and beginning to take on Margery Kempe's story again, so they left and went to my room.

"Pilgrims don't write tragedy," Christine said. "Pilgrims write letters. Like the letters Paula and Eustochium wrote from Jerusalem to their teacher Marcella in Rome. They don't try to tell a story. They itemize attractions on the pilgrim's route."

I told them I would have preferred spending more time in fewer places, letting history seep up through the soles of my feet, feeling it become a part of me.

Christine said the sort of travel I was describing was leisure, excursion, not classic pilgrimage. "When you're on a classic pilgrimage, you go here, stop, see if it's as it should be, quickly consider what you might encounter there and leave for another site where you stop, see if it's as it should be, consider what you might encounter there, and leave for another site."

"I couldn't write a decent paragraph in my journal," I protested. "I needed more time, time to sit there and write about how the place was affecting me, personally."

"Pilgrim literature is inspirational, not personal." She recited a line from one of Paula and Eustochium's letters: "Shall we see Lazarus come forth bound in his shroud, and the waters of the Jordan made purer by the Lord's baptism?"

"That's exactly where I wanted to spend more time. At the source of the Jordan, the stream where Greeks had once built a shrine to Pan." I told her how the Jungian said Pan was a reflection of the green man like St. George, how that reminded me of the Green Knight and the Grail stories, and how I would have liked to absorb that to see if there was something there that my mother had reacted to.

"Be careful with St. George," Marguerite cautioned. "He demonstrated so much antagonism toward the dragon."

Christine said St. George was like Hippolytus, the bishop some said her town in France was named after. He refuted all the heresies, and he had grave difficulty with Pan. Of course, he was pretty hard on dragons and all pagan things and probably wouldn't have had much patience for drawings like the ones the art teacher had done in her journal. She didn't know what he'd think of Hildegard's drawings; they were of gardens, and she was forever talking of greening and vegetation, which could be interpreted in many ways. Christine thought Hildegard was fortunate that the authorities agreed with her interpretations. The drawings, however, were simply there, evidence of mystical information that needn't always be interpreted the same way. Personal revelation like bar Yochai was talking about. People came along and saw totally new things in Hildegard's gardens every day. Of course, that was touchy. One had to be careful with mysticism. It was good for Hildegard that the authorities believed her visions were straight from God. Marguerite murmured in the background, and Christine reminded me Marguerite had never called herself a prophet, never claimed to recite the divine. Everything Marguerite wrote, she wrote in her own name.

"That was both your genius and your undoing," Christine said to Marguerite.

"It was the times," Marguerite said with a trace of resignation.

Christine thought I should tell the art professor about Hildegard, if I hadn't already, and about a woman named Thamaris, who painted the image of Diana. "And tell her about Irene, and Marcia the Roman, now that I think about it." Traveling with Christine was like traveling with a reference librarian.

Christine thought of herself more as an editor, an encyclopedist, a literary historian. "Your students did a good job as beginners at 'Pilgrim's Lit,'" she announced. "Especially the woman who itemized places. Her language had some of the quality of the chanson, limitless traveling, like Egeria in her 'Peregrination.'"

"Egeria?"

"Aetheria's another name for her. Such controversy over our

179

identities. I wonder if it interferes with an understanding of our work."

"I've never had that problem," said Marguerite. "Usually our identities are simply ignored."

Who was Egeria, I wondered. What did she do?

"She stood on the hill where Moses was a shepherd," Marguerite said. "She wrote about a church, the cells of holy men, good water, a fair garden—roses and broom bush, the burning bush."

"Egeria's repetitive. Processional. Almost liturgical. Imitation, that is the office of the perfect pilgrim," Christine insisted.

It reminded me of how we used to walk in the garden at the college at Easter time, chanting the stations of the cross.

"Exactly," Marguerite agreed. "Traveling to the land of the song and repeating the song—one hour singing, another chanting—until it lives again in you. 'Crossing the sea to suck the marrow of the high cedar.'"

I wondered if that was a line from Paula, Eustochium, or Egeria.

"A line from me—paraphrasing Ezekiel—who is, in my opinion, paraphrasing someone else," said Marguerite.

I looked around. I was half expecting to find another dead woman writer in the shower. "Am I going to meet Egeria or the others?"

"Perhaps if you travel far enough and long enough," Marguerite answered.

I told Marguerite and Christine I had spent the day trying to distinguish between tourists and pilgrims and travel and pilgrimage and far and near, and had not achieved any clarity on the issue whatsoever.

Marguerite thought that was part of my problem: it was a very long road to the land of the forgotten ones, the naked annihilated ones, the clarified ones, and I had only been a pilgrim for one day.

Forensics: IV

I was enjoying this pilgrimage most when Marguerite and Christine were along. At breakfast, however, they disappeared again. They apologized for cutting out on my birthday, but Christine was still in search of "fruits and fresh water," which they expected to find easily, and they promised to join me as soon as they could. I hoped they didn't take a long side trip; I wanted them with me when I found Brother Hugh, whom I would have called that morning if the phones had been operating, but they weren't expected to be fixed until midmorning and by that time—especially at the rate our pilgrimage was going—we would have visited Capernaum and be on our way somewhere else.

Meanwhile, I was trying to fit my notes from the first day's pilgrimage into my mother's categories of gestures: Grail, Ulysses, and Other. So far, everything went under "other," so I started a new list and divided it up in a way that made sense to me: things and verbs. "Things" were what I could smell, taste, touch, see, and hear, just like Sister Hildegard's friend Marguerite d'Oingt was after. "Verbs" told me how everything ran, where it went, why. I was doing all this as I sat on a white Adirondack chair at the edge of the sea, my bare feet in the water, my notebook on the wide arm, a pencil in my right hand, a cup of coffee in my left. And Gala right behind me.

I read my list of things—tombs, caves, hills, windows, bread, oil, flames, waves, sails, birds, fishes, dragons, splendour . . .

"You smell splendour?" Gala asked.

"Sometimes," I responded, "but mostly I hear it."

"What does it sound like?"

"Like music." I didn't know what kind of music, but I knew it had to be music, and I didn't know how I knew.

Gala wondered if "splendour" were a verb. "Let's hear the sound of your verbs," she asked.

I read the verbs. There was running and hiding, and going up and coming down, and flying and sailing, and living and dying, and feeling naked and covering up, and weeping. Verbs also had color. Running, for instance, was green, and hiding was blue; sailing was red, it poured like wine; purple was the color of weeping. I was coming to understand why my mother was interested in gestures, for what was a gesture if not the coincidence of a thing and its motion? No wonder she was always looking for gestures. Making bread. Sipping sacred drinks. How many things we did every day were once sacred gestures?

Gala said a gesture was a political act. A simple sign in one culture would get you in trouble in another. Sometimes, people had to hide the simplest of gestures, just to be safe.

"How do you hide a gesture?" I asked.

"By making it so common nobody objects, like a 'Hail Mary pass' in a football game. The people in the stands never dispute a 'Hail Mary pass,' no matter what their beliefs." Gala insisted politics required the presence of people who were willing to become embroiled in argument, and she wondered where the people were on my lists. She stood there, watching, waiting for me to add a column of people. I listed the names that had come up on the pilgrimage: Joseph, Jacob, Pan, St. George, and Jesus, the rabbis, a shepherd, pilgrims and tourists and soul mates, heads and faces, Dinah and Magdalene.

"Only two specific women? See, I told you. Identify people, and you find politics. Politics is what allows one to understand gesture."

I added the words "Lazarus" and "dead women writers" to my list.

Gala said Lazarus was a man and wanted to know if I was putting a critical skew on this, bending Lazarus' gender, like Sylvia Plath did. Did I mean Plath's Lazarus? Was that why I added "dead women writers?"

I told her I didn't think so.

Gala said Plath was her favorite poet. She brought along a volume of her collected works, and she suspected I knew that and dropped an allusion to Plath into our conversation on purpose. She was convinced I wrote "dead women writers" on my list because she had brought Plath along. Did I know Plath?

Not personally, I said, not yet, anyway. I was about to tell Gala exactly what I did mean, because I felt comfortable enough with her to let her know about Christine and Marguerite, but Kathryn came and announced that everyone was waiting for us in the parking lot. It was time to go to Capernaum and back down to Tiberias.

Capernaum had been there all the time, right behind the guest house, a short hop and skip away. We left the van in the parking lot and went to the kiosk at the edge of the lot, where a young boy was selling tickets and souvenirs. The souvenirs reminded me of the holy goods stores where Andrew and I spent our days when we were kids. He would have loved that stand. It was better than a holy goods store. There was olive oil in plastic containers molded into the body of Jesus and empty plastic Jesus bottles as well, for those who wanted to fill them with water from the Sea of Galilee or the River Jordan. Also there were bath salts from the Dead Sea. And rosaries: hand-carved wooden rosaries, blue crystal rosaries, dark brown rosaries made from the hips of dried roses. Hats and veils and books and slides and cards and jump ropes. Secular and sacred, sublime and profane, next to one another, blended together.

"Jump ropes," I said aloud.

"You want one, a jump rope, for the children?" the boy asked.

Everybody spoke English, everywhere. I took one because I thought I might use it for exercise that night, when we were back at the convent. I could jump in my room like Sister Hildegard did in the convent at home, like Rose and Nancy did every morning. No wonder they brought their own ropes. Perhaps that's why my mother had a jump rope. It must have been part of her daily routine, skipping rope. We all skipped rope when we were children. I twisted my rope so it was easy to hold and walked toward the site.

There, at the entrance gate, was a low stone building with a statue of St. Francis and his birds. It had to be the Franciscan monastery. I told Veronica to go on without me, I had to speak to Brother Hugh, I would meet them later. They went in through the gate while I walked to the heavy door of the monastery and knocked a bit too hard. My pounding puzzled the young man in a brown robe who came to the door. He thought there must have been an emergency. He was pleased that he was wrong, that I was all right. Would I like to come in? Yes, he said, there was a Brother

Hugh. Yes, he had once studied in Haifa. Yes, he was there. He would be leaving soon for the festival at Stella Maris, but he was still there at this time.

It was cool inside the stone rooms, and sound echoed as I walked with the young Franciscan down the tiled hall to a parlor. I explained who I was and why I wanted to talk to Brother Hugh. He left me alone, ten minutes perhaps, until a man whose body seemed older than it should have been finally came into the room. His skin was thin like Greek pastry, and it was wrinkled around his eyes and mouth. He was bent so that it seemed a strain for him to look up at me when I was standing. I sat down. He smiled as though he knew me.

"The-American-who-has-an-urgent-quest," he called me. Then he pointed at the rope I still had in my right hand; his smile became small and narrow, then faded altogether. "You carry this rope?" he asked.

"They sell them here," I said, smiling back at him. This was our warm-up. The talk was starting the way important talks always start—with trivialities, with weather, with sports. We were beginning with jump ropes. "The young man said they are for children, actually, but I bought it for myself. I'm in need of exercise."

"For exercise, for the children, of course. That is as it should be. A lovely children's game."

"My mother . . . " I started a sentence, but he broke in.

"Father Louis spoke of your father every day. There was never a day that passed that he didn't speak of your father."

"And my mother?" I asked. "The sisters at Stella Maris thought perhaps Father Louis had given you some books and some papers, things that belonged to my mother. She was working on something here in Israel . . . " I let the last part of the sentence hang, unfinished.

He smiled again, but it was a restrained smile.

I tried to be patient, to let him fill in the silent space.

He said nothing. The gap became uncomfortable. I finally spoke again.

"My mother's things. My father told me she came to Israel in part because of the lists she was making, some words, some unusual signs. We have only one of her notebooks. My father says Father Louis was going to send the others, and somehow he never did. I know there was a fire, and some things were lost, but I thought perhaps there might have been other things, and that you might have them. The sisters said you might. Do you?"

He shook his head.

"You don't?"

"No. I'm sorry, but I don't have anyone's notes. I never knew your mother, you understand. I only know *of* your father . . . "

"But what happened to her things?"

"There was a fire. If there was anything left, Father Louis would have sent it."

"And her grave? No one seems to know anything about her grave."

"That is the easy question," he said and stood to let me know our brief discussion was already coming to an end. "The graves are at Mount Carmel. Near the sacred place of Elijah. It is a beautiful place. It was a tribute to your father that his wife and mother-in-law were allowed to be buried in such lofty soil."

"The sisters said their graves were somewhere else, not at Stella Maris."

"No, not at Stella Maris, but up above, where Elijah fought the great battle with Jezebel's priests and the pagan god."

"Not Pan, but the other one?"

"You don't remember the story of Ahab and Jezebel? You must read your scriptures more often." He shook his head, then took my hand. "One—Kings—Eighteen. The place of fire." He was leading me through the hallway toward the door. "I am sorry I have no memories for you; there is nothing I can give you that will help you find your mother."

"This festival, the one at Elijah's tomb? Can you imagine why she was interested?"

He was looking at his sandals. He shook his head.

"People talk of Dog Days. Do you know what it means?"

"Now. The hot days. Summer."

"From the old calendars?"

"And the new."

"You never saw anything my mother was writing about Dog Days?"

"Everyone writes of Dog Days. It is the heat, the parching, the searing of the soul."

I told him that sounded like the words of a mystic. Did he know, was my mother a mystic, did she use that sort of language in her writings?

"Her things were gone before I arrived."

"But you know something about her things, don't you? About what she was trying to find? She was following the chain of custody of some everyday gestures. Did Father Louis mention that? Did he say which ones?"

"I have spoken without clarity. I must not mislead you. There is nothing of hers that you can find."

"Her grave? And that of her mother?"

"Other than that," he agreed. We were at the front door, and he had opened it. "When you go to the small church at the top of Carmel, you will see a grove to the Virgin. It is near the grotto, but you will need help. You will need someone to show you the graves." He lifted my hand, the one that was clutching the jump rope. It was a surprising move. He stared at my hand, then brushed my fingers against his lips, and let my arm drop. He smiled again, shook his head, and shut the door.

So, Annie had been right. I wasn't going to find anything.

I could see the top of Gala's straw fedora bobbing inside the synagogue ruins. The group had already walked through the church built over the walls of the house where Peter had lived, but I wasn't ready to join them yet. I sat in the garden in the middle of some sort of demonstration of antiquity—pieces of carved column and stone reliefs, eagles with garlands, grapes and vines, a shell surrounded by another garland. My inclination was to leave the group and go straight up to the graves, but we were already scheduled to go there tomorrow. That day, the group was going down to Tiberias, then back to the convent and the Elijah festival at Stella Maris. The festival had importance for my mother; my father said so. Besides, how could I go anywhere? Rent my own car? Hire a driver? Leave the group? I'd have to break my promise to Andrew. I could have used a talk with Marguerite, but she didn't materialize. It was an odd sensation, this knowing where my mother was buried, this being close to her, and yet, this not knowing, this not being with her at all.

I walked over to the guides, who were telling history in English and French and Spanish. I hopped up on the smooth limestone wall and slid into a corner next to Gala, listening to the English-speaking guide.

"Pilgrims have been coming here since the fourth century to see this town where Peter and Andrew and James and John came from. And Mary, the mother of James and John. And Salome, too." the guide said.

"Finally," Gala said, only half whispering, "women for your list."

The wall behind us was yellow-white and three stories high. I touched the stone nearest me. It felt soft like the flesh of a young willow trunk, but right next to it was grey mortar and stone again, then a smooth whipped cream grout and something very sandy and rough, and finally the smooth toffee cement again. Someone

188

had been fixing this up, putting it back together the way Andrew and I once mended our back stairs, when we were young and couldn't imagine how it would look years later, when bonding the structure so it would hold was all that counted. We didn't notice the layers we created, fresh grey-green patching cement striped into white concrete stairs. We thought we'd done a good job.

Gala saw me running my hand over the concrete. "Sloppy archeology," she tried to keep her voice low, "tampering with history. Patchwork."

We walked out through the archeological gardens, where she was upset once again that pieces of the temple had been moved, not out of any attempt to understand the past but simply for display to tourists.

"Pilgrims," I said.

"Which Salome was she talking about?" Kathryn asked Gala. "Mary's midwife? Wouldn't she have been in Bethlehem?"

"Salome, the mother of the sons of Zebedee," Gala answered. "The one who traveled with Jesus in Galilee."

"The dancer?" asked Nancy, "the woman with seven veils, the one involved with John the Baptist?"

"Maybe they're all the same person," I observed.

Veronica, who had good color in her face from sun and exercise the day before, looked fragile suddenly, pale and bent, and she took her scarf from around her shoulders and wiped her eyes. She had begun to weep, again. Kathryn guided her back to the car, and we went on to Tiberias.

This time, we took a tour of the town. We walked around remnants of basalt walls in the Hammat synagogue; we skirted edges of a mosaic from the old synagogue built one layer earlier; on the mosaic, we caught a Roman name and read Greek and Hebrew at the same time and saw a bust of Helios the sun god and the zodiac. Along with milk and sweet food cooking in oil, there was a new smell at that edge of town, sulfur from mineral baths. We saw the tomb of Rabbi Meir Ba'al Ha'ness. We saw the tomb of Rabbi Akiva. Finally, we arrived at the tomb of Maimonides.

There, right across the street from Maimonides' tomb, were phones, a bank of three public telephones at the edge of a small park. I crossed and stood and watched as a woman lifted the receiver, slipped her phone card into the slot, and dialed a number. It was simple. I went to the next phone and repeated the motions. It was 8 a.m. in Vermont. Three rings and Aurelia answered. Andrew was fine; he was finished with his roots and on his way home. He sent his love. He'd be reachable that night. My father was well. He was at the college for an early-morning work session. Someone was breaking into his e-mail "Thomas line" and posting messages, debating Thomas' theories. The messages were all about women, but Sister Hildegard insisted it wasn't me, and he was quite stirred up. He'd be sorry he wasn't home.

"Aurelia. I'm going to the graves. Tomorrow. I'm going to spend the day at the graves."

"Annie says you should stay away from the graves."

"Annie is negative. Besides, it's apparently all that's here. No one has any idea where her writings are; no one even knows what she was thinking about, what gesture she was concerned with."

Aurelia said I should take my own notes. Follow my own curiosity. Investigate my own gestures. That's what she thought it was all about. "The Morgan girls were never much for establishing creeds." She laughed when she realized what she had said. "You're Creed enough," she laughed again, "you and Sister Annie."

I told Aurelia I hadn't seen any porches here, certainly not porches with women singing and dancing on them, but Aurelia said she was sure there was one there somewhere. I said good-bye. Veronica had left Maimonides' tomb and was standing behind me.

"Do you know that man?" Veronica asked me and pointed

toward the large man, the one who had been at my father's reading, the authority with the radiant figure pinned to his lapel, but this time he was wearing the white robes of a Dominican. She had no idea who he was, but he was asking about me, what I was wearing. "Odd for him to be fixating on you like that. He asked for you by name, so there's no doubt he's looking specifically for you."

He was standing under the red iron structure, staring at us. Then he turned and disappeared in the bushes behind a kiosk where they sold yarmulkes. I told Veronica he had been in Johanna's Cape, the day she and Gala and Divany and the others came to my father's book signing. I walked back across the street and past the kiosks and into the monument, but I couldn't find him. I wandered around inside the monument until I saw Gala and Astrid studying the writing on Maimonides' tomb.

"Since Moses no Moses has been so Moses." Astrid said those were the words inscribed on the part of the tomb I was looking at. It was in Hebrew, but Astrid had asked a young woman to translate it for her. "You see, his name was Moses."

My mind was on the large man, not on Maimonides.

He'd told Gala he was looking for me, too. "He's a Dominican. You can tell from his robe and his tonsure. He claims to have proof you've been fooling with some material on the ethernet. I told him you've done no such thing. We haven't even been near a working phone. It must have been your poem; you seem to have upset one of the dogs of god," she chuckled. "I wish Divany were here."

The man couldn't have been upset by my poem being on the Internet. He'd heard me recite it at my father's party. He must have been talking about the same messages that had disturbed my father and sent him over to the college for an early-morning work session. Who was this fellow? How had he found me in Israel? Everyone saw him, so he wasn't another one of my visions. No wonder Sister Hildegard called him a specter, the way he intruded and disappeared.

How could he be there, and then suddenly not be there?

"It was Maimonides who noted the spiritual can emerge where matter is no matter," the guttural voice right next to me seemed to be coming from the jowls of the Dominican.

"Who are you?" I asked.

"A humble priest, a philosopher, a scholar like your father. I have come to talk to you because of what you're doing to my Thomas web site."

I told him I wasn't doing anything to his web site. He bowed. He said he would be glad to explain the works of Maimonides to me. I said I appreciated Maimonides, but with all due respect to the man whose grave I was standing near, his tomb was not the most interesting tomb on my tour. I told him I was more inter-ested in the tombs of certain women. In fact, I told him I was only interested in women and said I was making a list of women's things. I offered him my notebook, open to my lists.

"Dog Days? Ropes? Hills? Caves? Birds? Trees? Fire?" He looked perplexed. "The things of women? Will we be subjected to these trivialities of nature now on the Thomas line? Will you and your women be teaching this sort of thing on the Internet?"

I pulled my notebook away and informed him I didn't appre-ciate being followed and harassed and called trivial, and if he didn't stop interfering with my pilgrimage, I was going to call the *real* authorities.

He bowed again and disappeared into the crowd of pilgrims at Maimonides' tomb.

His presence was damaging the day, spoiling the fresh aroma of carnival. All that lingered in the midafternoon heat was the scent of milk, beginning to curdle. I tried to shake the Dominican's disdain and leave it there, stuck in the spaces between pavement blocks like the bits of tobacco and cigarette filters congealing in spilled Coca-Cola on the sidewalk in front of me. What had he published? Why had my father found his arguments interesting?

At the van, Gala sighed deeply. "Only two more tombs," she said and asked me to drive. She was beginning to feel the heat. She sat behind me, directing me, insisting no one knew the way until they drove it—up away from the seaside, onto a hill, between the half-built apartment building and the row of houses, behind the stores, down the alley, up the gravel drive. Stop. We would walk the rest of the way.

She pointed at a circle of poured concrete slabs, iron reinforcing rods rusting at the edges, tucked in behind a garage. It was the tomb of the matriarchs, sixteen flat pillars, circled like Stonehenge around the graves of Moses' sister and mother, Miriam and Yochevet. And Aaron's wife, Elisheva, as well as Zipporah and Bilha and Zilpah. Famous men named again in the obituaries. I was glad that three of the women were identified only as themselves, not as the wives and sisters of dead prophets.

I set a stone on the blue sarcophagus, lit a candle, placed it next to the fire, and made a note with the names of my mother and grandmother—Faith Morgan and Grace Morgan, no reference to any men. I had never really heard about the Morgan men, so the Morgan name seemed pure and feminine. On another paper, I wrote Miriam and Yochevet and Elisheva and pushed the folded names of women into cracks between the rocks. It was a simple gesture.

"Is this meant to resemble Stonehenge?"

Veronica laughed. "No. It is merely unfinished. Someday, it will be complete."

When I pulled back onto the road at the edge of the sea, I saw the Dominican following us in a small, white Escort. Gala saw him, too, as he pulled out around us and sped on ahead. I was determined to ignore him. I kept driving, following Gala's directions, toward the baptismal area on the banks of the Jordan. I turned off the road into a cemetery and parked at the edge of a gravel path. The path skirted the edge of the sea, then went up a small hill. Veronica was leading us, telling us there was no time for baptism. We were going to see one last grave. There were palm trees, oleander bushes, grave markers, and thorns. We stopped at a marble stone that said only "Rachel."

It wasn't the biblical Rachel; it was Rachel Blobstein, a Russian immigrant who moved to Israel when she was nineteen years old. Her grave was raised from the ground, and mourners had left flowers and stones on it. There was an extra arm of marble that bent around the side of her tomb; in the arm was a steel-lined well, about eight inches deep. A young woman lifted its square black marble lid and removed a book with a yellow vinyl cover, on it a postcard photograph of a window looking out at the Sea of Galilee. When she saw us watching her, she spoke to us in English about the tomb and this Rachel who had come there to till the soil of Israel. Rachel was a poet and an artist who dreamed of a place where scholars would live from the soil. She believed in a religion of work. She dug and pruned and sowed in the earth and in her poems; she was in love with nature. She and the land were one. The yellow vinyl book was a collection of Rachel's poems.

The young woman read:

Only a tree have my hands planted
On the peaceful banks of the Jordan

Only a path have my legs beaten
Through your fields

Gala fretted about identifying a woman poet with nature, such a female stereotype: woman as nature, matter, controlled. Men always ended up being culture, mind, controller. The young woman reading and translating at Rachel's tomb smiled. She thought it was a curious thing to worry about. Nature was never controllable. Consider Rachel. She got tuberculosis and had to leave her kibbutz. She was only forty-one when she died.

"This poet is not well-known outside of Israel, but here she is almost a cult figure," said Veronica. "Her readers are pilgrims."

I had never seen a grave like this one, poems buried there beside poet in a small marble crypt with her verse rising daily, every time a reader came with a stone or a flower and lifted the lid and opened the yellow book. I was hoping my mother's tomb would be the same; all her papers sorted neatly in a metal-lined bin at the side of her grave. I imagined a container like the tackle box where my father had kept her stones and photographs and skipping rope. Waiting to find her grave was becoming a burden.

I stood to stretch and looked at the sky. It was empty, except for the light that came in shards from a large white sun, like rays from heaven in Bible stories. The woman was still reading Rachel's poem. "My mother, I know how meager is this gift of your daughter's creation . . . " There was a roar like thunder, far away. I turned toward the sound. Maybe it was a sign, a vision like one of Sister Hildegard's. Something was beginning to shimmer in the light on the water, a form, shaking out of the sea, growing bigger, coming closer, louder, a boat, aiming straight for the cemetery, heading for us. The boat slowed and relaxed in the water. I could see there was no miracle; it was just the way light fell on the Sea of Galilee, and the sound of thunder in the sun was a boat with a canvas awning and nine fishing poles propped at the back. It was piloted by a tanned man in a black T-shirt, and the large Dominican was standing next to him, robe flapping in the wind. They didn't come to a full stop; they cruised by, turned around, and cruised by again. We were under surveillance. I remembered Sister Fides' belief that the Pope had troops following Divany Schulman. Were they after me now?

"It's that meddlesome man again," Gala said. "Has he been fishing?"

"It might be us he's looking for. " It was Marguerite's voice, whispering. She was standing behind a small hill, by a palm tree.

"He started a quarrel over at Maimonides' tomb," Christine added.

I thought Christine was talking about his argument with me. "I've been trying to shake off the effect ever since."

But Christine said she and Marguerite had been carrying on their own joust with him. "They're all getting involved. One writes from Paris, another from Salonika. All the old boys are joining the debate. Hildegard told them they were drying up."

"Sister Hildegard was there at Maimonides' tomb?"

Not exactly. "We were talking to her on the net," Marguerite answered.

So it was them, breaking into the Internet. How did they do it without a computer and modem and phone?

They said they didn't need machines. They'd never needed machines. They had *gnaden und wunder* . . . graces and miracles. They could always communicate with one another, it was just easier now that they could piggyback on the ethernet.

And who did they mean by Hildegard? Sister Hildegard? My father's friend? The one in Vermont?

Yes and no. Not exactly. Not the way I think of her.

"Hildegard von Bingen then?"

"Best to let that one alone." Marguerite did not want to answer that question. "In any case, it's quite obvious the Dominican is looking for us. We could have guessed he'd come here. He's hung up on man's power over nature. Rachel's poetry must be vexing."

Kathryn came up beside me. Was I having another one of my visionary spells? Should we all get out of the sun?

196

Later, I found out more about the row they were having on the Internet. Aurelia said that when my father, Sister Hildegard, and the college's computer specialist were talking to security specialists in Washington, D.C., the prior of the Dominican House at the University of Paris sent a message: pirates had once again broken into the Thomas web site and were using the MUD for their own pseudo debate.

Date: Seventh Month, '00
X-Sender: thomaquin@paris.summa
To: vonbingen@mystik.illum; christine@pizan. cite; porète@farnear.nil
Subject: feminea forma (Citè des Dames, Le mirouer des simples ames)

Now women by nature are of less virtue and dignity than men, for "That which acts is more honorable than that which is acted upon" as Augustine says. (Summa Theologiae and Augustine on Genesis)

Date: Seventh Month, '00
X-Sender: aristotle@salonika.edu
To: thomaquin@paris.summa
Subject: feminea forma

I am in agreement with your assessment. The female provides the matter, and the male the principle of movement, the male is the carpenter, the female the wood. (Generation of Animals)

Date: Seventh Month, '00
X-Sender: socrates@plato.repub
To: aristotle@salonika.edu;thomaquin@paris. summa
Subject: feminea forma

Do you know any human activity in which the male sex does not surpass the female? (Republic,V)

197

Date: Seventh Month, '00
X-Sender:christine@pizan.cite
To:thomaquin@paris.summa; aristotle@
salonika.edu; socrates@plato.repub
Subject: Summa Theologiae and Augustine on
Genesis; Generation of Animals; Republic,V

God has given women such beautiful minds
to apply themselves, if they want to, in
any of the fields where glorious and
excellent men are active, which are neither more nor less accessible to them as
compared to men if they wished to study
them. (Citè des Dames)

Date: Seventh Month, '00
X-Sender:socrates@plato.repub
To:aristotle@salonika.edu;thomaquin@paris.
summa
Subject:trivialities

Let's not waste our time talking about
weaving and making pancakes or boiling
stews, things at which women appear to
have some talent and about which people
would laugh if a woman were bested by a
man (Republic,V)

Date: Seventh Month, '00
X-Sender:christine@pizan.cite
To:thomaquin@paris.summa; aristotle@
salonika.edu; socrates@plato.repub
Subject:de philosophia

It was Minerva, Ceres, and Isis who knew
of grains, weaving, and gardening. It
seems to me that neither in the teaching
of Aristotle . . . nor in that of all the

other philosophers who have ever lived, could an equal benefit for the world be found as that which has been accrued and still accrues through the works accomplished by virtue of knowledge possessed by Minerva, Ceres, and Isis. (Citè des Dames)

Date: Seventh Month, '00
X-Sender: thomaquin@paris.summa
To: christine@pizan.cite; porète@farnear.nil; vonbingen@mystik.illum
Subject: Cite des Dames, Q. 1.28.1

. . . there would have been a lack of proper order in human society if some were not governed by others who were wiser than they. Woman is naturally subject to man in this kind of subjection because by nature man possesses more discernment of the reason. (Summa Theologiae)

Date: Seventh Month, '00
X-Sender: porète@farnear.nil
To: thomaquin@paris.summa
Subject: freedom and subjection

This soul, says Love, is free, yet more free, yet very free, yet finally supremely free, in the root, in the stock, in all her branches and all the fruits of her branches. The Soul has her portion of purified freeness, each aspect has its full measure of it. She responds to no one if she does not wish to. (Le mirouer des simples ames)

Date: Seventh Month, '00
X-Sender:vonbingen@mystik.illum
To:thomaquin@paris.summa; aristotle@
salonika.edu; socrates@plato.repub.
Subject:power

. . . the soul is the freshness of the
flesh, for the body grows and thrives
through it just as the earth becomes
fruitful through moisture . . . The earth
sweats germinating power from its very
pores . . . (Illumination 3)

Date: Seventh Month, '00
X-Sender:tacitus@history.rom
To:socrates@plato.repub; aristotle@
salonika.edu; thomaquin@paris.summa
Subject: Roots, fruits, branches; grains,
weaving, and gardening

Your argument with women reminds me of what
I said in Germania: They are protected by
forests and rivers . . . they worship in
common Mother Earth and conceive her as
intervening in human affairs and riding in
procession through the cities of men.
(Germania)

Date: Seventh Month, '00
X-Sender:thomaquin@paris.summa
To:vonbingen@mystik.illum; christine@pizan.
cite; porète@farnear.nil
Subject: Mother Earth (river and sea) is
subject to man

Let me repeat what I have written: . . .
in the order of nature established by God,
lower elements in nature must be subject
to higher ones . . . Woman is naturally
subject to man . . . and God said to man
that he would have dominion over the fish
of the sea. (Summa Theologiae)

Date: Seventh Month, `00
X-Sender:vonbingen@mystik.illum
To:thomaquin@paris.summa, et al.
Subject:women, fish, the sea, power, dry-
ing up

As I have said to others: Pay careful
attention lest with all the fluctuations
of your thoughts the greening power which
you have from God dries up in you.
(Illumination 12)

Forensics: V

The evening air was full. Roasting nuts, lamb cooking on open fires, corn bubbling in pots of boiling water, oil—hot for sweet cinnamon bread and falafel. Campsites in tents and on blankets. Dart games in front of the church, by the graves of the Frenchmen. Wooden milk bottles to knock down at a shekel a throw. A stage on a metal scaffold and pop music pouring from hanging speakers. Stella Maris on the night of July 19 was not the Stella Maris we'd left. The nuns who had been unwilling to open their doors after dark to pilgrims two nights before had opened the courtyard to a carnival. No one was dancing, but teenagers were parading back and forth, boys to the right, girls to the left, ignoring one another, carefully, the way we used to when we went to high school parties called mixers because no one came with a date, and everyone was supposed to mix. I honked and blinked my lights, and the teenagers opened a space so I could drive through. It was the feast of Elijah. This was his tomb, and people were there to celebrate. Since we were there to write the stories of our souls, Veronica said we should graze from the stands, munch in the streets, head into the crowds, sing, dance, talk, flirt.

"It's my birthday," I announced.

"Precisely," she said and threw her hands toward the sky. "Become a participant observer."

It was exactly what I had wanted. A chance to wander. There didn't seem to be anywhere at Stella Maris that was off limits that night, except the sisters' cloister. I decided to start at the edge of prohibited territory, next to the cloister, in the rooms Aurelia said had been assigned to my mother and grandmother. There was another group staying at the convent, pilgrims from Spain, and they were assigned to some of these rooms, but they were outside enjoying the festival, and I knew I could be in and out before they returned. I removed my Visa card from my Filofax and slipped the thin plastic card between the frame and the door of the room at the top of the hall, the room occupying the space Aurelia had described as the parlor, and the door fell open. Inside, it hardly looked like a parlor. It was a big square room, but nothing more than a larger version of the room I had been assigned: three single beds and two built-in wardrobes, an old metal fan hanging from the ceiling. There was a double window at the back overlooking a playground, and the breeze coming through was hot and dry. The floor was black linoleum with grey marble streaks. Three of the walls were painted pale green, the other wallpapered with Kelly green swirls like shooting stars or dancing fairies. Someone had tacked a foot-high color photo of fishermen over the wallpaper, so the fishermen seemed to be casting amidst ancient lures.

I tried to imagine this as a comfortable parlor, where an English woman would serve Earl Grey and scones and sit in a soft chair to read the mystics, but there was no comfort left. I took one last look around and blew a kiss to the two women that coincidence had made me miss by moments, and I closed the door and went on to the other rooms. They varied little except in size and shape until the last one, my grandmother's, the most interesting room I had seen in the convent. It was made of two small squares, zigzagging around the intrusion of hallway linen cupboards and a balcony at the top of an exterior staircase. The bathroom cabinet was empty. There was no clothing in the wardrobe. The bed had been made, and no bodily hollow had been impressed on the taut, tucked linens. I went back to my room and packed everything into my little black suitcase and wheeled it down the hall, into this room. I unpacked my things and walked down to the kitchen where I had left the sister the morning before. She was there, once again, because she was the one assigned to be in charge of pilgrims. I told her I had switched rooms, pretending I had an allergy to some substance in mine. I sneezed—five, six, seven times. I told her I had moved to the room at the end of the hall, the zig zag room.

"You can't stay there," she admonished. "There is a door and an outside staircase. It's not safe. No one sleeps in that room."

I told her it was the only room in which I didn't sneeze, and I asked for the key. She said there was no key to that room. I assured her that was fine. I would leave it open.

"Not the outside," she said. "You must not open the door to the balcony."

I promised I wouldn't, thanked her, and went back up to the room and directly to the balcony door. It was triple locked. I opened each of the three bolts and walked out and stood on what could have been called a porch. It was the closest thing to a porch I had seen in Israel. So, it was here my grandmother had danced. I did a pirouette and bowed to her memory and climbed down the wooden staircase to the playground below, where children from the festival were swinging high and climbing and sliding down. Two slides had been welded to the jungle gym so children could compete at climbing to the top and flying down again. It was a 1950s gym, rust-proofed metal, bolted and welded together, just like the one we had in our backyard when I was growing up. Annie and I used to run round and round, scrambling up to the top, which we called the sky rocket, and hurtling to the earth down the slides. Standing in the sky rocket at the top of this jungle gym were two red-haired girls, twins.

"Hi," one said. "I see you're American, and you think you can dance."

I asked how she knew, and she pointed to my grandmother's porch. I asked how she knew I was American, and she said it was my shoes. I was wearing my NIKEs because I'd planned to go for a run. I asked how she happened to speak English with a hint of Brooklyn in it. She said her father grew up in New York, and she had lived there until she was five. Now she (and her sister) were eight. The one who was talking had long hair, braided from a part in the middle. The other had short curly hair, which—I was informed—was always trimmed on the feast of Elijah. Otherwise, they were identical. They had been playing a game they called "great women of the Bible," and the silent one was imitating Rachel, and that's why she wasn't talking because Rachel had just died. When their mother and father came, they were going down to the cave of Elijah and then to the top of Mount Carmel to sleep outside so they could see the star in the morning. She thought I really ought to go there, too.

I asked what star, and she said the famous dog star. I asked if that was like Dog Days, and she said it was what put the dog in Dog Days.

"The star that's as wild as Elijah in the hills," said the other twin, who had come back to life as herself.

"Now I'll be the star. I'll be a famous shooting star," said the first, and the two young girls slipped down the slide and waved and ran around to the front of the church to find their parents. I followed the path through a patch of mint and stepped around a thorn bush and came to the booth where you were supposed to throw a ball to knock down wooden milk jugs. I paid a shekel for each of two hard rubber balls and took aim. I missed completely the first time; the second time, I hit only one wooden bottle. I nodded and smiled, and the young boy wanted me to try again, but I shook my head.

On the other side of the fishpond, there was an open door into the church, and I could see tables filled with flickering candlelight. Inside, I genuflected for the first time in twenty-five years, entered a pew halfway up the center aisle, and knelt down. I had been there two nights before to sleep, and I looked carefully now at the rose lady and the wooden man, who had become cloudy in my memory. The rose virgin was seated, a child facing forward on her lap, like the mother and child depicted as the seat of wisdom. Two cherubs sat at her feet. Nine angel heads circled around her, a bird I could identify easily as a white dove over her head. Her gown was very light blue, but there was pink marble all around her, and that, along with red pillars against the white and yellow stone of the church, was what gave her the rose cast.

There were gold-trimmed plaques on the walls. On one side of the rose lady was a plaque with a picture of a castle with gold windows and a dove in the middle of seven tiers of radiance. At the bottom of the castle were wolves or dogs, spirits flying. This

207

plaque said "*El Castillo Interior, S. Teresa.*" On the other side was a plaque with seven small tombstones and three paths, two winding, one straight. On the straight path was written "*Nada, Nada, Nada.*" At the bottom of this plaque it said "*Subida del Monte Carmelo, S. Juan de la Cruz.*" So, Prudence Rodney's words belonged to St. John of the Cross before they belonged to Hemingway. In between these two plaques, the rose lady continued to sit on top of the cave, open to the rock of the hill, on top of the tomb of the dark brown wooden statue of the prophet Elijah. Perhaps the wooden man was hiding there in his smoky niche hewn out of the rock, as Elijah hid when he was on the run.

Around him were pieces of paper with writing covered in plastic to preserve them. I walked to the altar and discovered I couldn't read the writing. I was standing next to the wooden man on a floor of simple rock, rubbed smooth by the feet of pilgrims. I lit tapers for him and the rose woman again as I had two nights before. Now, the table next to the altar was full. It was hard to find space for my two flickering lights. I pushed someone else's candle aside an inch or two and guided mine into a space where I could keep them together. I noticed the grotto was dirty with candle smoke. I took my silk scarf from around my waist and rubbed the scarf against the rock to collect some of the wooden man's soot.

I went out the side door into a small museum. It was one narrow room with glass cupboards on either side. There were figurines, stamps, coins, bracelets, cups and bowls, heads—women's heads like the one I was charmed into buying in Qazrin—pots and mosaics, time running backward in these glass windows as I walked around the room past relics of Greeks, relics of Romans, relics of Egyptians, relics of David and Solomon and Abraham, and two pieces of brown clay, one no more than three inches high, broken on the right side, the other a bit smaller and curved as though it had been cylindrical in form. A corner was crumbled, but impressed into the rest of the clay were stars, tiny trumpets, darts, and arrows with inverted tips, all crisscrossing each other.

A woman wearing a name tag came to my side and asked if she could help me. She said I had been staring quite awhile at the pieces of clay, could she tell me something about them?

"What are they?" I said.

She said it was cuneiform. Two small pieces of Mesopotamian history left years ago at Mount Carmel.

Could she read this writing? She shook her head. She understood a couple of people could read them: a woman who died suddenly, back in the fifties, and perhaps Brother Hugh, a Franciscan who came from time to time.

"A woman who died?" I asked, but I did not tell her the woman was my mother or that I had been with Brother Hugh in the morning or that he had neglected to mention this scholarly link between their souls.

"Yes, quite tragically. On the feast of Elijah. Today."

"Does everyone know this story?" I asked.

"I should think so. If you live here in Haifa, you hear such stories. There are so many feast days, so many pilgrims. Tragedy can happen."

There was something about identifying my need to know about my mother's work that made everyone mute, so I tried to behave in a disinterested fashion, like a tourist, like a pilgrim. This woman was museum staff; it was her job to talk about these pieces, and she was telling me more than anyone else had been willing to tell.

She thought the tablets were from well before Abraham's time. "But of course they came into the hands of the church quite recently, perhaps during the crusades; there is a legend that these tablets—and others—were hidden by the Templars when Akko fell."

"Where are the others?"

"You're expecting a lot from history," she said. "It's seven hundred years and several monasteries and destructions later."

"Why would the Templars want these?" I asked.

"We don't really know. We've had scholars look at them, and they say they are fragments. Since we don't know where the Templars found them, we can't place them, really. We know they're not economic texts. They appear to be related to kings and gods and the wife of a god, a lady of heaven, some sort of festival, and some sort of coming and going. With the fire in the fifties, we're lucky to have any of this material at all."

I asked what burned. Did she know? The whole convent? The church?

"Not at all. Only the office of a famous priest who used to be here. Not his office, really, but a storage shed on Ha Carmel." She thought the convent originally had three tablets and a cone. The priest died, and he never knew these pieces were rescued. Archeology students found them up there in the crevices. The tablets had blended in; no one had noticed them. They looked just like all the other rocks, except for the bent one. The students were so excited, they'd begun to excavate up there, only a surface excavation; they couldn't be allowed to dig up the top of Mount Carmel. Brother Hugh had told them the history, that these tablets were not native to that hill, that finding them had been a matter of chance, an accident, a recent and modern accident. "But they're still up there, using only noninvasive tools, radiography or ultrasound. Something that gives them pictures," she said.

"The other pieces? Could they still be there?"

The woman shrugged. "They are stones. Stones survive fire. Stones survive rain. They may still be up there. Or they may have been discarded like the simple lumps of earth they are." She asked if I would like to make a donation to the museum, that way perhaps the monastery could afford to bring in scholars; perhaps more could be learned. She offered me an envelope and pointed to a box where I could deposit it. She left me and went over to talk to a man who was admiring a pair of Byzantine earrings.

I opened my backpack and took out my mother's black ring binder and flipped to the page I called arrows and stars and trumpets. I tried to compare the clusters of inverted arrows penciled between the boxes on her graph paper to those pressed into the clay. I couldn't. The tablets were impossible to focus on in that light. They were streaked with shadows from the relics next to them in the case. I tapped the woman on the shoulder and asked her if she could open the case for me so I could see the tablets close up. She looked at the pages in my mother's book.

"Are you a Sumerologist?" she asked.

No, I said, I was simply a writer, interested in writing. She said if I came back in the morning, she would open the case for me. Right now it was too busy. Tomorrow, before Mass, at 7 a.m., she would let me gaze at the tablets in natural light. It was almost ten. I was sure the sisters were asleep and would not get to her before morning to warn her not to show me the tablets, so I agreed. I would come back, I said. She nodded and smiled. It was time for me to talk to my father.

Outside, the crowd was growing in front of the church; with the doors open, I could see the rose virgin seated on her throne while pilgrims moved up and down the street in front of her. I thought I saw Gala's hat going by, but when I ran after it, it was a man whose head was in a straw fedora. Behind him were two men carrying small drums, tapping out rhythms, and a woman whose hair was covered by four long scarves of different colors rippling gently in the hot dry air. I took out a brush and brushed my own hair that was straight from the heat and wind, and I noticed a black-headed man walk by, leading a sheep and a goat. There was a woman carrying a pitcher of wine, and three older women moving together, carrying baskets of bread and fruit.

Finally, I saw the accupressurist and the candle woman. They were wearing long capes, and Liz was near them with colored ribbons in her hair. Children were skipping rope behind her, and then I saw Gala, who had bought some sort of double-edged ax at one of the curio stands. Stephanie and BeeBee were sitting with people drinking dark beer and eating dates; Astrid was leaning over a bowl of something that gave off a light smoke, like incense. Kathryn was attending to Veronica, who had begun to weep.

Then I noticed the large Dominican, standing in the crowd on the other side of the street. He was staring directly at me. He looked angry, and I was tired of him. So, I left the churchyard and went to the bank of pay phones next to the cafe where I'd sat sipping water before I fell asleep inside the church. There was an odd sound next to the phones, like sirens or voices whining, trying to get inside the receivers. It was already ten o'clock at night—three in the afternoon in Vermont—my father had to be home from his emergency meeting about the Thomas line, and I wanted to talk to him about the annoying man who had been stalking me ever since his book party. And about the clay tablets as well.

He picked up the phone on the first ring. He was in his spy room, in the attic. "Nina! Sweetheart! Happy birthday. Are you all right?"

I told him I was, but I was very upset about the lack of coop-eration from the sisters and this fellow, Brother Hugh. I told him I had to sleep in Elijah's tomb, and I still hadn't seen the graves, but I was going in the morning, and why was that large man following me? The Dominican. The one who had quizzed me at his party. The authority fellow.

My father had forgotten I'd seen the Dominican at his party.

"He asked about my poem, remember? And he's been following me ever since. This afternoon he claimed to be checking on
—'pirates'— on the Thomas line . . . "

"How could he be in Israel so quickly?" my father asked.

"You sent him?"

"Not at all. Last time I heard from him, he was at the
University of Paris. He's taking the piracy troubles on the Thomas
web site very personally." My father apologized for his friend and
said he'd try to reach him and tell him to leave me alone. "He can
be a bit schoolish sometimes."

"Schoolboyish, if you ask me."

"Really, Nina, if you saw the way he fashions a syllogism, you'd
be impressed. Believe me, you would."

I told him the fellow's syllogisms hadn't been helpful here. In
fact, no one had been helpful here. No one wanted to talk about
my mother, no one except a volunteer in the little museum who
told me about two clay tablets and said the last person at the convent who could read them was a woman who had died suddenly
in the fifties. "It was Mother, wasn't it?"

"Yes," he said. It probably was. He sounded extremely hesitant.
She used to read clay tablets, he said, but he was surprised the
monastery had acquired new ones.

I told him that they hadn't, that archeology students had
found them up on the top of Carmel the month before.

"How many?"

"Two."

His voice was nearly inaudible as he repeated "two." Then he
cleared his throat. "There were four in the Templar's collection.
Four. Your mother liked to call them 'philosophers' stones.'"

So, he knew. All along. He knew more than he had told me.
Why?

"We were worried about you," he explained.

213

"Who's we?"

"Me and your sister Annie."

"She knew, too? Why did you tell her and not me?"

"I didn't tell her. She was there."

"Where? When?"

"On Ha Carmel, when we buried your mother and grand-mother, when we accidentally burned the papers and the tablets."

"*You* burned them?"

"Father Louis and Annie and I. After the funeral, the night before we all left."

"Why would you burn mother's things?" I was whispering. I always whisper when I mean to scream. "Why would a scholar burn another scholar's work, even if she wasn't his wife, but especially if she was his dead wife, who wasn't going to be able to complete the work herself?"

He insisted it was an accident. They had packed her things, and Father Louis suggested they store them in his new office up on top of Carmel where they were building the new church. It would be a good thing to do until my father was settled. They moved the Templar stones up there, too, because Father Louis was going to have Brother Hugh, a Franciscan who would be his new assistant, copy them and send the copies along.

"Brother Hugh? I talked to him this morning. He's about as helpful as Annie. Why would he copy the stones?"

"Because he's an Assyriologist himself."

"Did he know what the tablets said?"

Only from what my mother had told Father Louis and Father Louis told Brother Hugh because Brother Hugh didn't arrive until after we were gone, after my mother's work had been destroyed. After the stones disappeared in the fire.

I asked my father to run through that again, how was her work burned?

"Father Louis wanted Annie to have a chance to celebrate the battle of Elijah against the pagan gods. She'd been looking forward to the festival; your mother and grandmother had spoken of little else for weeks, and then Annie spent the time in hospital rooms and in mourning instead. And Father Louis thought she should have a bonfire on Mount Carmel. So, the night before we left, we packed up your mother's papers and books into boxes and put them in the monastery truck and went up there and unloaded the books into the storage shed. While I was looking one last time at your mother's grave, Father Louis made a bonfire for Annie, and the next thing we knew, the sparks—the winds, it was dry, it was windy—the sparks flew to the shed, and suddenly it was on fire. An amazing fire, the air was so hot and dry that when the shed caught fire, it just blew up. My first instinct was to run into the shed and retrieve your mother's work, but it was a hellfire, Nina, like I've never seen. Father Louis and a young man I didn't know, a gardener who was working there, held me back from the flames."

I couldn't speak. He'd kept this from me so long, I didn't even know what to bother asking next.

He began again. "Somehow I've always feared you would think I hadn't tried to save her things, but I tried. I did, Nina."

"I only wish you had decided to bring her papers with you. Especially since it was something she was excited about."

"That was what Father Louis said, too, only he saw it the other way, get away from the material for a while, get away from her passion and my sadness. He thought the work had killed her, obsession with the work; it made her careless, made both of them careless—your mother and your grandmother. They were behaving like schoolgirls, shouting to children about games. She was seven months pregnant, and she was skipping across the street as though she were seven years old. Father Louis said sometimes the brilliant suffer lunacy over work. He'd seen it before, especially among scholars of antiquities. Especially in the Middle East."

"Mental illness?"

"No. Something more like zealous empathy. I guess they call it the Jerusalem syndrome now."

"You weren't in Jerusalem."

"Haifa's close enough. You get there, and you begin to relive the old stories, and you become one of the characters, and you get into some sort of bliss and can't get out."

Was that why he thought my mother's gestures and rituals were powerful?

Exactly. He'd seen people who thought they were Jesus, carrying crosses around, people who thought they were John the Baptist. "And look what happened to the Templars."

"What happened to the Templars?" I asked.

"The rituals. The processions they brought back from the Holy Land. They didn't go over well with the authorities. For some it was harmless, the whole grail thing, but Father Louis was worried your mother was stirring something up."

"Stirring up the grail?"

"Because she believed she had found it."

I took a deep breath. "Where? Did she say?"

"She said only that it was in the events of every day, in those gestures of hers."

I was finally beginning to understand my mother's notes about the grail and to wonder if, in Father Louis' solicitous kindness, my mother's things had been burned intentionally. "How badly did the Templars end?"

"The ones in France, they were burned at the stake."

"No accident that time," I said. I knew he got my drift.

"Father Louis thought the family needed to get away from the intensity of it all. After all, I had two girls to raise alone. Father Louis wouldn't have stopped scholarship. No matter what Annie says."

"What does Annie say?"

"She was only three years old. She couldn't remember it right."

"What does Annie remember?"

"It's all mixed with Aurelia's talk of the Morgans."

The way he could delay discussing the sadness. I wanted to shout at him, make him respond, but I couldn't muster anger toward him. He believed he was doing the right thing; he always believed he was doing the right thing. What good did it do me to be angry? I simply had to repeat my question, "What does Annie remember?"

"Annie says Father Louis was happy everything was burning, because your mother and grandmother had accidentally called up the Morgans, the spirits of death, by reading those tablets and singing and dancing on balconies."

"Called up the Morgans? How could you believe that?" I asked him. "Annie and you, a mathematician and a world-renowned exponent of the rational, you believed that?"

"Father Louis said nothing to me, only to Annie, and she was a child. I had no opportunity for belief or disbelief. I just wanted to put it all behind."

"I suppose Annie and I are lucky he didn't burn us." The small message pad on the phone was blinking, telling me I had only one minute left on my phone card. I asked if he would make sure Andrew received the Internet message we had made on the eyeball camera. "Send him a message now, please. Tell him I'm going up to the graves." My voice was slow, deliberate, and demanding.

Of course, he would try, but the system was behaving erratically, the whole college network. He was afraid it might be some sort of virus. Or the storm. That's why he was up in the attic. Tinkering with the system, hoping he'd figure it out. He told me to be careful. He said I shouldn't go to the graves until morning—and then not alone.

I told him not to worry; there were no spirits, at least not any that would hurt me. "I'm going to try to find the other two tablets. You can't burn stone." The message pad blinked zero seconds, and the phone went dead. I said a polite good-bye into the silent receiver, and hung it up as BeeBee and Liz came out of the café behind me. They'd been down to Elijah's cave at the bottom of the hill, on the cable car; it was running until midnight for the festival. They thought I should see it.

"You still have time," Liz said, "the nuns aren't going to lock us out until twelve."

"It's a holy place. For everybody," BeeBee was elated. "Elijah's hiding place when he was on the run. The spot where he went to prepare for his fight against Baal. The school of the prophets. The cave of the green one. A place where the holy family rested. If you wear a scarf and a skirt, you can't offend anyone."

Liz wondered what you had to do to offend pagans. "Baal, Tammuz, Helios, Pan," said Liz. "In paintings, you see one taking over for another, each one becoming the one he supplants."

"And eventually Elijah becomes a feral fellow. And John the Baptist and Jesus and St. George. I love it," said BeeBee, who was in a state of bliss.

Liz said everyone was down there, everyone except Rose and Nancy, who had gone back to the convent early.

I was dispirited after my conversation with my father, and I needed an activity to shift my mood. I went into the cable car station and looked at the crystal globes, running up and down the mountain. I had seen this contraption from below as we drove into the city; the cars looked like ornaments loosely strung together, blowing up and down Mount Carmel in the hot, dry wind. I paid four shekels for a round-trip ticket and sat down in the sphere. It swung back and forth from my weight, as though I were on a Ferris wheel with Annie, who used to make the seat swing before the carnival man in grey work clothes sealed us in with the safety bar. No one came to seal me in so all the way down I worried the door would fling itself open and scatter me against the side of the hill. We made it safely down to the station at the edge of the sea with no incident, and the voice that had been giving a thumbnail tour of Haifa on the way down the hill warned us all to be back at the station in time for the last run at 11:45.

Elijah's cave was across the road from the cable car station, up a stone staircase that wound under trees around the base of the hill. Old people were sitting on the steps, each with something different to give. An old man gave me a bag of incense, and a woman tied a red cord around my right hand.

"Rachel's blessing," she said and smiled.

I had a pocketful of half-shekels, and I dropped one in the coin boxes. At the top of the stairs, there was a man who shouted at people who tried to enter the cave without the proper attire. I pulled my skirt out of my bag and put it on over my loose trousers. I covered my head out of Catholic-woman instinct, and I realized that I was crossing gender lines. The cave guard had been shouting at a bareheaded man; for him, only men needed to cover their heads. I was trying not to offend anyone, not Jewish or Muslim or Christian. Hopefully not pagan either, I thought, as I went into the cave dressed as both a man and a woman.

There were deep blue and red velvet curtains on the cave walls and people standing behind them, leaning on the rock. I stood in the middle. I listened to the prayers. The red-headed twins were there with their parents. They waved and showed me the red strings on their wrists. I wiggled my fingers back and showed them mine. One of the velvet curtains moved, and Astrid appeared; she held the drape away from the wall for a moment, and Gala and Veronica and Kathryn all came from behind it. Veronica was weeping openly. She was making no attempt to stop.

It was 11:40. We left the cave. Gala and I lit candles outside. Gala was lighting for Elijah, I supposed. I was lighting for green men and feral women who sang and danced on balconies and read obscure tablets, no matter who their god was. We walked back down the stairs and across the road to the cable car, and sat down in the glass sphere. When we were in the globe and moving up the hill, Veronica's sobbing turned into short gasps and muffled snorts. She had her eyes shut and her head on Kathryn's shoulder. Gala had taken her hand in her own.

"Sister Hildegard seems to think Veronica is devoted to Margery Kempe," I remembered.

Gala said she and Divany believed the same thing, and since there weren't many people who appreciated Margery Kempe, they felt Veronica had to be nurtured and cherished.

"Is this Jerusalem syndrome?" I asked.

Kathryn nodded. "Perhaps."

"Maybe she is struck by the women who weep in the Bible," said Astrid. She believed a special burden came with the name Veronica, like the woman who dried Christ's own tears on her veil.

"Ezekiel," sobbed Veronica, "8:14."

Astrid had a pocket Bible. She opened it. "They're weeping for Tammuz, an idol like the one Elijah struck down."

I told her that Liz and BeeBee mentioned somebody named Tammuz, too.

"I don't think so," said Astrid. She said Veronica couldn't be serious about Ezekiel 8:14. Not BeeBee or Liz, either. "The world stopped weeping for Tammuz long ago."

Forensics: VI

$\mathcal{M}$y father was experiencing intermittent power surges and transmission failures, but sometime after I talked to him—during the middle of the night in Israel, early in the evening in Vermont—this message came through the Thomas line into his Multi-User Dungeon:

Date: Seventh Month, '00
X-Sender:thomaquin@paris.summa;
aristotle@salonika.edu;
To:christine@pizan.cite; vonbingen@mystik.
illum; porète@farnear.nil, et al
Subject:moisture

The causal relationship between moisture
(of winds) and lesser perfection (as in the

creation of the female) has already been documented. (Summa Theologiae, Generation of Animals)

It was quickly followed by a second message:

Date: Seventh Month, '00
X-Sender:christine@pizan.cite
To:thomaquin@paris.summa; aristotle@ salonika.edu; socrates@plato.repub; tacitus@history.rom, et al.
Subject:silence

I indeed understand the enormous ingrat- itude, not to say ignorance, of these men who malign women, for although it seems to me that the fact that the mother of every man is a woman is reason enough not to attack them, not to mention the other good deeds which one can clearly see that women do for men, truly, one can see here the many benefits afforded by women with the greatest generosity to men which they have accepted and continue to accept. Henceforth, let all writers be silent who speak badly of women, let all of them be silent--those who have attacked women and who still attack them in their books and poems, and all their accomplices and sup- porters, too--let them lower their eyes, ashamed for having dared to speak so badly, in view of the truth which runs counter to their poems. (Cité des Dames)

When my father tried to e-mail Sister Hildegard to see what she thought about the messages, he discovered his computer had stopped working altogether. He called Sister Hildegard on the phone to see if she was having computer problems, and she said she'd unplugged her machine because she was in a contemplative mood. She hadn't been online since morning. She hadn't read any of the new messages.

It was apparent the network had been targeted by some virus or by the storm that had raged all day, or both. The storm-virus had created noise on the lines, which effectively silenced everyone with access to the Multi-User Dungeon of the Thomas Aquinas Web Site at 6:42 p.m., Eastern Standard Time. When it was all over, the computer experts said the damage was so extensive the only remedy would be to return all the machines for new motherboards.

Sister Hildegard, whose computer had been unplugged by sheer chance, was the only user of the Thomas Aquinas MUD who came safely through the crash.

Forensics: VII

The crystal globe transported my group up Mount Carmel to Stella Maris. We walked across the street of my mother and grandmother and through the crowd of camping pilgrims. With all our scarves and ribbons and robes, we looked like a troupe of medieval mendicants. I think that's why I didn't notice Marguerite walking right next to me until we came to the church doors, which were closing as we approached them. Marguerite pulled me in quickly and spun me around to face a priest I hadn't seen before. She whispered in my ear, "Tell him you forgot something." He was about to lock the door I had just squeezed through. I told him I had left my bag inside, he asked where, and

Marguerite pointed toward the museum.

"In the museum."

He said it was fine for me to go back in; I could leave by the museum door because that would be the last one he would lock. I followed Marguerite into the museum, expecting to see the volunteer, but she was gone. The room was dark except for light coming in from the courtyard, enough light for me to see what Marguerite wanted me to see. The glass case was open. The stone tablets were there. I had on so many clothes, it was easy to slip the narrow tablets into pockets, only one per pocket so the thin clay pieces wouldn't bump against each other and crack or peel. I shut the glass door and went outside as I had promised the priest I would.

"Now what?" I said to Marguerite. "Now that I'm guilty of pilfering antiquities, now what?"

"Happy birthday. Spend the rest of it reading. Copy them. We can always put them somewhere so that the proper people find them in the morning."

"I can't believe I took these." We walked around to the staircase leading to my grandmother's balcony.

"A bird in the hand," said Christine, who was waiting by the jungle gym. "Does that bird think of bygone times as it flies singing over the spring by the tree?"

With Christine, I had learned to wait for attributions.

Christine unfolded a sheet of paper and pointed to a spot halfway from the top. She'd been working her way back through the dead writers list and was delighted to find a reference to Princess Nukada. "She wrote in Japan," she said. "long before Marguerite and I were born."

"Nin has the tablets." Marguerite was extremely pleased with her lawlessness.

"Even flaming fire can be snatched up, smothered, and carried in a bag."

"The tablets are in my *pockets.*"

Christine said she could tell the way I had my hands cupped over the open edges that the stones were in my pockets, but she thought the essence of the issue could be caught in the lines of another early Japanese poem by Empress Jito. "When I found her, I tried to convince her to come with us. Princess Nukada, too, but they weren't able to get away right then. In the end, it turns out Beatrice won't be able to stop by either."

"You haven't been around much yourselves," I pointed out. "Now it appears you're leaving again." Christine and Marguerite were walking away from me, away from the staircase and the convent, back toward the front of the church and the bank of telephones at the top of the hill by the restaurant and the cable car.

"Soon," Marguerite called back.

"We have more to do, but we'll be with you soon," said Christine.

I stepped gingerly up the wooden stairs, through unlocked doors on the balcony into my grandmother's room. Although it was hot and dry, I was comfortable with the doors and windows open, especially after I took off my scarf and my long-sleeved shirt and the skirt I'd put on to go into Elijah's cave. I still had on my trousers and a waist-skimming T-shirt I bought back in Burlington when the clerk convinced me it would be perfect for Middle Eastern heat. I felt a breeze at my waist where the T-shirt hovered and another at my ankles, and I shivered in the heat that seemed oddly clammy. I poured a glass of water and drank some and sat down at the table near the window.

I propped the tablet fragments against my Israel guide and aimed my flashlight at the ruts and grooves. I opened my mother's black binder and began to study and compare the lines. I had no idea what I was looking for except coincidence of pattern, repetition of design. I wished I had a copy machine; I would copy my mother's work so I could circle the patterns that I thought I saw repeated, but I didn't want to write on the only copy of my mother's notes so instead I counted down the lines on my mother's pencil draft and numbered a blank page, then I counted the lines on the clay and did the same on another page. I marked the new pages "Mother" and "Antiquity," and each time I saw a corresponding sign, I copied it in the proper place on both pages.

No wonder she liked graph paper. I sharpened my pencil with my travel knife. I was finding more and more coincidences. I worked, copying the wedges into the tiny squares of graph paper until I remembered the twins who had invited me to the top of Mount Carmel to see the dawn. I was suddenly overcome by the poetic notion of seeing day begin at the grave of my mother whose days had ended too soon. I still had the keys to the van; there was nothing to stop me.

I wrapped each of the pieces of clay in a washcloth and tied them into two plastic bags, tucking them—with my mother's folder—into my backpack, in the folds of my sweater, my devotional skirt, and the scarf I'd rubbed with Elijah's soot. I was prepared for the dress requirements of all orthodoxies and for the strange chill that seemed to be following me as well. I went down to the van. Gala's small bag was there. I looked inside: a flashlight, a bag of rice cakes, and surprisingly, a bottle of dark beer. I checked the map the rental agency stuffed in the glove compartment and decided I could easily drive up and get back down before anyone at the museum missed the fragments in my bag. I pulled carefully out of the parking lot, past families of pilgrims who were sitting on their blankets now, eating charred lamb and flat bread and talking in hushed tones. I pulled out on the street of my mother and grandmother and drove up to the spur on the hill to see sunrise where there had several times been fire.

I was no more than a quarter of a mile from Stella Maris when

I noticed lights in my rearview mirror, a small, light-colored car, a large man inside. I thought it was the Dominican's Escort, that he was following me again. Suddenly, the small car pulled to the side of the road, made a U-turn, and went back down the hill, as though it had been called back. Was he doing his disappearing act, or was he simply stalking my imagination? I checked the clock on the dashboard. It said 1:42 a.m. I looked in the mirror again; no one was following me, except the night.

The road became gravel, dark red in my headlights, winding 'round the hill into a grove of cedars and tall pines and stone benches and two huge square stone monuments. My lights caught the vision of Elijah wielding a sword—wild man, foot on the neck of his rival.

There was a wide space where I parked the van. I took Gala's flashlight and tucked her cloth bag inside my backpack, in case there was something else I might need. I began to walk, past a grotto and a statue of the virgin to the front of the church. My father said they were building it when they were here that last night making Annie's fire. The architecture seemed too recent, post-fifties, more like the 1960s. The church door was locked. It was 2 a.m. I wondered where the red-headed girls were, perhaps around the other side. I found a staircase, which I climbed. As I took each step, I could see more bright heaven, more dark earth. There were no clouds, but the night outlined everything in heavy tincture, deep blue. Sky, moon, stars, hills, hills, hills, and the sea. This was the top of the world. It was also a small blue-green garden, and there were people, blurred in the night ink against the wall of the church, some awake watching the sky, others asleep on the grass. I saw the girls, heads on the lap of a woman, her red hair swinging from her shoulders in the wind. I walked toward them, thinking she might know where there was a dig and where the graves were. Did she know where either one was?

Yes, she did, but this was not the time. Morning was better.

I told her morning was fine but now was preferred, and she pointed, toward the grotto. "Behind, where rocks change from grey to pink. In the morning, colors are clear. The dig and the graves both, not far from each other, but entirely easier in the morning."

I thanked her. I had decided to go to the graves in the night, no matter what everyone said. I went back down the stairs and flicked on Gala's flashlight. There was the grotto again with the virgin, her foot on a serpent, both of them on the top of the world. I headed toward her. Rocks were all grey there, like the grey stone bench I bumped my shin against in the dark. I stopped and sat on the bench for a moment. It was going to be darker yet in the cedars, so I switched off the flashlight and waited for my night vision. There seemed to be a path worn just to the left of the virgin's statue, and I thought I saw a flicker of ribbon curling in the air, tape perhaps, marking the site. I walked slowly in the dark; there were small cedars, medium cedars, large cedars growing alongside each other like unnested dolls. The ground under my feet was spongy, as though this woods had a subfloor. Roots, pushing through the needles and leaves, thin ones winding out from the tree trunks, bulging up from the ground, hooking across my path, foot catchers. And rocks, emerging suddenly from the earth like stairs. Was I imagining it, or was the stone picking up a rosy cast? I had not yet come to whatever it was that had seemed to be ribbon flashing. I kept walking.

The trees closed in over me, and I felt the curious cool again, blowing gentle breaths against my neck. I'd felt something like this in my grandmother's room. It was familiar, but it wasn't till now in the woods that I knew what it was. It was the breeze in the forest next to Memphremagog, the chill in the copper moss woods next to Lake Superior. Cold in the midst of heat. It was a sensation I knew well, and it was comforting. I felt at home. I stepped gingerly on the spongy ground. Reverence was called for. And caution. The chilly woods were at the top of a dry, stone mountain, not next to a lake, and I had no intention of falling off.

What I didn't expect to do was to fall in, which is exactly what happened. Without warning, the spongy loam gave way under me, and I went down, down, straight down into the velvet ground. When I finally stopped falling, I expected to see bones jutting out of my limbs, but I wasn't hurt. The earth was soft and yielding, and I was muddy, oddly muddy rather than dusty like the world up above. I still had my backpack and Gala's flashlight. I switched the beam on and turned in a circle, having the eerie feeling that I had dropped into someone's grave. The space had been squared off, but now it was empty. There was no one there, except me. When I tried to climb up out of the hole, earth came off in clumps in my hands and crumbled under the weight of my feet. I was in trouble.

I called. I called again. Nothing. If I kept climbing, I might pull a slide in on top of me or block my air. The grass already seemed to have closed over me after I fell in, and I could see the sky only from one corner, through a slit in the sod up above. If the red-headed girls were right, their dog star would rise in a few hours and along with it, the sun. Then, if I yelled, people would hear me, and they would come looking for me and find me and help me out. Until then, continuing to scream was useless and disturbing and energy-depleting, especially since the chill was more obvious to me in the cave.

Carefully, I extricated the spare clothing I'd stuffed in my pack and put it all on—scarf over sweater, skirt over trousers. I was stuck in a hole in the ground, and there didn't seem to be any way that I was going to get out and sneak the clay tablets back into the museum before 7 a.m. I unwrapped the tablets and focused the flashlight on them. They were all right. They hadn't chipped in the fall. I turned the light off to preserve the batteries and let my fingers dance over the marks in the clay, wondering if anyone had learned to read these signs with their fingers. It might have been possible. I could feel every ridge. I began to trace the signs slowly, redrawing them one by one, my forefinger sketching each dart, each arrow, each star, outlining the dents and turns, seeking form, shape, gesture. Someone had arranged these signs to compose a message entirely in gestures.

⧗ ⧗ ⧗

Shatapda's signs were understood. Her message was clear. And she was fortunate. Her habit of writing from the heart had impressed the authorities, and her people survived the war. They came through the bloodshed without plague, even though they'd been turned out of their homes, torn from their culture, left like fish discarded on the beach. The new government paid attention to what Shatapda wrote, gave her people some green space, let them have their music again. It took five years to have peace restored, and historians said it never would have happened if Shatapda hadn't taken the step, written her letter, managed to communicate directly. They made her letter a part of the canon and used it in the writing school as an example, and she was famous for a while.

Some people called her a historian because she put the facts down so well. Some called her a journalist, for the same reason. She should have been happy to have been named to the top writers' list, but she always wished they'd put her work in the proper category. Her letter wasn't history or journalism, although she knew how to write in those forms; she'd been to school herself, she knew the rules, consulted the stylebook. Her letter was a poem. The effort she'd gone through. The subtlety she'd achieved. The allusions to earlier texts. Where she'd broken with poetic form was in her broad gestures, her line length, pushing her signs all across the clay, and that may have been what made them regard it as prose. She was ahead of her time.

It seemed everyone had benefited from her writing, except herself. After five years away, she'd never really gone back into society. She became a recluse. Life in the city no longer attracted her. Being alone had its pleasures. She had no desire to talk to strangers, to talk to people she knew, to talk.

This was a fine time for her to be invited to a writers' conference. She hadn't wanted to go, but they kept calling her, playing with her metaphors, speaking of her work as poetry. To be honest, the notion of other writers redrawing her images was exciting. They were noticing her intertextuality. Perhaps they would keep the echo going. Yet, she'd been wandering in the hills so long, she had no decent clothing, no cosmetics, no bracelets to hang on her wrists. She looked dead, the way she'd been walking around, all twisted and bowed and used up. It had been forever since she braided the crown of her hair and turned her long black curls into an easy roll that touched her jawbones and skimmed around her neck in back. She'd let her hair go natural, and it was wild and springing from her head like leeks.

Now that was something—the notion that hair could look like leeks; it just didn't work as a metaphor anymore. Not that hair didn't still look like leeks, but nowadays so few people ate leeks, planted them, watched them grow from the earth. Who sliced them anymore, let them curl in hot oil? Most people saw leeks cleaned up and bunched unnaturally in the market, like over-grown onions. Or boiled to a puree in soup. And nobody had hair that looked like a bunch of overgrown onions reduced to liquid in soup. Luckily, she hadn't used that metaphor, although it had been popular once. She believed the images she used were still working: the storm, the ritual, the echo, the decaying of walls, the moaning of pigeons, the scattering of birds, the scattering of honor, and she, herself, a woman in the window watching her life set before twilight, her song subdued, her soul unrevealed. Was she sacred or was she taboo?

She still felt strong; how had she become so overwhelmingly obsolete? That may have been what convinced her to come out of exile. The calls about her letter, the questions about her metaphors. The possibility of extending her day.

Even so, she wouldn't have made the sailboat trip over to Israel if it weren't for Heduanna, who was invited, too. Her mentor, her teacher—Heduanna, the mother of all writers. Heduanna wasn't really her name, just a nickname, like her own, Shatapda. They'd dreamed up the names for this trip. Their full names had tones of cultural obscurity and chthonic elitism written all through them: enheduanna and ninshatapada. The shortened versions were to be pronounced Hed-yanna and Sh'táhp'da. Well, no one knew how to pronounce their names anyway, since Sumerian was a dead language. It had been dead even when she and Heduanna had written in it. They were classicists in their time, like the monks and nuns who preserved Latin and Greek, educated in the old literature, dedicated to preserving the old culture. And it was a language done in signs, rather than sounds.

So, when it came to drawing up a pronunciation guide, Shatapda felt free to suggest the "not-too-many-vowels" sound that she'd come up with. It had a modern urban tone. Like Japanese. Of course, they'd keep their full names on their work, but this was the turn of a new century, a new millennium, and there was the possibility they'd meet Americans, people who had trouble with honorifics. Shatapda had been warned, introducing themselves with the titles *en* and *nin* in front of their names would be off-putting, like asking a new acquaintance to refer to your

Ph.D. or wearing a Phi Beta Kappa key or casually referring to yourself as royalty.

They had decided to introduce themselves as simply Heduanna and Shatapda, names with both presence and historical weight. They were not overly difficult names, simple but dignified. At first, they'd considered shortening even further to Heddy and Shtopdy, but those names were whimsical. And it was important not to be overly whimsical. Scholars had been known to check for scribal whimsy, suggesting a display of error rather than aesthetics. After all, they were not only poets, they were regents and priests. They had to behave with decorum. Thank the gods Heduanna still had a closetful of clothes, a basketful of makeup, more than enough jewelry for two chieftains, and a strong enough voice for two cantors, two preachers, two bishops. That made coming out of exile a good deal easier for Shatapda.

⧗ ⧗ ⧗

Heduanna was below deck, fastening the clasp on her necklace and arranging the ornament in her hair. First the lapis beads, winding them around the bun at the crown of her head, the cluster of roses on top of that, and finally the gold leaves and circles that fell to her forehead and cascaded over her heavy black curls. This was called a *tiara*, but the word *tiara* had pretensions; *ornament* was what they were saying now.

Heduanna straightened the layers of her skirt. She loved every inch of her girth. When she chanted hymns, her whole body moved in cadence. Now she was swaying, arms extended in the night air, humming. She was stimulated by the prospect of audience, anxious to read from her work.

They'd come to Israel in their boat with carnelian sails, carrying crates of food and drink to give to everyone who extended them hospitality. Heduanna felt as though she were on a trade mission, but this was more important than economics. She was going to have a chance to talk about things invented in the old culture, Sumerian improvisations, not just sailboats and vehicles with wheels and cities and the brewing of beer, but the festivals of Inanna and the practice of an author signing her work. Actually, she was the one who came up with that, the idea of an author signing her work. No one had done it before her. If there was a cult of the author, she was the one who had started it by signing her "Hymn to Inanna."

In retrospect, she'd started a good deal more. She started debates over the custody of expression, arguments about authorship, copyright battles, even this whole dead authors thing. She wondered what would happen if the trend reversed itself, and all authors actually were dead, only texts and audiences remained alive. Would it be the way it used to be when every story belonged to the folk? Maybe it would be better, for a while. The problem was, when writers left work unsigned, anybody could claim authorship. Biography was disregarded, personal mythology had no meaning, and mythology, stripped of the existential *now*, stiffened and solidified.

Slowly at first, and then with the suddenness of a dry desert storm, men took over, as though writing were a male trait, as though the schools hadn't been full of female scribes, as though the canon hadn't been full of their work, as though the god of writing weren't female, as though their male pronouns even existed in the first writing, as though you could tell who was who in Sumerian by virtue of grammar. Heduanna knew better. She knew you couldn't tell a man from a woman, not by the language. There was no "he." There was no "she." When Heduanna wrote, the distinction was a simple one: some things were alive and some things were not alive. That was all. You had to catch gender by what she referred to as *context*. You couldn't always tell by clothes, people dressed half-male and half-female for parades, not exactly cross-dressing, more like double-dressing. In Sumerian, the only way you knew for sure who was male and who was female was by their body parts.

So, it was a good thing they didn't have sexual hang-ups like some people did today. And it was a good thing she signed that piece she wrote about Inanna. It was hard enough for people to understand about women writers these days. She heard one scholar admit she, Heduanna, was the first writer to sign a text—in the history of the world—and then he said, "But that's all." What did he mean? "That's all?" If she'd been a man, they'd have come up with a syllogism that proved if the first writer was a male, all writers must be males.

She'd been snubbed by women, too, the ones who said she just happened to have the right father at the right time. Not her fault he'd been the most powerful man in Mesopotamia. It's not as though she were the first woman to get the high priest job, not the last either, not by five hundred years. She came in on the cusp of the two societies. She was Akkadian on her father's side, Sumerian on her mother's, but her mother's side was good enough. In memory of her mother, she wrote in Sumerian. In memory of her father and her mother, she named her sailboat Tiamat, after the Akkadian first mother, Mother Sea. That mother had ended up slain by her son, which wasn't good, of course, but it certainly demonstrated what kind of cusp Heduanna grew up on.

Sometimes, they called her a collaborator—the same label they gave to Inanna—a collaborator because when men took over, they diluted the power of female gods like Inanna and weakened the women who wrote about them as well. But that Inanna—hehzooah! Inanna rode the wild dogs! In her prime, nobody could dilute her force, her squall, her thunder. Inanna was a sister. She was a woman. She was heavenly, earthy, open like a day, calm as the sea, wild as a tempest. She could be a dragon. She breathed fire. She baptized herself in fire, but she knew the ropes—when to twist, when to tangle, when to untangle. And when she went down to the other land, when she went up to the other land, when they scattered her at the seven gates, when they hung her like a piece of wood, she was still a sister. Heduanna knew, she'd had the experience, she'd felt ash on her cheeks, been covered in sand 'til words were pests on her lips, crawled through thorns in a land full of strangers, but Inanna came out of it. And Inanna taught Heduanna how to sail through the abyss. Dream. Moan. Birth. Quiet. Food. Water. Exit. Chase. Twist. Skip. Balance.

Inanna needed a larger audience, a more supportive audience. Women needed to help each other get better press. Women needed to help each other.

Heduanna moved around the cabin of the Tiamat, checking everything she and Shatapda had brought with them. The basket, woven out of goat hair, was filled with food and drink: dates, cheese, a tasty paté made from chickpeas and onions and garlic, a pot of mustard, a tray of barley cakes, and beer—sweet dark beer that smelled like caramel and danced on your tongue and slipped down your throat like cream. She poured the beer into a pottery cup and watched the half inch of foam evaporate into a thin white line. She didn't sip it, she didn't need to taste things anymore. Sight and smell and sound were enough. She bent over it and smelled the bitter sweetness and watched the core pull away, leaving a light rope of bubbles whispering at the edges and a thin cream design at the center—a hill, globes rising over it, one circle high in the sky like the moon. She had read omens in the cast of oil in water, the flight of birds in the sky, the markings on the livers of sheep, but never before in the pale foam of beer. She had invented again. It made her feel as good as she felt years ago when

238

she coined phrases in her dead language. Heduanna had a sense of invigoration. It was time to go to the mountain. They would get there while it was still night.

She tied her lapis and carnelian belt around her waist and put on her rings: gold, green bloodstone, lapis. Two gold bracelets on each arm. Earrings almost the same size. Then she circled her eyes with a faint line of grey-black kohl, used tufts of lamb's wool to dust rose amber on her cheekbones, and painted her lips with a soft ruby cream. She was as beautiful as the rising moon and equally alluring, and that's the look Heduanna wanted because, from her point of view, it was godly to be seductive, just like it was godly to be wild, godly to be powerful, godly to be a woman, and godly to write about it.

Comedy

Deep musty smells, dry world wet from the underside, damp earth. Dark grey roof of a sky. Still not morning, but I was hungry. I remembered Gala's rice cakes and beer and was ready to have a snack when I began a debate with myself. Would the rice sustain me as it sustained the people of China? Would the alcohol in the beer fool me into thinking I was warm, speeding me toward hypothermia? But I needed liquid, didn't I? Even so, how much did I dare drink? Would they come for me at dawn? Would I spend days in that tomb? Should I begin to ration my supplies?

"I don't see any need for you to ration anything," came a woman's voice from the other side of the hole.

Unique sounds. Unique tones. I had not heard English sound like that before. The person talking to me had an accent which was not French and not Italian, but who could it be but Marguerite or Christine? I whispered, "Marguerite? Christine?"

"It's me, Heduanna." The voice was coming closer. It was a heavy accent, not the one I'd been listening to since I arrived, not Israeli. "Shatapda and I have enough in our basket for you to last in here indefinitely."

I reached for the flashlight and flicked it on. There were two women standing in the dark; one was slightly larger than the other and wore some sort of crown. She was holding a clay pitcher. The smaller woman was holding a square basket, made of a tightly woven material, almost like wood, a hairy sort of wood. She opened it, and I could see dates or figs and cheese.

The one with the pitcher said, "Try this. I think ours is better beer."

"Better beer?" I asked.

"The original," she said. "I understand the recipe's been modified since. Not that the essentials aren't still there, not that yours is bad, but when good things get passed down for so many years without access to original recipes and ingredients, some of the original zest is lost."

She poured her dark beer into a pottery cup. It had the scent of Saturday afternoon tea with the sisters. It was dark brown with beige foam, not white. I smelled again. "Guinness. It smells like Guinness Stout."

"Some haven't been away from the original as long as others," said the smaller woman. "Drink."

I couldn't bring myself to drink what these people were giving me. Who were they? Was this a terrorist kidnapping? Were they threatening me when they said they could keep me indefinitely? Was I a hostage? Is this why the State Department put that warning on the Internet? Was the beer poisoned or drugged?

"You seem frightened," observed the smaller one.

Worried. I admitted to being worried. This was an odd experience. I had promised my family not to leave my group, and when I went off on my own, look, here I was, in some sort of tiger trap, being offered something strange to drink by women who appeared friendly but could be spies or agents or people with underworld ties. Underworld is the word that they seemed to hear.

"Everyone worries about the myths," said the one with the figs.

"Everybody knows the Greek and Roman versions. You panic about eating something as small as a pomegranate seed. Instead, you should be pleased that we brought you this. Food and drink are what keep people alive. In our stories, food and drink are good."

"Who are you?"

"We are Heduanna and Shatapda. Writers from Sumer. Mesopotamia. You know, the Tigris and Euphrates. Maybe you call it Babylon, although that's not precise. I understand it's called Iraq now."

Iraq was not what I wanted to hear, but these people didn't fit my image of Iraqis. I had a sense of Byzantium, Phoenicia, but not quite. I didn't know what to make of them.

"Who are you?" asked the one called Shatapda.

"Nin Creed."

She was surprised. She thought I was American. She didn't know Americans used honorifics.

I asked what she meant by an honorific, and she said the title *nin*. I explained that it was my name. "I never thought Nin was an honorific. What's it mean?"

"Depends," Heduanna said. "Sovereign, regent, priest, sister . . ."

"So, is it a man's title or a woman's?"

"Depends," Shatapda responded. "Actually, it's part of my

name—nin-shatapada. But there are a lot of men—not really men, sort of men, gods, male ones—with nin in their names." She said the same went for Heduanna; her name was really en-heduannna, no caps. "The sign for *en* means priest and chief and lord and governor and that sort of thing because women did everything in our time, made the beer, ran the tavern, became the king."

"They used to say my mother was a king." I wondered if this meant Aurelia's story had some fact behind it.

"Women used to do more. Orchestrated the temple. Wrote the poems; read them. Wrote the songs; sang them. Gender issues were different in the old days, except for child care, seems women have always been in charge of children. We used to have to take the kids to work with us back then."

She was like Aurelia, the way she made up the rules for stories. "nin-shatapada," I said, uttering the syllables slowly.

She explained that her name could mean sister who speaks from the heart or priest who reveals the soul or woman who conjures from innards. It was all related, really—heart, soul, innards, speaking, revealing, conjuring—all part of the poet's work. She said they'd come by invitation to a festival of dead writers. Up to this point, however, the only person they'd met was me, and I didn't appear to be dead at all. "We don't know if you're a writer, but you're obviously a reader because we've been watching you for a while, and you seem to have been reading our work."

Heduanna said I had been touching the sign for *nin*, that *nin* was the very mark my thumb was resting on, the first sign of the first line of indentations in the hard clay. She said, "nin-me-šár-ra, u-dalla-è-a. Sister who is all of us, all of us who are opening like a day, surging like a storm . . . "

So that was it. I handed Heduanna the clay fragments I'd been fingering. "This is who you are?" Yes, these women were from Iraq but from Iraq before it was Iraq, and they looked ancient because they *were* ancient, and they were another of my dreams, another one of my spells, as Veronica's nurse called them. These were the lower-cased names from Marguerite and Christina's writers' group. I wondered whether I was awake or asleep. Perhaps I'd been hurt when I fell. Maybe I hit my head. I looked at the two of them. They were elegantly dressed. Their hair was black and curly and full. They were wearing blue and red and green stones and gold, quantities of gold. They were smiling. They had brought me gifts, and they were offering them while I was being American and fussy and impolite. I smiled back. I took a sip of their beer. It was strong, malty, wild.

"We were hoping to find Marguerite Porète and Christine de Pizan. Perhaps Beatrice of Nazareth, have you seen them?"

I told them I had not seen Beatrice, although I had heard a great deal of her, and I had seen Marguerite and Christine, but not for a while. Not since Marguerite convinced me that there was more to life than rules, and I stole antiquities out of a museum. I apologized for having taken their work. They said I wasn't the first. We sat down on the ground. I drank more. I offered them a taste of Gala's beer and rice cakes; they examined them closely, looking, sniffing, listening, but they didn't eat.

"It's nothing to worry about," said Shatapda. "You must have noticed that Marguerite and Christine don't eat either." She said it had to do with being dead.

I told them I had noticed because I was very interested in dead women, especially my mother and my grandmother, who were buried right near us somewhere in this woods. I explained that my mother was the one who could actually read their texts, that she had been working on a comparative study in the 1950s in Haifa when she died. And my grandmother died at the same moment. The very same moment when I was born.

"What was her name?" Heduanna asked.

"Faith. Faith Morgan DeLacey Creed. My grandmother was Grace Morgan DeLacey."

"Fata Morgana? The ancient one? When did she die?"

I told them 1951.

"It's not the same one, then, and it's too soon for you to meet them here," Shatapda stated.

I explained that I hadn't hoped to meet them. I really hadn't considered anything like a séance. I had simply wanted to find my mother's work. I wanted to know what she had been reading. Everything on her desk when she died had been destroyed in a fire, except the notes I had in the black binder, the two fragments of their work, and the other two tablets that I'd come up here hoping to find.

"It's possible you will find them someday. Our work has lasted a long while. It's hard to destroy," said Shatapda.

"But what do you want to know?" asked Heduanna.

I told her I wanted to know every word on her tablet, every word on Shatapda's tablet.

"These are more than just words. They are signs. Every sign has many meanings, and all the meanings apply."

"How many meanings?" I asked.

"Many."

"And you mean them all, at the same time?"

"We're poets," said Shatapda, as if that explained everything. "That's how we see the world. The jumping, the skipping from one image to another. Even the allusions we make by accident are intentional." She indicated that I was the same sort of accidental allusion. "Consider your name."

I told her that I was sensitive to the issue of being called an accident. "And besides, the priest baptized me Nina, not Nin."

"Close enough for truth to seep through. They call you *nin*, and you're here with us," Heduanna paused. She passed me a handful of dates and a barley cake. "You may not understand your hunger; it's a hunger deep in the earth, but even without understanding, you've been craving us all your life. Eat."

The dates were sweet. And the cakes were better than Gala's rice cakes, which were salt-free. The ancient cakes, they told me, were from sprouted barley, malty, prepared in vats where beer had been brewed.

"Energy squeezed in my fist," I said.

Heduanna looked at me oddly when I said that.

I told them I needed to make lists of words. That my mother had been making lists of words when she died. I showed them her lists, and I showed them mine. "She was looking for gestures," I said. "She seemed to think there was a connection between the Holy Grail and the ceremonies of everyday life in Haifa. She had many questions . . . but they all boil down to this, some common gesture and its chain of custody."

"What gesture?" asked Heduanna.

"The grail itself." I told them the story I had pulled from my father, how my mother thought she had found the grail itself. "But now, nobody understands what she found."

"It is interesting that she calls the grail a gesture," Shatapda said.

"I've been thinking it may be a cup." I lifted my mug of dark Sumerian ale. "Perhaps the gesture is drinking from a designated cup."

"The cult object," said Heduanna. "You, and your mother, have been seeking the cult object. Do you know this grail story?" She wanted to see my mother's notes, to find out about the grail, and to see what my mother had been reading in Sumerian literature. When she began to turn the pages of the black ring binder, she shook her head. Speaking English was easy because she was a seer and a prophet, but reading this new writing was something else. Where was Marguerite? And why wasn't Hildegard there?

And Marie de France, of all people to be missing. "I have to look very hard to see pictures in your letters. You're stuck on words. If you're having a problem, it may stem from the way you write." She thought words like these must have grown from the influence of rationalists. She paged through my mother's notes, skipping everything but the pages of cuneiform. Those she read carefully. So did Shatapda. They were hoping my mother had transcribed the two lost tablets so we could see what, other than their works, she was examining.

"That will tell us what she found," Shatapda said.

When they had read all the cuneiform transcribed into little squares on graph paper, they conferred in their own language. The sounds seemed to be short bursts—consonant-vowel-consonant-vowel-consonant-vowel—as though all ideas were made up of one-syllable sounds, as though all syllables were hyphenated, as though staccato were the cadence, and repetition a major poetic device. Sometimes, the repetitions were double, the beats double, the sounds double, the syllables coming doubly fast. They drew signs in the air, as though they were pressing them into clay. Large gestures, fat signs, pregnant signs. When they were finished, they seemed sad. And tired. They looked at each other, not at me. Heduanna said the only complete works in my mother's notebook were the two she had suspected, Heduanna's *nin-me-šár-ra* and Shatapda's *lugal-mu-ra*—the clay tablets I had taken from the museum.

"These are significant works; don't think we're saying she had nothing here," said Shatapda. "Heduanna's poem is the first signed work in the history of people, and mine is a significant letter prayer, like a psalm, and she has them here, transcribed, well done, but she did not transcribe the other works. If there were two other pieces, she didn't have a chance to write those down."

Silence filled the cave. I didn't know what else to ask these women. The sky above me was all purple grey. I had fallen into a pit; I had come close to finding the answer to my mother's question, and still I knew nothing. Annie was going to be pleased. She was going to be right.

I clapped my hands together, there was no sound. I waved my hands over my face. No bird, not even a fan. Let it fly. Let me name the echo I was hearing. But I could not. I was in the brambles, caged in a place of the living and the dying. I was fading like a weak storm.

"You're thinking my words, translating my work," Shatapda said.

"I can't be," I said. "I can't read your work."

"Then you're recomposing it, rewriting it . . . "

"I can't write anymore. From the time I left home, I haven't been able to write. My thoughts are wooden. I have no more poems."

"You may not have any poems of your own, but you're coming very close to translating mine," she insisted. "That last thought was line 49, I'd swear. It's not me, not a hundred percent, but about as close as most translations get."

"My mouth is speaking tangled chants. Words crawl out of my mouth like bugs on my lips. Look at me, squatting in the dust. All I understand is gravel pouring through my hands."

Heduanna rubbed her hand across my shoulders. "Young one, I know you've learned to read cuneiform because now you are reading my lines. Either that, or you are reading my mind, which means you are an *en* or a *nin*, which—of course—you are."

The two women seemed both affected by my sadness and pleased at my new clairvoyance. They exhorted me to read the English part of my mother's notes, to tell them the story of the grail. I told them no one really needs to read the story of the grail; people simply know one version or another.

"It's part of the folk literature, then?" asked Heduanna. "It changes a little bit here, a little bit there?"

I told them the grail story was like stories you tell at camp or things we call urban legends now. They were very interested in the notion of an urban legend, especially since their people had invented cities, and they felt responsibility for what goes on in cities. They wanted to know if an urban legend was a story about the founding of cities, and I said, no, it was just a story somebody tells somebody and somebody tells somebody and somebody tells somebody else.

"The oral tradition," Heduanna said. "Is it coming back?"

Maybe yes, maybe no, I said. I told them there was something going on electronically, in something called the etherworld. That confused them so I said it was like an oral tradition but in a different form—like electricity—which is like fire. They understood fire. I told them the grail stories were started long before electricity; they came from Marguerite's time and before. Heduanna and Shatapda sat cross-legged on the ground. Heduanna motioned toward a spot on the other side of the woven box where she wanted me to sit. The woven box was between us, as though it were a campfire. "Tell us the story."

I began.

Somebody, sometimes called the "Fisher King," I never know if the king fishes or *is* a fish, has something that Joseph of Arimathea took from Israel and dropped in a well in Glastonbury, which is, coincidentally, where my mother and grandmother were from. Maybe it was Jesus' cup. Maybe it was the philosopher's stone. Aurelia said my mother liked to talk about the philosopher's stone. No, Aurelia was not part of the original story. She was my father's housekeeper, more than that, really; Aurelia was our Nanny, like your mother, when she's away.

Anyway, this king, the Fisher King, is sick, and his land is drying up from a drought, and nothing works while the king's in trouble so somebody has to go and find the king and get Joseph's grail. Before the journey starts, there's a fight over an outfit, a costume, red armor. A young man, a wild sort of boy, who's not well-dressed and not ready for a quest, strips the red armor off the knight and puts it on over his own rough clothes. Then, he heads off to find the castle and the Fisher King and the grail. But to do this right, to meet the Fisher King and get out of the land with the grail, special words have to be said. There's a question that must be asked, or else the knight who's seeking the grail will be sent away empty-handed.

A wise old person tells this feral boy knight about the special words, and the boy goes to the castle, and there's a huge procession, a parade with people carrying a spear and a two-headed axe, candles, fire, and wine. Wine is spilled somewhere along the way. Sometimes, there's even a head on a platter in the parade, but don't think about that. It's not in every version. But there's always weeping and moaning and shrieking. And in the end, if the seeker says the right words and gets the cup or the stone or whatever, then everything is as it should be, the land turns green again, and the hero is guardian of the grail.

When I stopped talking, Shatapda asked, "Who's in this parade? Other than the head?"

"A man with a spear, lots of people shrieking and weeping, women and men carrying candles, someone with a mace, people with burning balsam. Basins of water, special cloths, and the queen, who has the grail."

"There's food?" asked Heduanna.

"There's food."

"There's drink?"

"There's drink."

"There's dance?"

"There's dance—sometimes with swords, sometimes with colored scarves and ribbons and bows and knots and people dressed every which way."

They opened my mother's book again and paged through her copies of cuneiform signs, slowly. Again they spoke the quick one-syllable sounds to each other, but this time when they were finished, they looked me straight in the eye. They seemed to have come to a different conclusion.

Heduanna spoke. "What happened to your mother is this. She was not able to transcribe the other two tablets, but her last two pages—which at first reading seem to be repetitions, a study page, bits and pieces, signs from our two works—may instead be a list of coincidences of sign from Shatapda's to mine, to yet another and to yet another. So now we suspect that the last pages are—in cuneiform—lists, ideas, images, gestures. Not only from our works but also from the other two tablets, gestures she thought were repeated in this grail story."

This appeared to please them. "Is this good? Does it mean something?"

Yes, of course, it meant something. Everything meant something. My mother was correct in looking for the story in the gestures. In Shatapda's view, stuff and action were thoroughly intertwined; my mother's concern with gesture showed a remarkable Mesopotamian sensibility, but multiplicity and ensemble must be kept in mind-soul-body. She said it as though it were hyphenated, and she drew in the air at the same time. Separation was to be avoided. Separation could lead to fall.

But philosophy aside, could they tell from the gestures what stories my mother had? What the stories on the other two tablets were?

They could. Yes. To them, it was obvious.

I asked Heduanna to read the signs on my mother's list, but

she said that that was dangerous, separating sign from story; it tended to limit allusion, which as Shatapda had pointed out, lead to separation of stuff and action and, eventually, to inaccuracy and drainage of power. Separation was exile. She was still sitting cross-legged, moving forward and backward and side to side as she spoke.

Shatapda, on the other hand, was sitting very still, as though she were bound, as though she were caught in an invisible net. She announced, "This isn't documentary writing."

"You see, taken all together, it's the same story as yours," Heduanna added.

I didn't know how to take it all together. I didn't see.

"Somebody took Inanna's story and turned it into yours," said Shatapda. "Of course, we did the same thing. That's accepted; that's done—calling up old text, adding new text, new life."

"What story?" I asked. "The story of the woman who goes to the mountain and loses everything?"

"It's dangerous to separate such gestures," Shatapda repeated, still not moving anything but her lips, "Separation is exile. That may be what stopped your mother."

"Death stopped my mother."

"Except it obviously didn't because here you are—telling us her story," said Heduanna. "The same goes for Inanna's story. I allude to it in my poem, Shatapda alludes to it in hers, and now that you tell us the grail story, it's obvious it was alluded to again. Inanna's story is dead. Long live her story."

I asked if they could tell me Inanna's story, in once-there-was-a-goddess-named-Inanna style, like I told them about the grail. Heduanna said they couldn't because Inanna wasn't a goddess, she was a god. There wasn't any sign for goddess in her language. "All we have are gods. Some gods have vulvas and some have penises."

Shatapda said perhaps they should be careful not to be so

specific about genitalia, even godly ones. She had heard Americans were squeamish about body parts, especially in regard to divinity, and after all, I was American.

"It's hard to tell Inanna stories and avoid body parts," Heduanna pointed out.

I assured them I didn't mind. Go ahead. Be specific. Shatapda shook her head. So, despite my asking them to be as true to the sign as possible, I think Heduanna and Shatapda couched their stories in metaphor. Whether what they did happened naturally because in their language one sign could have so many meanings, or whether they resorted to euphemism for my sake, I've never been sure. But this is the way they told two of the many stories about Inanna, the two they believed my mother had been working on.

Heduanna went first.

Inanna rules heaven. Inanna rules earth. She cocks her ear like a dog and listens to the great earth, cocks her ear to the sound, listens, decides to go up-down the mountain. Before she begins her journey, she puts on her cloth of power, she puts on egg stones, gold rings, cords, lapis, crown. She carries wisdom. Someone is ill, someone is dying.

She tells her good friend, "If I am not back, come for me."

There is confusion at the gates, she is not expected. Her cloth, her stones, her ring, her lapis line, she is stripped of everything, including her wisdom and her power. This mountain is sacred, it is somewhere else, she must become nothing to enter. While she is gone, nothing works—no one makes love, animals die, plants whither. She is chaos. She is pause. She is hung on wood. She is dead. Someone must find her.

Her friend goes to a god who once gave Inanna wisdom, and this god gives again: water of life, plants of life, words of life, beings neither male nor female. They march to the mountain, to the other world. There is weeping and moaning. They weep and moan. They speak the words of life. They ask for the body of Inanna. Inanna is given to them, and they feed Inanna plants of life. They give her water of life. She is reborn.

They parade out of the mountain, gods who are not alive, but they march. Gods who are not warriors, but they carry spear and mace. Gods who try to take Inanna's friend, and Inanna says, "No, she is weeping and moaning, wearing dust and ashes." Gods who try to take Inanna's daughter, and Inanna says, "No, she is weeping and moaning, wearing dust and ashes." Gods who try to take Inanna's son, and Inanna says, "No, he is weeping and moaning, wearing dust and ashes." And they are spared. But finally they come to Inanna's house, and Inanna's husband—his name is Dumuzi—is sitting on a throne. He is not weeping and he is not moaning. He is having a party. He is not wearing dust and ashes. The gods of death say, "We'll take Dumuzi," and Inanna says, "Be my guest."

I gasped and whispered, "Head on the platter." Shatapda whispered back, "The story isn't over yet." Heduanna told how Dumuzi runs, how he hides in caves, how some gods help him, how some are on his side while some are on Inanna's. There is a chase. Dumuzi begs to turn into a snake. There's a fly. That's the end.

"The end?"

"Of that part. Of course, there are sequels."

"What happens in the very last sequel?" I asked.

Neither one answered, at first. Heduanna cocked her head as I imagined Inanna must have. "I don't think we're the authorities on the last sequel. We're better at original story. But if you mean the last one in our series, in the end he's caught, there's chaos again, but someone—some say his sister, some say Inanna—agrees to share the burden of the time in the mountain."

"Six months up, six months down," Shatapda inserted.

"Balance," said Heduanna.

"Like Persephone?" I asked.

Heduanna called the Persephone story derivative but acknow-leged it as a good story anyway, pointing out that in the older story, Inanna went to the other world of her own free will. "Nobody made Inanna do anything. It was all her own idea."

The running and hiding in caves, that reminded me of Elijah and the famous rabbis and George and Pan."

"And Tammuz. The last time Dumuzi's people get his story across is in the Bible, and by then, they're calling him Tammuz," said Shatapda.

"We looked the Tammuz story up. In the Bible, the women are weeping for him, not for his wife," I said.

Shatapda shrugged, saying it was hard to tell with folktales. "Maybe those women aren't weeping for him at all, maybe they're weeping for Inanna because they know what happens to people who don't."

"Or maybe she changes gender," Heduanna suggested.

"Inanna's fond of gender bending," Shatapda agreed.

"And the appropriation factor. Gods don't always end up the same sex they start out as. Men have a way of taking things over," Heduanna added.

"Look what they did with Heduanna's creative theory. Aside from the folk stories, Heduanna was the first to mention creative theory and certainly the first to compare it to birth. It's in her text, right there in signs, bold as can be—creation of a text, of a song, of a story is the same as birth. And the next thing you know, Plato portrays Socrates as a midwife and calls the act of questioning labor, and men are giving birth to ideas all over the place."

Heduanna refilled my cup. "Same thing happened with beer from what I hear about the world these days."

"Appropriation. That's why it gets complicated with Inanna," Shatapda mused. "She could be in your stories, disguised as a man."

"We saw them celebrating Tammuz down there at Stella Maris," said Heduanna. "On our way up here. The ceremonies seemed authentic, complete with a weeping woman."

"The woman is a friend of mine. A good woman, suffering from Jerusalem syndrome. She identifies with Margery Kempe."

"Looked like Inanna's friend," said Heduanna, "She was called Ninšubur."

"But it's not really a celebration of Tammuz; it's all about Elijah. Up here, too."

"Up here, it's the Baal thing," said Shatapda. "But no matter, they're all related. Inanna has this death experience and rises again and pretty soon people forget about her and forget what Dumuzi was doing when she rose from the dead and what led to his death and rebirth. So, Dumuzi becomes Tammuz becomes Baal, and if you read any of the writing on the wall around here, you know how Baal ended. Baal's gone, the land is drying up, so his people parade around, there's a lot of dancing and a huge party with food, and they try to raise Baal up, but Elijah wins the day. Elijah takes over. Elijah makes the rains come. Elijah makes the earth green again. Story sound familiar?"

I took a sip of Heduanna's beer, tasted another of her dates, and gazed through the opening in the earth. The sky was becoming three shades of grey, pink silver at the top, in the east. In the west it was still purple drab. A gull flew over, its wings twisting in the wind. Or was it a bat? It couldn't have been a bat in the morning; it had to be a gull, wings folding and unfolding like maple leaves. Trees shivered against the sky. I had come in search of a gesture and had been told I needed a cauldron full of gestures. I was lost, in a cave, in the ground on top of the mountain where it seemed Elijah defeated the very gods these women were telling me were the source of his story. This was chaos. There was no distinction, no differentiation. There was *nothing* because everything was the same. No story, because every story was the same. Pause. Chaos. Ocean. They are the same thing, in a way, nothing, yet both—everything.

"I think that's my line," the voice with a different inflection came from behind me. I turned around. It was Marguerite. " . . . she would be like a body of water which flows from the sea . . . and when this water or river returns into the sea, it loses its course and its name . . . "

"Nin has become a seer," said Heduanna. "She is able to read thoughts in the past, as did Christine."

Christine, of course, was there, too, and the four dead women writers seemed pleased to see one another. How was the sailing? Tiamat was comfortable. Where was Beatrice? Consumed by her thoughts. Where was Hildegard? Minding the debate. How was the debate? Over for a while, never finished. Christine told how lightning struck the Thomas line.

"There won't be any more Thomas Aquinas and Aristotle and Tacitus and Plato online," said Christine, "not for a while. Not even Plato, after all his talking about equality and then trivializing everything women do well."

My father's web site. His work. It was gone. These women were my visions; did that mean I was responsible? Was I in control of what they had done to my father's electronic society, to the group of thinkers who met in his Multi-User Dungeon? Had I destroyed his MUD?

Christine apologized for interrupting my father's life, but she said they really had no choice. The debate had taken a turn, which was long overdue.

Marguerite and Christine sat down and began to pick through the dates and figs and cheese and barley cakes in Heduanna's basket. "Shatapda was about to tell more of Inanna," Heduanna said. "Tell us about the parade."

Shatapda said she believed the fourth tablet my mother was studying was about a procession, a celebration, a march often marched, a story often told. It was about Inanna and the land and the king and greenness and life. It was about splendour. It was about the marriage of Inanna to her beloved.

"Ill-fated like the last?" I interrupted.

"You must wait to the end to see," she said.

Inanna is happy, as happy as a wild cow. She is the sun and moon. She shines. Her people walk before her. They beat the drum. They play the harp. They have the silver instrument. They walk before her. They comb their hair. They wear colored cords. They wear the cloak of divinity. They wear the sword belt. They carry the sword. They grasp the spear. They have the double-edged ax. Their left sides they cover with women's clothing; their right sides they cover with men's clothing. They carry hoops. They have the ropes. They skip the ropes, they dance, they leap.

"That's what got the Templars in trouble," said Marguerite. "Cross-dressing and dancing around. That and banking."

My mother's interest in the Templars' parade was coming into focus.

Shatapda continued.

They walk before Inanna. The one who covers the sword with blood, he sprinkles blood. They walk before the pure Inanna. They pour blood on the dais of the throne room . . . beat the drum, mark the time, sing, lament. Beasts, orchards, gardens, green reeds, fish in the deep, birds in the heavens. Dates and cheese and fruits, dark beer, bread, and honey and wine. The king, like the sun, fills his space next to her. They make love on the bed. You are surely my beloved—to bring food, to perform the rites, to carry the bowls.

"To whom is the grail brought?" asked Marguerite.

All four women nodded and smiled at the question.

"Inanna is the Venus star. She is the ornament of the assembly. Everything is made abundant. The people spend the day in plenty. Sweet sound," said Shatapda, ending the tale.

"Well spoken." Christine clapped her hands together.

Marguerite stood and bowed to Shatapda, "The Templars who were in prison with me were telling that story all the time, but I enjoyed this presentation more than any I've heard before."

Whether or not I was supposed to, whether or not it separated the ensemble or drained the poetics, I made a list of gestures while Heduanna and Shatapda talked. For me, the existence of the story was in the images and actions that grew around the characters, what my mother called gestures. Here's my list from Heduanna's story of Inanna's journey up-down the mountain: sister, dress, lapis, crown, line, up, down, gate, undress, chaos, ocean, life-plant, life-water, weep, parade, husband, wild, green, chase, balance. And Shatapda's parade list: wild cow, cloak, moon, harp, colored cords, drum, like women, like men, ropes, skip, gardens, food, rites, sweet sound.

"So, the grail is food and love, brought to Inanna?" I paused and waited for them to answer. At first they were quiet, then they began talking, but to one another, not to me, and I realized they were tracing the chain of custody for themselves. How did the gesture go from one god to another, from one gender to another, one folk to another. The Templars? The Romans? The Byzantines and the Greeks?

Yes, all of the above, and Abraham, of course. Abraham brought the story from Ur, with his family. Ur. Where Heduanna was from.

"But listen, I think I was right about what the grail was. It is the cup, of food and love, and that must be what my mother was looking for. "

"Nin," Christine admonished gently. "It's part of the protocol.

One never defines the grail. It is not something that's done. Not even under oath."

"Especially not," Marguerite emphasized.

I looked at Heduanna and Shatapda. Their wisdom was less encumbered by rules, wasn't it? But then, was anyone's less encumbered than Marguerite's? Why were they still so unwilling to separate? Why couldn't one gesture be named as the most important?

"What survives is the spectacle," explained Shatapda. "And that must often be practiced behind a curtain of triviality."

"Triviality?" The gesture I was seeking was trivial?

"As you said, common. Hidden in everyday use."

"And thank the gods for that," Heduanna said. "The veil of triviality has kept people from studying it, exposing it, fearing it, destroying it."

"And what about understanding it?" I asked.

"What matters is that we use it. We don't need to understand why."

I stood in my corner and strained my face toward the air above. They were telling me that knowledge was dangerous, not simply to the knower but to the wisdom itself. Were they suggesting I not seek or simply not find? Or maybe just not mention? Or be careful to whom I mentioned it? What kind of marketplace was that? What sort of free spirit lived that way? I felt that I was being driven down. My soul was being eaten. I was breathing like a bird trapped in a hole. I began to weep.

Shatapda noticed. "You don't need to analyze it. The gesture is everywhere."

"Far, but near," said Marguerite.

"Not the mace, not the scepter," was Christine's contribution.

"Not the castle, not the mountain," said Marguerite.

"It is present in the going up and coming down," stated Heduanna.

"What did I come down, and when did I go up? Where exactly have I been? And where am I now?" I asked.

Marguerite said I was seated on the throne of peace, in the book of life. I was where the soul remains after the work of the ravishing farnearness . . . When she said that, her voice trailed off at the end, as though she herself were somewhere far and near.

"Here," said Heduanna. "Nin, you're here with us. Come sit and listen. What you seek is here. The folk always have it."

What I heard was rain. Drops beginning to hit the soft earth that roofed over this grave I was sharing with ancient women. Rain, striking the dry ground of Mount Carmel, in the heat of Dog Days. And then I heard wind. It whistled around the break in the ground above me. And children's voices, girls' voices, singing in rhyme, their feet skipping lightly above me. Something tapping at the ground. Cuffing. Hitting. Rhythmically slapping. And children again, singing rhymes. That's all I heard. It seemed to be nothing. Is this nothing? Is that all I need to hear?

"You are free now," Heduanna announced.

"What do you mean by free?" I asked. I didn't feel free. I felt empty. I was coming away with nothing, yet they were telling me there was nothing more I needed to receive.

"The understanding of nothingness releases and frees. When you will nothing, you lack nothing," said Marguerite.

"You have done it, you have committed freedom," said Shatapda.

Heduanna stood. "You have returned to the mother, and in our language, returning to the mother means to become free, *ama* is mother, *gi* is return. You have done it: *ama-ar-gi*."

Christine said I had finished my task. It was time for me to leave. And it was time for them to leave me. They had nothing more to impart. The four women pushed their backs against the soft loam to make it firm, so I could catch a toehold. They insisted I kiss each of them twice, first on the right cheek, then the left. Heduanna motioned toward the goat-hair crate, suggesting I use it as my first step up out of the cave.

As I was climbing, my backpack opened, and the jump rope I had bought at Capernaum fell back down into the pit.

Marguerite held it a moment, then tossed it back into my bag. "I knew you had the gesture in your custody all along. Search for the unknown, find the familiar."

Shatapda said it was the turning, the tying, the untying, the jumping, the skipping. "She who twists the straight cord, she who straightens the twisted."

"Not the grail, but the procession," affirmed Christine.

"The bending," Heduanna added. "Not the philosopher's stone or even your mother's clay tablet, but the circle, the hoop, the rope, the dance. Balance. We all have it. We all have had it, all along."

"It's not the grail, it's a jump rope?" I asked. "Joseph of Arimathea went to Glastonbury and threw a jump rope into the well?"

"I wouldn't want to answer that directly," said Heduanna, "but have you ever seen a rope next to a well?"

Of course, I had. Well, actually, I hadn't seen very many wells, if they wanted to know. People didn't have wells anymore; a few, in the country, up in the woods, not many. But in the old stories, yes, when I thought about it, there was always a rope next to the well.

Shatapda shrugged her shoulders, as if to say that was proof enough. I did have it all along. Every woman had it. We'd always had it. Girls had always skipped rope. In every culture. In every time.

"And no one has ever tried to stop us," Heduanna was exhilarated.

"A practice safeguarded from the burnings by a curtain of triviality," said Marguerite.

"From all destruction," added Christine, as if to remind us of Marguerite's special interest in trial by fire.

"But can a skipping rope be the Holy Grail?" I asked.

"You needn't answer that question," Marguerite scolded gently. "You simply need to jump."

That was the last I heard of them. I was above ground, and the rain had become stronger, and the earth was moist to the point of muddiness. There was a gentle breeze, and the red-headed girls and their friends who had been skipping rope a few feet away were there at the edge of the cave. Andrew was holding onto my wrists, and he was crying. He was sobbing. He was covered in dust and mud, and he had scraped his face against roots that gouged and scratched him as he reached for me. Gala and Veronica and the others, they were there waiting, too, happy to see that I hadn't destroyed the Ram in the night and that I'd survived. Brother Hugh was there, bending over the pit, and there was a young man with short black hair and deep brown eyes, wearing a uniform and peering at me, then at the bottom of the hole, then back at me. Andrew pulled me up over the edge and twined his legs around mine and rolled so I wouldn't fall back.

"What are you doing here?" I asked.

He said he came to Haifa early that morning and found Brother Hugh, who said I was separated from the group. The Ram was gone, and there were clay tablets missing, so he found the archeology team, and they all set out to search. They had been using their impulse machine, and they had images of bones underground, but not just one set of bones, several, hard to tell how many, and there was movement, a great deal of movement, and he knew it was me, there, in my mother's grave.

I told him it wasn't my mother's tomb, but he pointed to the stones. Faith Morgan DeLacey Creed. Grace Morgan DeLacey. I told him it was empty, and he didn't argue. It was the practice to remove remains after a number of years. Bones were placed in a single, small crate, to make room for the future. He flashed a light into the grave. The place where I had spent the night, telling stories with four women, had been abandoned like the houses of Machu Pichu or Pompei, leaving evidence of recent use and sudden exile: a small crate, a beer bottle, broken rice cakes, and a handful of something that looked like date pits. Next to those, what we had been reading, three clay tablets and a fragment of cylinder seal. Four fragments altogether. Four, all four. So, the women had located the other two after all.

It turned out that the young, black-haired man who looked like a policeman or a soldier was the archeologist in charge of the site, and he dropped a rope ladder, carefully climbing down to retrieve the fragments. When he came up, I told him what each one said.

"I believe you are right," said Brother Hugh. "I didn't know you could read these." I told them I couldn't. But I could tell them what they said because they were pieces of a story everybody knows, although sometimes we tell it with slightly different details, slightly different gestures.

The archeologist was happy I'd found the missing fragments for him. He insisted they be examined by scholars, first at the museum in Haifa, then at the university in Jerusalem. Maybe eventually, they'd invite scholars from Paris and Pennsylvania and Yale, and they'd all look at them. The tablets should be scrutinized, said the archeologist; after all, there was a possibility that they had come with Abraham from Ur. On top of that, the way I was reading them, the tablets had a certain lilt, something reminiscent of the Kabbala.

Brother Hugh was puzzling over the sudden rain and the cool wind in the middle of the Dog Days. He suggested the chilled wet air was actually a cloud, slipping over us, that soon it would be burned off by the sun, and the day would be warm again, as usual. He was so absorbed in the question of weather that he readily submitted the texts to the authority of the state. Maybe that's why no one threatened to charge me with stealing antiquities. The archeologist handed me the half-finished beer and rice cakes.

I picked two flowers, blue as lapis, from a bush growing amidst the cedars, and two round fruits, red as carnelian, and I put them with the rice cakes and beer on a hollow piece of cedar that looked like a dugout canoe. I thought no one was looking when I slipped the boat into the grave, but Gala had been watching. She said I was an odd one, slipping pomegranates back into the underworld. I gave her the keys to the Ram and her bag. She reached into the bottom of the bag and pulled out a small paperback volume of Sylvia Plath poems. I wondered for a moment what would have happened if I had read those in the night, but then I remembered what Shatapda said about time. It was too soon. Veronica had stopped weeping, and she was walking toward the van. But Andrew had not stopped crying. He was sitting at the edge of the tomb, his head in his hands. We were safe and away from the trench. In the pause, his body began to heave, and he began to sigh. I had never seen him like that. I had never seen him cry. I had never seen any man weep in that fashion.

"How did it happen that you came for me?"

He said he couldn't help but come. It was simply the way the story goes.

I told him I had just heard the story, and the man doesn't weep at all at the end, he doesn't even miss the woman, he doesn't look for her. He doesn't get his clothes all dirty and scratch himself up. In the story, the husband puts on a good outfit and calls up some friends, and they're all sitting around having a party. He couldn't care less.

"And then what happens?"

"The wife gets there with the angels of death, and they ask if they can take her husband, and she says 'Be my guest' and fastens the green eye on him. He runs and runs and runs and begs to be turned into a snake and hides in caves and ends up spending six months out of every year in the netherworld. The other six months, she goes away."

Andrew didn't like that ending. Was I going to leave it that way? Wasn't I going to revise it? Hadn't I already? Hadn't he?

Revise a myth? Could I have done that? Can a person do that? I knew I intended to, but how many parades, how many people dancing and singing and skipping and playing music, how many bowls of food and wine, and how much attention to the garden does a writer have to come up with to change a story like this one? How much tangling of straight cords and untangling of twisted ones, skipping and jumping among the colored threads? And the weeping and moaning at the proper moment? And the understanding of when the proper moment is?

When we got to the airport in Tel Aviv, I called my father, but he wasn't home. Aurelia said he'd had such a shock when Annie told him about my falling into our mother's tomb, the poor man, and he didn't have the computer to occupy him. The machine had a virus, and a lightning strike damaged his network. He'd been told he needed a new motherboard, and he wasn't going to be able to get the Thomas line up again for weeks. Sister Hildegard had suggested they go over to the Aquinas Center and spend the free time putting the garden in shape, and that's where they were. Aurelia said Annie would be relieved that I was all right.

Was Annie still perturbed? No more than usual, but she was convinced no one could have told me anything I didn't already know about our mother. I told Aurelia to tell her she was right, no one did give me anything I didn't have. Aurelia said she'd tell her when she came over for tea, Annie and the sisters, all except Sister Hildegard, who wasn't going to be able to join them because when she finished gardening with my father, she was going to visit with old friends from far away.

I thought I knew who the friends were and what the lightning was, but there was one piece of the story I didn't understand. "Aurelia," I asked, "if lightning struck the computer system, who got the message to Andrew? Was it you?"

"Who else?" Aurelia asked.

She was simply always there, taking care of everything, so important, so easy to ignore. I told her I loved her. I don't know if I'd ever told her that before. I thought I might as well get her advice in advance, so I asked her what she thought of our plan to take a long trip home. We were considering two options: one, go to Greece, try to figure out what my mother was looking for in the Ulysses story, maybe even retrace Ulysses' travels, at least the path his travels took in my mother's head; two, come home the same way I had come the first time I left Haifa, retracing my father's steps, going out all the gates I had come in, stopping in Rome, stopping in Glastonbury, stopping to see her and my father and Annie and Sister Hildegard and Lake Memphremagog.

Aurelia didn't think much of either option. She said there really was only one journey to think about, and yes, it was my mother's journey, and it seemed to her I had already completed that one. She thought I should go home, get out of the heat, breathe northern air, sit by an icy lake. "Sing, dance, eat, drink, and sleep in a good cool bed. And take Andrew with you."

In the end, I agreed with Aurelia. Maybe the heat of Dog Days was too much for me. My knapsack was heavy; I felt as though I were carrying all the gates I'd ever opened, right there on my back. It was time to go home. So, we flew from Tel Aviv back to New York, caught the first plane to Minneapolis, and then went straight up to Duluth. As soon as we were home, I changed into my running clothes, and Andrew ran with me, down to the promenade next to the lake where people walk and jog and Rollerblade, along the pier, out to the lighthouse, and back up to the park. We stopped at a garden tap, and a woman served us Guinness; the froth melted into designs, and we tried to read our futures in the foam, the way Aurelia read tea leaves. It was sundown, and I saw a sailboat moving across the skyline. It was an ancient blue schooner with a green bloodstone cabin and carnelian sails like the one that skirted across the Sea of Galilee.

We walked home, and I worked next to Andrew, pulling weeds, digging in the moist earth, breaking clots of black soil, and planting the wild roots of roses and berries he brought from his trip to the woods. When we finished, we went into the house and opened all the windows and breathed in fresh air from the lake and listened to children singing outside. They were spinning ropes and jumping and repeating an old rhyme I'd sung as a child.

On the mountain stands a woman
Who she is I do not know
In her hair are beads of lapis
At her feet is ice and snow

Mother . . . Sister . . . Auntie, come and sing
Once upon a time a woman was king . . .

She goes riding with the wild dogs
Scattering light across the sky
Opening morning, spinning daybreak
Dragon woman, flying high

Mother . . . Sister . . . Auntie, go and shout
Woman's in the mountain, can't get out

In the mountain, sleeps the woman
Bed of cedar, bitter stand
Ocean's desert, river's dusty
Fish lie dying in the sand.

Mother . . . Sister . . . Auntie, start the dance
Wake up the woman, now we have a chance

From the mountain comes the woman
Skipping ropes and making scrolls
Twisting straight cords, smoothing tangled
Threading spindles, braiding rolls

Mother . . . Sister . . . Auntie, can you see
Woman rising from the dead, flying from the tree?

On the mountain sits the woman
There amidst the wind and rain
She is mother, she is sister
She is freedom back again.

Fragments:

A partial list of writers invited to the
Dead Women Writers' Conference.

Adele de Blois
Aelffled
Agnes
Akasome Emon
Alais
Almucs
Almucs de Castelnau
Andrea Acciaiuoli
Angela da Foligno
Anna Bijns
Anna Maria von Schurmann

Arete
Atalise
Aude Faure
Azalais de Pourcairagues
Bathsua Pell Makin
Beatrice d'Ornacieux
Beatrice of Nazareth
Berthgyth
Bieiris of Roman
Birgetta of Sweden
Brunhilda
Bugga
Caesaria
Carenza
Catherine of Alexandria
Catherine of Aragon
Catherine of Genoa
Catherine of Siena
Christine de Pizan
Christine Ebner
Chu shu-chen
Clare of Assisi
Clare of Rimini
Constance
Costanza Varana
Countess of Die
Cynehild
Dhuoda
Eangyth
Egburg
Egeria
Elizabeth of Allde

Elizabeth of Thuringia
Empress Anastasia
Empress Jito
enheduanna
Esclarmonde
Eucheria
Euphrosine of Vendome
Eva
Eynehild
Deborah Ascarelli
Gertrude
Gio
Grazida
Grazida Lizier
Guillemette Bathegan
Gunhild
Gwerful Mechain
Hadewijch
Heloise
Herchenefreda
Hildegard of Bingen
Hrotswitha
Hugeburc
Ibn Zaydun
Irene
Isotta Nogarola
Isume Shikibu
J
Jadewijch
Jane Sharp
Juliana Bemers
Julian of Norwich

Kasa no Iratsume
Kubatum
La Castelloza
Lady Horikawa
Lady Ise
Lady Kii
Lady Murasaki
Lady Sarashina
Lady Ukon
Lioba
Marcia the Roman
Margaret of Cortona
Margaret Ebner
Margery Kempe
Margherite d'Oingt
Marguerite Porète
Maria de Ventadour
Marie de France
Marie Guyard
Marie le Jars de Gourney
Maysun
Mechthild of Hackebon
Mechthild of Magdeburg
Mengarde Buscalh
Murasaki Shikibu
Muriel
ninshatapada
Ono no Komachi
Otomo no Sakanoe no Riatsume
Paula and Eustochium
Paulina
Perpetua

Philaenis
Princess Nukada
Radegunde
Raziya
Rotagund
Rosanensis
Sappho
Sei Shonagin
Sempronia from Rome
Shirome
Shizuka
Sor Juana Inez de la Cruz
Sybille Peire
Thamaris
Tibors
Trotula of Salerno
Wallada al-Mustakfi
Yosami
Yselda
and
the beguines
the naditu
the nuns
the troubadours
the women at Regensburg
the women of the 18th century
the women of the 19th century
the women of the 20th century
others whose work is lost or unknown: erased, ignored, dismissed,
suppressed, marginalized, misunderstood.
(Please use the next pages to continue this list . . .)

A Conversation with Cass Dalglish

Q. *Nin* is a mystical, mythical, magical fable. Nin Creed, a feminist poet embarking upon a quixotic quest to recover the lost writings of her late mother, finds herself accompanied by a few of the legions of women writers who lived and wrote centuries ago and whose work, too, was lost. How did this story begin for you?

Cass: Nin's story actually had roots that were deep and personal. The personal story for me is that within days of my birth, the grandmothers on both sides of my family died, so that I grew up without actual memory of any of the older women in my family. I had only a few artifacts—one grandmother's guitar, another's marriage license, a few photos of the family band, tales from the Irish, Scottish, and Welsh sides, and stories of earlier grandmothers crossing the country in the 1800s from Vermont to Minnesota to New Mexico, mixing with silver miners and outlaws and politicians. I really had very little, other than a strong desire to know these women. At one point when I was studying in Vermont, I made weekly searches through drawers of vital statistics records in Montpelier, looking for something that might mention my great-grandmother and her mother, a woman I'd heard had a red wig and smoked a pipe. Finally, I was told that laws hadn't always required that a female's birth be recorded.

Around that same time, I began an academic search for the beginnings of women's literature, and I started my hunt for the earliest texts—much as a spiritual feminist might begin, with a faith that in ancient times, "when God was a woman," things must have been better. I thought women would have been spiritual leaders, rulers, and deities, and, of course, they would have been writers and editors as well. I wanted to know those women, and I wanted to read what they had written.

I wanted to share these ancient women's stories with others, to record them in our memories, to make up for all the grandmothers whose stories had never been written down.

Q. As you were writing this novel, you learned how to read cuneiform texts. Why did you do that?

Cass: Since I was determined to read the earliest of women's writing, I thought I'd better learn the earliest written languages in history. I was convinced that once I could read the languages I would find women's work. This was around the same time that I was teaching a seminar on writers who got into trouble for telling "secrets" about their own cultural groups: James Joyce, Philip

Roth, Salman Rushdie, Mary Daly, Spike Lee. In criticizing Roth, one reviewer expressed shock that Roth knew Yiddish and still wrote revealing fiction about his people. I looked at it a different way. I thought only writers who *did* know their people's vernacular could write honest stories. And since my own writing was steeped in what I felt was a "female culture" and I often found myself writing stories that involved "intra-feminist" critiques, I thought I'd better learn to read what women were writing back "when God was female."

Q. And you found texts that were written by women?

Cass: I was a college English professor, enrolled in Sumerian cuneiform 101, studying with a scholar in ancient languages, and one day he asked me why I was doing it. I told him I wanted to know when writing became women's work. He said he knew of one Sumerian woman writer, a priest named enheduanna who was the first author in history to sign a text, more than four thousand years ago, ". . . but that was all." His remark, ". . . but that was all," reminded me how women always accept lesser roles. Good grief, I thought, if anyone said a man had been the first author in history to sign his text, we would presume all early writers were men, in fact, we presume all writers were men without any evidence at all. And here we had proof that the first author in history was female and we were still taking a back seat to male writers. It turned out that my professor didn't really mean "that was all" because he went on to help me locate other writers, like ninshatapada who wrote in an epistolary, psalm-like style. We began to read the texts together, and he connected me with a scholar whose doctoral work linked feminist studies and ancient studies. She and I have continued to read early texts and, with two other feminist scholars, we have founded the "Edubba," an organization that focuses on ancient feminist literature and Sumerian poetics. "Edubba" means the house of clay, which is what Sumerians called their writing schools.

Q. Why would Sumerian be a language of interest to contemporary women?

Cass: The land of Sumer was located in Mesopotamia—the land between two rivers, the Tigris and the Euphrates. There, writing was done by scribes—women among them—who used strong reeds that grew in the currents of two rivers to impress pictographic signs into clay tablets. The Sumerian culture is also interesting because the deity in charge of writing is Nidaba, a female god who appears in one story holding a golden stylus and a clay tablet, and the first-recorded female regent was Ku Baba, King of Kish. Ku Baba is mentioned on the Sumerian King list; she was a tavern keeper who became king in her own right, not by descent or by marriage. She reigned more than two centuries before Queen Nitokris of Egypt. And there is also archeological proof that women were part of the regular workforce in Sumer, scenes of women at work with children at their breast. This piece of evidence has double meaning because it tells us women were fully employed outside the home, and it also reminds us that women have had daycare problems for more than four thousand years.

The language itself is interesting too. Sumerian might be called a non-gendered language because it doesn't differentiate for male and female in pronouns, in deities, or in falsely gendered occupational titles like judge or king. Some deities are male; some are female. But all are gods; there are no goddettes or goddesses. There was apparently no need to use the diminutive to mark the female and to diminish feminine power.

Q. What does the title mean? Is the book named after the protagonist Nin Creed?

Cass: Nin is the name of the main character who is on a quest to find the work of her mother, a linguist who died on the day of Nin's birth. "Nin" is also one way to decipher a specific Sumerian pictograph, the first sign in enheduanna's poem. In Sumerian, a single pictographic sign can have multiple meanings, five, ten, even more, and the sign that designates "nin" has many meanings attached to it. It can mean "sovereign" or "lord." It can be a sign for a deity or ruler. It can also mean "sister." In my translation of enheduanna's poem I use the word "sister," but I like to keep all the meanings in mind when I consider a Sumerian sign, especially when I consider the signs in these early women's poetic texts. A poet's ambiguity is intentional.

Q. When Nin Creed begins to time travel, she meets women writers who aren't quite as ancient as the Mesopotamian poets. How did the medieval writers get into the story?

Cass: enheduanna's theory of the "birth of creative thought" precedes Socrates' "midwifery of ideas" by quite some time, yet Socrates gives no credit to enheduanna. Once I discovered a "canon" of early women writers whose works were obviously significant, I began to wonder why women's work was removed from the canon in the first place. What had rendered women's writing invisible? When I reread some of the philosophers whose work had remained in the canon, I found a common theme: women's work was trivial; women were lesser beings. Aquinas even wonders why God created women in the first place. This is the same sort of rereading of Thomas Aquinas that provides my character Nin Creed with an epiphany. Aquinas is the philosophical hero and mentor of her father, and when Nin begins a debate with her father about Aquinas' attitude toward women, she asks why such offensive writing about women isn't considered pornography, why we don't apply community standards to these ideas, why we don't consider what women said when Aquinas asked if they should have been created. That's where the medieval women come into the story—to help Nin remember what women were writing and thinking about.

Q. What made you decide to take historical figures like Hildegard of Bingen, Christine de Pizan, and Marguerite Porète and turn them into fictional characters?

Cass: As I was researching and writing this novel, I decided it was important to get inside the body and mind of my main character Nin Creed as often as possible. Since she was a poet (and I was writing her poems), I began to read her work publicly to see how audiences reacted to her. When I traveled to Israel to research archetypal theory and the Haifa scenes, I made a commitment to travel in character. Treating yourself like a fictional character is only a short hop from recognizing historical figures as live people in your fiction. At times, writing this story became a contemplative exercise because reading these women's work opened me to meditation on their themes and images. Hildegard of Bingen was a substantial, scholarly, and political presence as well as a visionary artist and musician. Christine de Pizan was at the center of one of the most significant academic debates in history about the roles of men and women. Marguerite Porète's independence and her belief in the value of her own work eventually resulted in her death at the hands of the Inquisition. I found myself talking to these women, and eventually they were talking back to me. That's when it became important for me as a writer to follow Hildegard of Bingen's advice—to listen, to turn my ear to their words, to set my gaze on what they wanted me to see. In building their characters, I have attempted to be true to their themes, their metaphors, their use of imagery, to give them another chance at a public forum.

Q. *Nin* is not just a legend; it's an "on-the-road" adventure, set in the high-tech, modern-day world of air travel, telephones, computers, and the World Wide Web. What made you connect these ancient and medieval women with their detractors via the Internet?

Cass: Many of my characters were coming from the otherworld, from a land of mystical reality. The ancient characters were writing in a language in which multiple interpretations could twist and spin simultaneous meanings in a way that resembled contemporary hypertextual poetry. And the medieval women had mystical bents that allowed them to see visions and have dialogues with deities and allegorical figures in what we might call an "asynchronous" manner. Then there were the contemporary characters who were hooked on the virtues of virtual reality and were spending a good deal of both their professional and free time on the web. To me, there seemed to be very little difference between the mystical impulses of the otherworld and the electrical impulses of the etherworld and I wondered if the two hadn't occasionally become linked in virtual space.

Q. And the ideas and words in the e-mail debate, did you write that Internet dialogue?

Cass: Actually, the comments made by both the women and the men in the Internet debate are their own. Nin Creed asked for a public debate, a real-time confrontation between mysogynist philosophers and the women writers who were their contemporaries. Members of the Dead Women Writers' Group complied. Since this is perhaps the first forum in which these women have been able to engage publicly with their detractors since Christine de Pizan's argument in the early days of the 15th Century, direct quotation was essential. The comments in the e-mails are all from published works. Because the characters wanted readers to be able to learn more about their ideas, they included source lines at the end of every e-mail entry they wrote.

Q. *Nin* seems to be a revisionist sort of novel in which philosophers are challenged and myths are rewritten. What happens when we approach the ancients and retell their stories as though they were our own?

Cass. We do this all the time. We retell stories that have been lived before, especially when there's something in a story we still don't understand. Over the years, I've realized that strangely similar tales come steaming up out of the fabric of many cultures. One notion that steams up through the millennia is the recurring story of a woman who appears and disappears, who is powerful and loses her power—Inanna journeying to the otherworld, the lady at Guadalupe, the muses at the mouths of caves, La Llorona who wanders the hills at night. When I was a Peace Corps volunteer living on the eroding edges of an Andean town, I was awakened one night by wind moaning, howling like a Minnesota timber wolf. The next morning, the air was heavy with the smell of dead animals, and I looked up into the trees to see if our neighborhood birds—the vultures—were there on the branches, sunning themselves like starlings at home. Just then a neighbor dropped by and asked if I heard La Llorona wandering along the hills the night before. "She looks for her dead children and she weeps," he said. "That's why she is called La Llorona." I found out later that La Llorona is a mythical person, that she's a character who resembles Lilith, and I realized that she must have passed by, that her scent had been in the air, that I had been given the privilege not only to retell mythology, but to smell it as well.

The story of a potent but liminal female presence is a story that gives us power as we interpret our lives as women, and fiction is another way that the mythical and the magical can become a part of our realities. When we read a story we agree to make room in our lives for places that might not exist, people we don't know, and thoughts we hadn't expected to have. When we connect to this kind of energy, we risk change, and so do the characters whose stories we tell and retell.

Bibliographic List of Works of Interest

Ahmed, Leila. *Women and Gender in Islam.* New Haven: Yale University Press, 1992.

Angela of Foligno, Complete Works. Trans. Paul Lachance, O.F.M. New York: Paulist Press, 1993.

Aquinas, Thomas. *Summa Theologica of St. Thomas Aquinas,* Vol. One. Trans.the Fathers of the English Dominican Province. Westminister, Maryland: Christian Classics, 1981.
— *Summa Theologica of St. Thomas Aquinas,* Vol. Five. Trans. the Fathers of the English Dominican Province. Westminister, Maryland: Christian Classics, 1981.

Aristotle. *Metaphysics.* Ann Arbor, Mich.: The University of Michigan Press, 1960.
— *On the Generation of Animals.* Trans. A.L. Peck. Cambridge, Mass.: London: Harvard University Press; W. Heinemann, 1990.

Babinski, Ellen, ed. and trans. *Marguerite Porète: The Mirror of Simple Souls.* New York: Paulist Press, 1993.

Balka, Ellen. Link to "Computer Networking: Spinsters on the Web." Canadian Research Institute for the Advancement of Women: Ottawa. 2 August 2000 <http://www.sfu.ca/~ebalka/publish.htm>

Berg, Temma F., ed. *Engendering the Word—Feminist Essays in Psychosexual Poetics.*Chicago: University of Illinois Press, 1989.

Bottéro, Jean. *Mesopotamia: Writing, Reasoning, and the Gods.* Trans. Zainab Bahrani and Marc Van De Mieroop. Chicago: University of Chicago Press, 1992.

Bruckman, Amy S. "Gender Swapping on the Internet." 2 August 2000 <http://www.cc.gatech.edu/fac/Amy.Bruckman/papers/index.html>

Bullock, William. *Beautiful Waters: Devoted to the Memphremagog Region.* Memphremagog Pr., 1926.

Bundtzen, Linda. *Plath's Incarnations: Women and the Creative Process.* Ann Arbor: The University of Michigan Press, 1983.

Campbell, Joseph. *Creative Mythology—The Masks of God.* New York: Penguin Books, 1985.
— *Myths to Live By.* New York: Penguin Arkana, 1972.
— *The Hero With a Thousand Faces,* Princeton: Bollingen Series, 1968.
— *Joseph Campbell on James Joyce.* Executive producer William Free, project director Stuart L. Brown. Oakland, Calif.: Mythology Ltd. and William Free Productions, 1990.

Carroll, Michael P. *The Cult of the Virgin Mary.* Princeton, N.J.: Princeton University Press, 1992.

Chrysostom, John. *John Chrysostom—On Virginity—Against Remarriage.* Trans. Sally Rieger Shore. New York: The Edwin Mellen Press, Studies in Women and Religion, Volume Nine, 1983.

Coghlan, Ronan. *Illustrated Encyclopedia of Arthurian Legends.* Rockport, Mass.: Element, Inc., 1993.

Cooper, Jerrold S. "Third Millennium Mesopotamia: An Introduction." *Women's Earliest Records.* Ed. Barbara S. Lesko. Atlanta: Scholars Press, 1989.

Copleston, Frederick, S.J. *Arthur Schopenhauer, Philosopher of Pessimism.* Bellarmine Series. The Holy See: Burns Oates and Washbourne, Ltd., 1947.

Daly, Mary. *Gyn Ecology.* Boston: Beacon Press, 1978.

De Lorris , Guillaume, Jean De Meun (Contributor), Charles Dahlberg (Translator), *The Romance of the Rose.* Princeton: Princeton University Press, 1995.

de Pizan, Christine. *The Book of the City of Ladies.* Trans. Jeffrey Richards. New York: Persea Books, 1998.
— *Selected Writings of Christine De Pizan : New Translations, Criticism.* Ed. Renate Blumenfeld-Kosinski. Trans. Kevin Brownlee. New

York: W.W. Norton & Company; 1997.

— *The Writings of Christine de Pizan.* Ed. Charity Cannon Willard. New York: Persea Books, 1994.

Donovan, Josephine, ed. *Feminist Literary Criticism.* Lexington, Ky: The University Press of Kentucky, 1989.

Dronke, Peter. *Women Writers of the Middle Ages.* Cambridge: Cambridge University Press, 1994.

Ebner, Margaret. *Margaret Ebner Major Works.* Ed. and trans. Leonard P. Hindsley. New York: Paulist Press, 1993.

Ecker, Gisela. *Feminist Aesthetics.* Boston: Beacon Press, 1985.

Eide-Tollefson, "Jesse Weston's Quest for the Holy Grail." *Mythos* No. 7, Spring 1998. Publication of the Mythos Institute, Frontenac, Minn.

Eisler, Riane. *The Chalice and the Blade.* San Francisco: Harper San Francisco, 1988.

Eliade, Mircea. *The Sacred and the Profane: The Nature of Religion.* Trans. Willard R. Trask. New York, NY: Harcourt Brace, 1968.

— *History of Religious Ideas: From the Stone Age to the Eleusinian Mysteries.* Chicago: University of Chicago Press, 1981.

enheduanna, *nin-me-šár-ra,* Various Cuneiform Texts: A-Q, S, U_1-U_5, , X-Z, a-d. (Translations by Cass Dalglish.)

Foucault, Michel. "What Is an Author?" *Textual Strategies: Perspectives in Post-Structuralist Criticism.* Ed.Josue V. Harari. Ithaca: Cornell University Press, 1979.

Gadamer, H.G. *Truth and Method.* New York: The Crossroad Publishing Co., 1989.

Gertrude of Helfta. *The Herald of Divine Love.* Ed. and trans. Margaret Winkworth. New York: The Paulist Press, 1993.

Gilbert, Sandra and Susan Gubar, eds. *No Man's Land: The Place of the Woman Writer in the Twentieth Century.* New Haven: Yale University Press, 1994.

Gilligan, Carol. *In a Different Voice.* Cambridge, Mass: Harvard University Press, 1982.

Gimbutas, Marija. *The Civilization of the Goddess.* New York: Harper Collins-HarperSanFrancisco, 1991.

Giovanni, Nikki. *Gemini.* Indianapolis and New York: The Bobbs-Merril Company, Inc., 1971.

Glassner, Jean-Jaques. "Women, Hospitality and Honor of the Family." *Women's Earliest Records.* Ed. Barbara S. Lesko. Atlanta: Scholars Press, 1989.

Graves, Robert. *The White Goddess.* New York: Farrar, Straus and Giroux, 1948.

Gubar, Susan. "The Blank Page and the Issues of Female Creativity." *Critical Inquiry* vol. 8, no. 2, Winter 1981.

Hallo, William W. "Individual Prayer in Sumerian: The Continuity of a Tradition." *Journal of the American Oriental Society* vol. 88, no. 1, 71-89.
— "Sumerian Historiography," *History, Historiography and Interpretation.* Ed. H. Tadmor and M. Weinfeld. Jerusalem: The Magnes Press, 1984.
— "The Royal Correspondence of Larsa: III. The Princess and the Plea." *Etudes sur la civilisation mesopotamienne offertes a P. Garelli,* Textes reunis par D. Charpin et F. Joannes. Paris, 1991.
— "Women of Sumer," *The Legacy of Sumer.* Ed. Denise Schmandt-Besserat. Malibu: Undena Publications, 1976.

Hallo, William W. and J.J.A. Van Dijk. *The Exaltation of Inanna.* New Haven: Yale University Press, 1968.

Haraway, Donna J. *Modest_Witness@Second_Millennium. FemaleMan_Meets_OncoMouse.* New York: Routledge, 1997.

Harris, Rivkah. "Gendered Old Age in Enuma Elish," in *The Tablet and The Scroll, Near Eastern Studies in Honor of William W. Hallo.* Eds.: Daniel C. Snell, Mark Cohen, David B. Weisberg. Bethesda, Md.: CDL Press, 1993.

— "Inanna-Ishtar as Paradox and a Coincidence of Opposites." *History of Religions* vol. 30, no. 3, February 1991, 261-278.

— "Independent Women in Ancient Mesopotamia." *Women's Earliest Records.* Barbara S. Lesko, ed. Atlanta: Scholars Press, 1989.

Heilbrun, Carolyn. *Writing a Woman's Life.* New York: Ballantine Books, 1988.

Heilbrun, Carolyn and Catharine Stimpson. "Theories of Feminist Criticism: A Dialogue." *Feminist Literary Criticism.* Ed. Josephine Donovan. Lexington, Ky: The University Press of Kentucky, 1989.

Hillman, James. *Archetypal Psychology.* Dallas: Spring Publications, Inc., 1993.

Hildegard of Bingen. *Hildegard of Bingen's Book of Divine Works.* Ed. Matthew Fox. Santa Fe, N.M.: Bear and Company, 1987.

— *Illuminations of Hildegard of Bingen.* Commentary by Matthew Fox. Santa Fe, N.M.: Bear and Company, 1985.

— *Scivias.* Trans. Mother Columba Hart and Jane Bishop. New York: Paulist Press, 1990.

Hoai-An Truong and others of the Bay Area Women in Telecom Bay Area Women in Telecommunications Group, "Gender issues in on-line communications." 2 August 2000 <http://www.cpsr.org/program/gender/papers.htm>

Hong, Howard V. and Edna H., editors and translators. *Soren Kierkegaard's Journals and Papers, Volume 4, S-Z.* Bloomington: Indiana University Press, 1975.

Howard-Gordon, Frances. *Glastonbury: Maker of Myths.* Glastonbury: Gothic Image, 1982.

Hyman, Arthur and James J. Walsh, eds. *Philosophy in the Middle Ages: The Christian, Islamic, and Jewish Tradition.* Indianapolis: Hackett Publishing Company, 1983.

Jacobsen, Thorkild. *Toward an Image of Tammuz.* Cambridge,
Massachusetts: Harvard University Press, 1970.
— "The Descent of Enki." *The Tablet and The Scroll, Near Eastern
Studies in Honor of William W. Hallo.* Eds. Daniel C. Snell, Mark E.
Cohen, David B. Weisberg. Bethesda, Md.: CDL Press, 1993.
— *The Harps That Once.* New Haven: Yale University Press, 1987.
— *The Sumerian King List.* Chicago: The University of Chicago Press,
1939.

Jeter, Kris. *The Archetypal Wild One in Mythology, Ritual, and Psychology:
A Book of Readings.* Compiled by Kris Jeter in collaboration with
Marjorie Bell Chambers, Cincinnati: The Union Institute, 1994.

Jito, Empress. Selected poems from *Women Poets of Japan.* Trans.
Kenneth Rexroth and Ikuko Atsumi. New York: New Directions
Books, 1977.

Jones, Deb Dale. "Gender Attribution in Sumerian: Some
Problems and Possibilities." Graduate Students in Women's Studies
Conference. University of Wisconsin, Madison: 1987.
— *She Spoke to Them with a Stormy Heart: The Politics of Reading,
Ancient (or Other) Narrative.* Dissertation Presented to the Faculty
of the Graduate School of the University of Minnesota for the
Degree of Doctor of Philosophy, 1993.

Jones, Kathy. *The Goddess in Glastonbury.* Glastonbury, England:
Ariadne Publications, 1990.

Joyce, James. *Ulysses.* Hans Walter Gabler, ed. New York: Vintage Books
Division of Random House, 1986.

Juhasz, Suzanne. *Naked and Firery Forms.* New York: Harper Colophon
Books, 1976.

Jung, Carl Gustav. *Aion: Researches into the Phenomenology of the Self.*
Trans. R.F.C. Hull. Princeton: Bollingen, 1959.
— *The Archetypes and the Collective Unconscious.* Second Edition.
Trans. R.F. C. Hull. Princeton: Princeton University Press, 1969.

Jung, Carl Gustav, M.L. von Franz et al. *Man and his Symbols.* New York: Doubleday and Company, Inc., 1983.

Jung, Emma and Marie Louise von Franz. *The Grail Legend.* Boston: Sigo Press, 1986.

Klapisch-Zuber, Christiane, ed. *A History of Women, Silences of the Middle Ages.* Cambridge, Mass. The Belknap Press of Harvard University Press, 1992.

Kramer, Samuel Noah, ed. *Mythologies of the Ancient World.* Garden City, New York: Anchor Books, Doubleday and Company, Inc., 1961.
— "Poets and Psalmists: Goddesses and Theologians." *The Legacy of Sumer.* Ed. Denise Schmandt-Besserat. Malibu, California: Undena Publications, 1976.
— *Sumerian Mythology—A Study of Spiritual and Literary Achievement in the Third Millennium B.C.* Philadelphia: University of Pennsylvania Press, 1972.
— *The Sumerians: Their History, Culture and Character.* Chicago: University of Chicago Press, 1963.

Kroll, Judith. *Chapters in a Mythology: The Poetry of Sylvia Plath.* New York: Harper and Row, 1976.

Kundera, Milan. *The Art of the Novel.* New York: Grove Press, 1986.

LaBatt, Rene. *Manuel D'Épigraphie Akkadienne.* Paris: Librairie Orientaliste Paul Geuthner, S.A. Nouvelle Édition, Revue et Corrigèe, 1976.

Lanham, R. *The Electronic Word: Democracy, Technology, and the Arts.* Chicago: University of Chicago Press, 1993.

Lauter, Estella, ed. *Women as Mythmakers—Poetry and Visual Art by Twentieth-Century Women.* Bloomington: Indiana University Press, 1984.

Lauter, Estella and Carol Schreier Rupprecht, eds. *Feminist Archetypal Theory.* Knoxville: The University of Tennessee Press, 1985.

Lorde, Audre. *From a Land Where Other People Live*. Detroit: Broadside Press, 1973.

— *Our Dead Behind Us*. New York: W.W. Norton and Company, 1986.

— "The Transformation of Silence into Language and Action," and "Poetry Is Not a Luxury," in *Sister Outsider*. Freedom, Calif.: the Crossing Press, 1984.

Lukács, Georg. *The Theory of the Novel*. Anna Bostack, trans. Cambridge: MIT Press, 1971.

Maggio, Rosalie. *The Dictionary of Bias Free Usage*. Phoenix: Oryx Press, 1991.

Martin, Joan M. "The Notion of Difference for Emerging Womanist Ethics: The Writings of Audre Lorde and bell hooks." *Journal of Feminist Studies in Religion* vol. 9, numbers 1-2, Spring/Fall 1993.

Matthews, Caitlin. *Arthur and the Sovereignity of Britain*. New York: Viking Penguin, 1989.

McLaughlin, Megan. "Gender Paradox and the Otherness of God." *Gender and History* vol. 3, no. 2 (1991) 147-159.

Meeker, Joe. *The Comedy of Survival*. Los Angeles: Guild of Tutors Press, 1980.

Metzger, Deena. *Writing for Your Life*. San Francisco: HarperSanFrancisco, 1992.

— "The Diary: The Ceremony of Knowing." *A Casebook on Anais Nin*, Ed. Robert Zaller. New York: New American Library, 1974.

Millay, Edna St. Vincent. *Selected Poems*. Colin Falck, ed. New York: Harper Collins, Foreword by Richard Eberhart, 1991.

Millett, Kate. *Sexual Politics*. New York: Avon, 1969.

Minnich, Elizabeth. *Transforming Knowledge*. Philadelphia: Temple University Press, 1982.

Moore, Marianne. *A Marianne Moore Reader*. New York: The Viking Press, 1961.
— *Collected Poems*. New York: The MacMillan Company, 1953.

Nakuda, Princess. Selected poems from *Women Poets of Japan*. Trans. Kenneth Rexroth and Ikuko Atsumi. New York: New Directions Books, 1977.

ninshatapada. "Oxford Editions of Cuneiform Texts." *Sumerian Texts in the Ashmolean Museum*. Ed. Oliver R. Gurney and Samuel Noah Kramer. Oxford: The Clarendon Press, 5:25 (lines 59-111). (Translations by Cass Dalglish.)
— "Textes Religieux Sumeriens." No. 46 (lines 36-58), No. 58 (lines 1-19), No. 59 (lines 20-35). (Translations by Cass Dalglish.)

Owen, Wendy. *A Riddle in Nine Syllables: Female Creativity in the Poetry of Sylvia Plath*. Ann Arbor, Mich.: University Microfilms International, 1985. Dissertation Presented to the Faculty of Yale University, 1985.

Page, Barbara. "Women Writers and the Restive Text: Feminism, Experimental Writing and Hypertext." *Postmodern Culture* vol. 6, no. 2, January 1996. Reprinted in *Cyberspace Textuality: Computer Technology and Literary Theory*. Ed. Marie-Laure Ryan. Bloomington: Indiana University Press, 1999.

Pantel, Pauline Schmitt, editor. *A History of Women, From Ancient Goddesses to Christian Saints*. Cambridge, Mass.: The Belknap Press of Harvard University Press, 1992.

Pardes, Ilana. *Countertraditions in the Bible, A Feminist Approach*. Cambridge, Mass.:Harvard University Press, 1992.

Parker, Dorothy. *The Collected Poetry of Dorothy Parker*. The Modern Library, 1944.

Pearce, Laurie E. "Statements of Purpose: Why the Scribes Wrote." *The Tablet and the Scroll, Near Eastern Studies in Honor of William W. Hallo*. Eds. Daniel C. Snell, Mark Cohen, David B. Weisberg. Bethesda, Md.: CDL Press, 1993.

Perera, Sylvia Brinton. *Descent to the Goddess, A Way of Initiation for Women*. Toronto, Canada: Inner City Books, 1981.
— *The Scapegoat Complex*. Toronto, Canada: Inner City Books, 1986.

Plath, Sylvia. *The Collected Poems*. Ted Hughes, ed. New York: Harper Perennial, 1992.
— *The Colossus*. New York: Vintage Books Edition, 1968.

Plato. *Craytylus*. Diotima's Perseus Links, WWW, Tufts, http://www.perseus. tufts.edu
— *Theaetetus*. 2 August 2000<http:www.perseus.tufts.edu/cgibin/ptext? doc=Perseus%3Aabo%3Atlg%2C0059%2C006&query=148e>.
— *The Republic*. Trans. Francis MacDonald Cornford. London: Oxford University Press, 1952.

Porète, Marguerite. *The Mirror of Simple Souls*. Ed. and trans. Ellen Babinsky. New York: Paulist Press, 1993.

Reade, Julian. *Mesopotamia*. London: The British Museum Press, 1991.

Reisman, Daniel. "Iddin-Dagan's Sacred Marriage Hymn." *Journal of Cuneiform Studies* XXV. No. 4 (1973) 185-202.

Rilke, Rainer Maria. *The Selected Poetry of Rainer Maria Rilke*. Ed. and trans. Stephen Mitchell. New York: Vintage International, 1989.

Rose, Gillian. *Feminism and Geography*. Minneapolis: University of Minnesota Press, 1993.

Rosenblatt, Jon. *Sylvia Plath, The Poetry of Initiation*. Chapel Hill: University of North Carolina Press, 1979.

Roth, Philip. *Reading Myself and Others*. New York: Farrar, Straus and Giroux 1975.

Sappho. *Sappho: A New Translation*, Trans. Mary Barnard, Dudley Fitts. University of California Press, 1999.

Sigmund, Paul E., ed. *St. Thomas Aquinas on Politics and Ethics*. New York: W.W. Norton and Company, 1988.

Sinclair, John D., trans. *Dante: The Divine Comedy, 2, Purgatorio.* New York and London: Oxford University Press, The Bodley Head, 1983.

— *Dante: The Divine Comedy, 2, Purgatorio.* New York and London: Oxford University Press, The Bodley Head, 1961.

— *The Divine Comedy, 3, Paradiso.* New York and London: Oxford University Press, The Bodley Head, 1961.

Snyder, W.C. "Mother Nature's Other Nature: Landscape in Women's Writing." *Women's Studies* vol. 21 (2) 143-162.

Starhawk. *Truth or Dare: Encounter with Power, Authority and Mystery.* Cambridge: Harper and Row, 1987.

Stone, Elizabeth C. "The Social Role of the Naditu Women in Old Babylonian Nippur." *Journal of the Economic and Social History of the Orient* XXV Part 1, 1982.

Stone, Merlin. *When God Was A Woman.* New York: A Harvest/HBJ Book, 1976.

Teresa of Avila—The Interior Castle. Trans. Kieran Kavanaugh, O.C.D., and Otilo Robriguez, O.C.D. New York: Paulist Press, 1979.

Thomsen, Marie-Louise. *The Sumerian Language,* Copenhagen: Akademisk Forlag, 1984.

Upjohn, Sheila. *In Search of Julian of Norwich.* London: Darton, Longman and Todd, 1989.

Van De Mieroop, Marc. "Women in the Economy of Sumer." *Women's Earliest Records.* Ed. Barbara S. Lesko. Atlanta: Scholars Press, 1989.

Wakeman, Mary K. "Ancient Sumer and the Women's Movement: The Process of Reaching Beyond, Encompassing and Going Beyond." *Journal of Feminist Studies* Fall 1985.

Walker, Barbara. *The Women's Dictionary of Symbols & Sacred Objects.* New York: Harper & Row, 1988.

— *The Women's Encyclopedia of Myths and Secrets*. New York: Harper & Row, 1983.

Weber, Samuel. *Mass Mediauras: form, technics, media*. Stanford: Stanford University Press, 1996.

Weston, Jessie. *From Ritual to Romance*. Gloucester, Mass.: Peter Smith, 1983.

Wolkstein, Diane and Samuel Noah Kramer. *Inanna Queen of Heaven and Earth*. New York: Harper and Row, 1983.

Woolf, Virginia. *A Room of One's Own*. New York: Harcourt Brace Jovanovich, Publishers, 1989.

Yutang, Lin, editor and translator. *The Wisdom of Confucius*. London: Michael Joseph, 1958.

Other Novels Available from Spinsters Ink

The Activist's Daughter, Ellen Bache. $10.95

Amazon Story Bones, Ellen Frye. $10.95

As You Desire, Madeline Moore. $9.95

Child of Her People, Anne Cameron. $10.95

Dreaming Under a Ton of Lizards, Marian Michener. $12.00

Fat Girl Dances with Rocks, Susan Stinson. $10.95

Finding Grace, Mary Saracino. $12.00

A Gift of the Emperor, Therese Parks. $10.95

Give Me Your Good Ear, 2nd ed., Maureen Brady $9.95

Goodness, Martha Roth $10.95

The Journey, Anne Cameron. $9.95

Living at Night, Mariana Romo-Carmona $10.95

Martha Moody, Susan Stinson $10.95

Modern Daughters and the Outlaw West, Melissa Kwasny . . . $9.95

No Matter What, Mary Saracino $9.95

Sugar Land, Joni Rodgers. $12.00

Those Jordan Girls, Joan M. Drury. $12.00

Trees Call for What They Need, Melissa Kwasny. $9.95

Turnip Blues, Helen Campbell $12.00

Vital Ties, Karen Kringle. $10.95

A Woman Determined, Jean Swallow. $12.00

Spinsters Ink was founded in 1978 to produce books for diverse women's communities. In 1986, we merged with Aunt Lute Books to become Spinsters/Aunt Lute. In 1990, the Aunt Lute Foundation became an independent nonprofit publishing program. In 1992, Spinsters moved to Minnesota

Spinsters Ink publishes novels and nonfiction works that deal with significant issues in women's lives from a feminist perspective: books that not only name these crucial issues, but—more important—encourage change and growth. We are committed to publishing works by women writing from the periphery: fat women, Jewish women, lesbians, old women, poor women, rural women, women examining classism, women of color, women with disabilities, women who are writing books that help make the best in our lives more possible.

Spinsters titles are available from your local bookseller or by mail order throught Spinsters Ink. A free catalog is available upon request. Please include $2.00 shipping for the first title ordered and .50¢ for every title thereafter. Visa and Mastercard are accepted.

Spinsters Ink
32 E. First St., #330
Duluth, MN 55802-2002
USA

(phone) 218-727-3222   (fax) 218-727-3119
(e-mail) spinster@spinsters-ink.com
(website) http://www.spinsters-ink.com

Louis Branca

Cass Dalglish is a former print and broadcast journalist, who has studied Sumerian and Akkadian cuneiform in her search for the earliest of women's literature. Her scholarly investigations have led her to compare ancient and contemporary women's poetry and to write and lecture on similarities between cuneiform text and hyptertext. She is at work on kinetic and choral translations of the first signed document in history, enheduanna's song to Inanna. She holds a doctorate in creative writing/ancient and archetypal women's literature from the Union Institute and an M.F.A. in writing from Vermont College. She lives in Minneapolis where she is associate professor of English at Augsburg College. Her first novel, *Sweetgrass*, was nominated for a Minnesota Book Award.